THE FALL FROM GRACE
OF HARRY ANGEL

Paul Wilson lives in Blackburn, Lancashire.
This is his first novel.

THE FALL FROM GRACE OF HARRY ANGEL

Paul Wilson

JONATHAN CAPE
LONDON

First published 1994

1 3 5 7 9 10 8 6 4 2

© Paul Wilson 1994

Paul Wilson has asserted his right under
the Copyright, Designs and Patents Act 1988
to be identified as the author of this work

First published in the United Kingdom in 1994 by Jonathan Cape
Random House, 20 Vauxhall Bridge Road, London SW1V 2SA

Random House Australia (Pty) Limited
20 Alfred Street, Milsons Point, Sydney,
New South Wales 2061, Australia

Random House New Zealand Limited
18 Poland Road, Glenfield,
Auckland 10, New Zealand

Random House South Africa (Pty) Limited
PO Box 337, Bergvlei, South Africa

Random House UK Limited Reg. No. 954009

A CIP catalogue record for this book is available from the British Library

ISBN 0–224–04041–3

Typeset by Pure Tech Corporation, Pondicherry, India
Printed in Great Britain by Mackays of Chatham PLC

For Doug – safe journey

I

My name is Harry Angel. Turkey neck and ears like the handles of a football trophy. Shirt collar rolled into rope around my tie however hard I try. Harry Angel isn't my real name, but it suffices. You could say I'm living a lie, but I've grown used to it. It causes me no loss of sleep.

I wanted to be a football player, join a travelling circus, but those were only dreams. I became an employee of the city. Each month the authorities pay me so I don't run out of fuel or starve or anything. In return I labour to turn this into a better place. This was once a fine town. The local politicians still dream of new starts, of old glories. I follow in giants' footsteps.

We officials of the city put these dreams into practice. We are nothing if not practical men. We map out the route to the promised land from warm offices, explain each new delay, each reasonable diversion.

We eye the politicians like children eye circus lions. Sometimes we prod them through the bars and run, laughing.

Up on the hill there is only the digging up of Sam Pound and an engine hum of unease in the bellies of my fellow men. I'm standing here, the pipe-sucking rising star called Drucker beside me, stamping my feet against the kind of cold that dawn brings. Hot breaths rise from us like we are horses steaming.

Sometimes I stand and watch such things go ticking by me like I'd buried treasure on a hill and was in the act of remembering where. It is a passing thing.

Our standing here is not some frivolous act. I am a public servant. I am here to see that good comes to the town. I am here to see the body of Sam Pound dug from the ground. You see, this is a cemetery.

2
—

The old priest would have known what to say to Mary Pound. He had known the Pounds all their long lives. Known me too from when I was a child. Longevity like that gives people a power over you. He knew my parents well. After my mother died he got in the habit of asking me how my father was managing on his own. I would tell him I could be doing more to help. He would say, 'I'm sure you're doing your best,' and in the end I gave up telling him the truth.

At any time, by sheer dint of memory, this man could picture me in short trousers doing things with worms and dung beetles, an authority to hold over any grown man. I figure that's why men like Drucker keep moving. History is a disadvantage. The old priest was a crabby Glaswegian with a constantly runny nose but he is dead now. Too much power is no good for any one man.

In his place they despatched a new man six months ago to rekindle Father Keam's dwindling east quarter parish of St Mary's. He arrived, as new men do, with a keen understanding of urban renewal. He had the sense not to go converting Jews and Muslims. They trained him well. I figure he'll be moving along soon. From the start he encouraged churchgoers to hold hands at the blessing. He has called the dead man 'Samuel' twice so far in talking to Mary Pound and she has eyeballed him each time with her piggy eyes.

3

The new man of God has bathed already this morning. Got up at four to do so. He has come at no particular request from her, to stand with her and offer the consolation of the Church. But he finds it difficult to know how to be with her and so he slides into an accommodating silence around her. It is a kind of comfort to offer. This he tells himself.

She is sometimes referred to as a rough diamond. Taken as she's seen. Sometimes she smells. He is clean and eager to learn. Eager to be liked and good at it for God's sake. Eager to forgive. He is another man rising. He calls her 'one of my little treasures around the church' – fat Mary Pound with the white face and the dead son. She thinks it a mean and little phrase for a man who could be her grandchild.

They are not the easiest of compatriots.

Priest and parishioner stand halfway down the hill. Lumpy carrier bags nestle like kittens at Mary Pound's feet. Men in overalls dig into the earth in front of them whilst others, supervising, watch. Further up the hill two men in heavy coats look on from a careful distance. One of them is me, the erroneously named Harry Angel, cold to the marrow. The other is the pipe-sucking Drucker. Around us is hush. Nods, signs. Falling whispers.

I feel edgy. It's not moral or anything. I'm not a religious man. It's just that life's hard enough without reminders like this. As with other men, I'm edgy around the dead and the signposts that they leave. Reminders of the journey's end. The final dumb practical joke still to come. The joke says, 'Christ, are you still here after forty-eight years, Angel? What dreams you had, boy!'

'Sod of a time to go digging up bodies,' Drucker says. I figure he is bored. Or anxious, or entertained. Something.

4

In my state of cold I am forced to risk movement and nod my turkey neck in agreement. Ears, like trophy handles, are raw red in this dry iced field.

4

This is a big year for the city – the city in which I live and work, in which my forty-eight years here have ebbed away one day by thieving day. It's three hundred years since its Charter of Incorporation was set out by the monarch as a tuppence-ha'penny market town crouched by the hills. There will be fireworks and things to mark the tercentenary. More signposts. More reminders of the journey's end.

In the year of our Charter's signing they were burning nineteen witches in the Yankee town of Salem for putting the evil eye on the children of the town, but we burned no witches here that year. Too busy building a town fit for heroes, signing charters and things.

It's been a bad time of late. They come, they go. A good show this year for the folks would make such a difference. The Leader is putting his heart and soul into it, despite the pending election. So are we, don't get me wrong. So are we. Men like Drucker and Harry Angel and the like labour to this end.

For its part the town has seen fit to promote me no less than three times since leaving my good friend Coleman Seer behind in the mill into which we had both gone as apprentices, since beginning my tutelage at City Hall under poor Vernon Smitts. The first time was when I got promoted to take over Vernon Smitts's job. The other occasions, you might say, have been more fortuitous.

Men like us shape the future, put into practice the harum scarum dreams of politicians. We are practical men. We make steady progress. It's not a bad town. Neither uglier nor prettier than others. Neither better nor worse. Just been having a blue spell. The Council Leader's done a lot to turn things round.

Outside of City Hall people go about their business. On the streets. In the park. Taking care to be out of the park by sunset. Sometimes after dark there is howling like a dog coming from in there. Taking care always to carry proof of identification whilst we weather the present troubles. People do the usual kind of jobs in the city. They make things. Bread and buildings and bowling alleys. They write reports and embezzle money and patrol the town, especially the east quarter where there is sometimes trouble. They mend things. Cars and telephones and bones. Good men and bad men. Day people making the city hum with life and its living.

At night the day people go to their homes. They have finished their work. They make supper and watch TV, and covet each others' wives, and dream of other things.

People are born, they die, they don't come back.

At night also the decision people make decisions at the Municipal City Hall, in its Council Chamber and in its narrow corridors that are not well lit. Night people drive taxis in the darkly lit city winking with lights. They guard warehouses and print the city newspapers and run all-night radio phone-ins for the troubled and the sleepless. They steal and they rape, but only the bad people do this. The night is full of the living and the dying.

The city is small and dark and far from the centre of things. Much like any other, you might say. Unremarkable under the shadow of the hills. Once men on their hands and knees dug for copper and silts of silver in these hills with their hands and hammers. We've come a long way since then and the hills are silent again. Dampness polishes the city's old blackstone buildings now until they shine like leather.

Like many towns, this one was once great. With some it has been forging steel or wrestling coal from the earth or building ships to sail the seas. With us it was cotton. Like all the others we seem to have had our turn at greatness, and now we are fallen from Eden. Believe me, we are working night and day to have it back again. Our people, the cityfolk, deserve nothing less. But first there are the problems to overcome. Not least, there is the digging up of Sam Pound.

5

I shove my hands deeper into my coat pockets, feeling for crumbs of warmth. The second man, taller and thicker set, watches intently beside me as the hole in the ground grows deeper. 'Child!' I am thinking. But Drucker is right. It's a sod of a time to go digging up bodies.

These things are always done at dawn with policemen standing guard discreetly. It's the ungodliness of the act. Here are deeds that no-one should chance upon by accident. Disturbing the bones of the dead. Not that I, Harry Angel, am a religious man.

I am here as Drucker's guide. All papers for exhumation, burial and cremation in the east quarter of the city fall on my desk for my signature. I stamp and record them, book the gravediggers and the little mechanical excavator they use these days until they get down near to the rotting coffin, amend the overtime payments and file the documents appropriately. The exercise also requires sufficient lime. For throwing into the opening hole.

Why lime?

Have you ever smelled decay? In days that have gone with their misdeeds, this lime mulch must have been often handy to cover the smell of decay.

Drucker is the Department's Director. He seems to think I attend each ceremony in person, that I am personally acquainted with each salvage of a decaying body. He keeps asking me questions. He stands beside me with the wooden-legged stiffness of a professional desk man. You get the impression I don't like Drucker, maybe?

'Its all rather Bu-Burke and Hare, isn't it,' he says. 'I'm glad I came. Important, you know, for the Senior to get out and about, see things. Do you suppose anyone will mind about me smoking? I feel quite lost without that damned pu-pipe.'

He will entertain friends over for dinner with ghoulie stories of the body he, Drucker, saw ripped from the ground. At dawn. With the bobbies standing guard. Whilst his wife clears the table for dessert.

Drucker stutters when he gets anxious. He is a PR man by trade. His first instinct is to smile, his second is to dislike you for it. I smile quickly. I am good at leading people surreptitiously in conversation. I lead them towards comfortable endings.

'Is there any mu-more of that coffee of yours in the car?' Drucker asks.

'There is . . . ' I am forced to hesitate, ' . . . but you might want to hang on another minute or two. It looks like they're ready to lift the box out.'

Drucker takes it as another sign of my familiarity with the routine. You see what I mean?

'Yu-yes, of course. We'll hu-hu-hang on, shall we?'

That bloody stutter.

Fifty yards away, the cluster of men begin the task of prizing out the coffin ready for its journey to the second autopsy that awaits it. There are pressmen here who write hurried shorthand squiggles to mark the significance of the moment. Not many. This is no pounding metropolis. As the body is winched out they look hard into the widow Pound's ordinary face.

When it is over, Mary Pound turns and leaves the priest, walking up the sloping field towards me. I am standing alone. I set up the ghost of a smile as she approaches.

'I'll nip off for that coffee now they're done if you'll give me the car keys,' Drucker had said. 'Hu-have a word with the woman if you get the chance. Su-sympathy from the City Council. I expect you're better at that kind of thing than me.' He had made it sound menial. I didn't much care. I was just happy to be left alone to face some day-old toothache the cold was egging on.

'Hullo, Harry.'

'Mrs Pound.'

She stands alongside me and we look together at the empty hole in the ground. Sometimes words are hard to come by. Hard to engineer without that hour to find a written-down phrase that will suffice.

'Left you to it, that boss of yours?' she says finally.

'He was cold,' I suggest meekly, not bothering to defend him. 'It's a sad business.'

She nods. 'They said it was important. Forensic tests

they can do now to tell me who did it. I expect the truth will out.'

I recognise the phrase. My mother had used it as well. It is, was, Father Keam's. Scottish. Runny nose. Dead now also. It is a phrase I always liked as a child. Like truth was a white rabbit to be plucked out from a tall black hat.

She was our neighbour on Beaker Street when we arrived in the city's east quarter. I was a child. She showed us what was what. Mary Pound knew everybody's rank including her own and she showed us how to play such games.

'After all those years of rearing him I'm better off knowing what killed him. You never stop fearing for them, you know.'

She is sixty-six. If I didn't know her I'd have said she was seventy-five easy. Sam Pound was her son. We were at school together. Beaker Street Primary. Getting set to run a million miles from here on the city's subway trams. Me, Coleman Seer, Sam Pound, Joe Mole and Sloopy Den Barton. Dreaming dreams of how we'd do things differently from our beaten parents in this brave new England.

Sure, they let me pretend I was English.

Sam Pound for one never got far. He had four kids himself. Of them, only Dooley is here, cowboy spurs and Jesse James hat and the morning off from the sheltered workshop where he bangs the ball and socket joints of wooden toys together for the orphanage and the hospital. It's a scheme the Leader started. I suppose the other Pounds are hanging out somewhere. Dooley stands alone, drawing pictures in the frosted earth with his heel. You don't know whether he reckons this to be a day out or what.

No-one much seems to leave this place. Few people, anyway. It's always been so. People like Drucker are the exception. Officials rising. People like him come, they do three years and they go, leaving barely a trace in the sand. The townsfolk are born here and they die here. By and large.

Up here on the hill the city's dead are buried. Small family groups, mute with respect, shuffle into the chapel through the oak Saxon doors and leave the back way through the rose gardens, having planted another generation down in the soil.

People's lives are punctuated by steady trips up the hill to this field of the dead. This field is rich in the compost of the cotton generations. The only route out of town was said not to be on the city's subway trams but to be through these oak doors. For me, as an outsider of sorts, it struck me as the biggest practical joke of all.

The subway trams seem to me like messengers from the outside world. It's not that people in the city don't know it's there, this other world. They know all about it. It zooms in from their TV screens through the day and the night. It paints pictures, histories, that they carry in their heads. Of other things beyond the damp green desert blackstone hills.

It isn't real life, though. Real life is here.

Mary Pound wears two cardigans everywhere she goes, and a wig the colour of straw that no-one knew why she wore. One time it fell off during a public meeting in the community centre in the east quarter. It would have been the funniest thing I ever saw except that she cried. Right there in the middle of the room. And underneath she was shiny bald. What about that! I'd known her all those years and this was news to me.

I ask her, 'Do you think it'll help. All this?'

She says, 'I think he's still dead when all's said and done. But I think I wouldn't mind a bit of revenge.'

'That sounds a bit extreme.'

'Not really. Revenge is simple, isn't it, love?' She wipes her face with the back of her mitten. 'It's the other options that are harder work.'

I can offer her only the same resolute smile I have offered Drucker all morning, but at least I'm good at it. The politics of silence. Everyone at fifty should have discovered at least one thing they can be good at.

'Anything I can do to help?' Another well-delivered phrase.

'You can get me out of that sodding flat, Harry. Out of that bloody east quarter. I've had no luck trying so far. I tell you, your mam wouldn't recognise it down there.'

'I'll have a word.'

Transfers out of that side of the city are near impossible these days, what with the Housing Commission starting to implement new instructions.

'You'll do your best, I know. I keep reckoning to go and visit your old dad, you know. They treating him well in that place?'

'Yes, they are, they are. But it's all downhill now I guess. I don't do enough really.'

'You do more than enough lad, I'm sure.'

I smile. Some people there's no telling.

6
—

I drive Drucker back through the city, the city that is not at ease with itself. But we are working on that, Daulman and Drucker and the rest of us. A single police car cruises past us. No noise. Friend or foe, the driver's glance across seems to ask. Or maybe it's just me being edgy. Christ, I've been up since four.

Three uniformed officers, Aratakis's men, keen to uncover plots afoot, sit motionless in the back. It is somehow more disconcerting than all the full-throated wails of last night. I live close to the east quarter. Sometimes I hear noises.

Drucker says, 'We'll need to be seen to be acting on this one. This isn't bu-bu-bloody New York.' The blasphemy seems unfamiliar on his lips. 'It's gu-getting out of hand. I'll have the Leader at my throat again.'

Beside me, I can feel Drucker's discomfort at the thought. Drucker is a smoother of feathers. Fussy and faddy. Action is not his forte. The smell of his aftershave fills the car. He has always taken a pride in his appearance. It is one of his best features. Cufflinks, tie-pin, fingernails evenly trimmed. Close up, Drucker has a boy's skin. It is clear and one-toned, but he sweats easily when he is under threat. Usually from City Councillors. Usually from the Council Leader. When he sucks on his pipe the boy's flesh around his jawline buckles into pouches. City Hall knows him as The Hu-Hu-Hamster.

We skirt the East River down where a housing scheme younger than Dumb Dooley Pound is falling into decay on the border of the city's east quarter. When Wiesel and his copper miners first set up out here to go scratching at the hills this area wasn't even recorded as part of the town's settlement. When Wiesel came, there was nothing but dark hills and the belly of rocks to scratch at. Men who'd gone out that far before had been turned into dogs and rabbits, the Parish Register says, because this was witches' land. A three-legged cat living wild that way had once been a deckhand out of Liverpool who'd lost a leg in his sailing days and who'd gone dredging thin seams of silver from the moors.

Now this place has a different silence. Now it seems to carry the bones of half the city's silent mills. Cotton finally made this town, then fled in the night. It left the monuments to its craft like giants' toys, sizes too big for those who by accident followed.

Halfway along Beaker Street a group of men circling a smouldering brazier look round at us. The brazier is a dustbin. I look across as I drive and see the men's faces and one face triggers a name – Jason Pound, eldest of Mary Pound's dependants since her son is, was, buried in the field on the hill. I don't want to watch them but my eyes are drawn from the road ahead. I'm tense like some animal that's hearing a noise that it can't rest with. The noise is a distance away but I'm wary all the same.

I write good social reports about this place when I'm back at City Hall. I can put the chaos into order on the pages. 'Because' and 'consequently' and 'understandable' draw the sting of what is in reality just quiet chaos. Just drifting. Just some wreckage of lives I'm driving through at pace.

As we speed by in the womb of the car I see others who I recognise from my dealings with these parts. Sloopy Den Barton. Joe Mole. Agitators in the uneasy life of the city's east quarter. An accident we are missing by driving hard, leaving them standing there as children stand expectantly around a bonfire. Drucker has not seen them. Not a perceptive man.

All of them are spare and lean and tight. Dreaming no dreams tonight. Old Sam Pound had four charges of his own like that, all of them now spread out somewhere in the city. Dreams are hard to come by in the east quarter. And then we are gone. Zoom! Like we turned off the TV or something.

7

In the lift back at City Hall that takes us up to the sixth floor, Drucker and I stand at the back of the group which has boarded the elevator. I nod to one or two as they step inside at floors on the way up. Casually. Just enough.

Undisciplined contact at close quarters can be so distressing. Eyelines criss-crossing the space to be avoided. The way to survive is to offer just enough of yourself. Fake it. It is as well to offer these small comforts. You never know.

Drucker's eyes stay down on the floor. You can tell a lot by the way a man rides in an elevator. I have sometimes prayed in positions such as this for the elevator to break down. Just for long enough. Have imagined Drucker running screaming through the city, naked, on his release.

Tee hee!

It hasn't happened. It doesn't. The metal box wheels us gently to the sixth floor, Drucker's eyes hard to the ground, sucking his pipe, cheeks like a hamster's, glad to be back in the nest.

My office is closest to the elevator doors.

There are no pictures on the plain white walls. No dead pictures of live things. There are no photographs of home on the walls, or of women. No scenes of past triumphs. Only a single pukka berry pot plant. It is a hobby of mine. I am uncomfortable with reminders of other things. Work is work.

What I have is junk. I don't throw things away too easily. You get like that? You don't know when things might come in useful, my mother said. They never do but it causes physical pain to throw out anything: pamphlets, reports, departmental briefs. Like these are barnacles carelessly grown to my soul.

Minutes from defunct committees lie collected in uneven stacks. There is a system but it is mine alone, impenetrable, built up of subtle nuances of 'ins' and 'outs' and 'pendings'.

I take off my coat and jacket and go to pour myself a coffee from the percolator in the lobby. The 'ongoings' stretch across a large 'L'-shaped desk in the centre of the office. Folders and files separate the layers of paper into slim slick volumes of information.

What do I do? Well now, let me tell you this. When I was taken on by City Hall in the spring of 1961 my mother lit a candle in the vestry of St Mary's. Maybe it burned brighter then than now. I found my mother sat alone one day at the kitchen table writing on a Woolworth exercise pad which I realised much later she used as an occasional diary. 'What are you writing?' I asked with all the fearlessness of youth.

'That maybe things will be alright after all,' she said.

Drucker thinks I sometimes empty ashtrays. He says, 'How goes it?' merrily enough. Daulman on his bad days pictures me as a Graphic Artist or the man from Stock Control. Maybe Stankill thinks I'm a spy. Who knows what Stankill thinks.

I'm the Miscellaneous Developments Officer. This far was I promoted most recently in service to Drucker's Department. People with ideas for improving the city which don't fit neatly into any one package come through me. 'Send it to Harry Angel,' they say. And it comes to me. I get odds and ends as well. Like exhumation orders. Like organising the replacement of citizens' lost ID cards. Like attending to the east quarter.

A PC keyboard sits on a smaller desk by the window, the VDU screen hanging above it. It is only used for nearly finished pieces or paragraphs. I am uncomfortable using it. I like the squeak of a nib and the soiling of clean paper with ink. Part of a last generation of foreigners to a world of screens.

My trade is words, spoken and especially written. Feasibilities, recommendations, briefs, monitoring studies, all charting the exquisitely balanced progress of the city in its struggle for improvement under the prevailing administration.

I can turn a mean phrase within the constraints of acceptable report structures. Explaining complex ideas in crisp phrases to dull citizens. They need a shorthand view of the world before they return to the TV window. To the eroticism of simplicity. To dead pictures of live things.

The latest report submitted by the Department of Corporate and Community Affairs to the Council does not gloss over the problems of the city. My own contribution to this report was, shall we say, peripheral. But necessary all the same. The report reviews the difficulties, for example in the east quarter. It acknowledges that bad things sometimes happen. Patterns of things. Like such things had a mind to them. But the report makes the point forcibly that there is much energy in the city, that partnership between people and the authorities is being vigorously and effectively pursued. (My own monthly liaison with the East Quarter Community Forum is one such cited example of this.) Sure, sure, this is miscellaneous. No-one else will go.

The document identifies courses of action and paints an elegantly phrased summation which seeks to direct the Council Leader, whose desk it landed on yesterday, towards the necessary conclusions.

What else does it do? It brings order to a wreckage of lives.

8

It is time for some truth.

I was not born Harry Angel. It is an irony not lost on me that a man who spends his days rejoicing in language was not born to speak English.

Truth is necessary, but like medicine it should only be dispensed in controlled amounts. I was born Harni Zelene-wycz in the back of a lorry near the village of Rajska where I had been conceived. I was born in a century destined to be remembered for two things, the rise of the TV game show and the production of human bonemeal. I know this from reading a Woolworth Exercise Pad but that's another story. Both require a basic mental dexterity from partici-pants. What the century has lacked in grandeur it has made up for in ingenuity.

My mother once said that if I ever made it to City Hall she would light a candle in the vestry of St Mary's. She was dazzled by the bright words of English democracy. She thought of City Hall as a dream factory. She saw the city to which we had come as a clean white wall on which to begin again our lives from scratch.

Harni Zelenewycz was born on a day when German troops were advancing on Leningrad. He was born, it seemed to his mother, by the grace of God and the favour of women, two months premature, a greasy blind mole and useless to the world. An absurd thing struggling for life amid the smell of new decay and old war, though there was no lime mulch to spare the sensibilities. 'Spare the child,' its mother screamed in labour. 'God give me one last thing in which to have faith!'

And here I am.

As a grown man in the city I know now that her praying thus to her God was like praying to an empty car park. But it held her together if nothing else, and unto her a child was born. A boy. He was born raw and bloody and with voices in his head in the back of a rattling truck too anxious in its haste to stop. The blood was mopped up by a toothless woman with a bright green ribbon in the straw that passed for hair on her head, but the voices remained.

At the age of two he was smuggled onto a contraband cargo ship bound for Alicante as it sailed west out of Salonica. Harni Zelenewycz was stowed in the bow by his mother, wrapped in a swaddling cloth of ship's linen.

I was finally christened four months later by a Polish army priest in a sturdy saxon city. Sanctuary.

It was VE Day. On the way home, giddy mothers threw me skywards in the street.

Eventually I grew old enough to tell my mother about the voices in my head. She said only, 'I think we should change your name now we are in England.' How else, she was thinking, was I going to make it to City Hall and mend this city which had welcomed us? A new start, she called it more than once.

At the mill they could not pronounce the name of my father, who had joined us in 1947, having collected a smattering of English from time he had spent with Allied troops in Central Europe. She asked me to think of names I might like.

My parents were still weathering the strictures of the Aliens Act whilst the voices in the head of Harni Zelenewycz persisted. My father had to report to the police station each time we left the city for a day, going maybe to the seaside or to the psychiatrist to find a cure for the voices in my head. 'This is England,' the police sergeant told him each time my father asked him why he needed to sign his way out of the city.

I told the priest about the voices in my head at my First Confession. Father Keam asked me what the voices said, so I told him. He said it was the angels trying to speak to me. I remember I could smell the whisky vapours spilling from his hot mouth. He never smiled and I remember that I thought he was the Devil. He said I spoke English like a real English boy. My mother asked me whether I'd decided on a new surname to write on the blank white wall of our new lives.

After my father joined us, he spent a lot of time in the shed at the end of our yard on Beaker Street when he wasn't out at work.

All the new arrivals went onto Beaker Street. We were outsiders, clustered together against the strangeness of the English way of things. 'Do you eat with a knife and fork?' they asked my father at the mill.

In the shed, he carved from wood with the steel-tipped chisels he had brought back with him from the war. I told my father about the voices in my head. He was carving a statue of Our Lady of Kocjelska from blackened beech. When I told him about the voices sounding in my head my father said, 'Me too.'

I made it to City Hall. I had been quick and keen at school. Good at maths, better at English. And a fleet-of-foot right winger on the football field, a Tom Finney who would one day play for England. There was little of Poland left in me now.

I ran and gasped around the playground with the other boys, chasing the marble or the tin can which in our febrile heads was a polished leather football. Darting like fish between girls playing more sombre, private games. It seems to me now that they were teaching themselves how to be women and we were teaching ourselves how to take the applause of other men in some electrified football stadium as we volleyed in the winner like we practised volleying marbles through the necks of milk bottles.

My mother had taken me to the city's voluntary-run

Polish Saturday School but my mind was ill-suited to languages, even to my parents' native tongue. Sunday Mass in Polish in the small chapel they had had converted was even more impenetrable. Two stained-glass windows looked down on the chapel altar, funded by the Beaker Street Poles. On the left was Our Lady of Kocjelska whose talismanic statue was carried by the Polish Second Brigade at Tobruk and at Normandy. On the right was Father Maximilian Kolbe, the priest who had bartered with the Germans to take him instead of others in the next batch of human meat to be butchered at Auschwitz or some such place.

The worship unsettled me, it was true to say. So did my mother's casual acceptance of risen saviours and weeping statues. My thoughts were easier when I could build them like blocks. Cause and effect. Languages were like fish slipping through my clumsy fingers.

Tom Finney came to play in the city and the young Harry Angel was passed over the heads of the crowd to the children's benches at the front down by the pitch and there he cheered with saxon lust as the Preston winger flew down the touchline. And my electric heart rippled in delirium and my cold feet stamped with the crowd as their shoes smacked the concrete steps of the terraces in an army roar of noise.

And oh to be in England now that the war was won and dreams of a town fit for heroes smoothed and clouded across the land.

Armed with my matriculation, I graduated with my

friend Coleman Seer to the City Technical College, destined it seemed to follow my father, the atheist, into textiles. But the mills were no longer the power they had been up to and just after the war. Cotton was no longer the life force of the city. Even then it was believed by some people that this was no accident, that the city's decline was so humdrum and remorseless that it had to have been plotted. It had a certain architecture – you know? The architects themselves were said to hang around Beaker Street and smirk but to be fair I never heard or saw much. What that means it's hard to say. I was young. I saw the city's recessionary fever as a drawing of breath before the onward march.

Once, the city had hummed to the workings of a hundred mills in every quarter. Half the dhootie cloth for India had sailed down our canal. A thousand crashing looms in every factory, the singing of *The Messiah* above the crash and clatter of the shuttles. It was a city at the centre of the Victorian world, but those days had gone and much of the cotton manufacture with it.

So they were easily swayed when I came home with news of vacancies at City Hall. My mother knew, had an instinct, that here was the new centre of things as the city was being shaped for the future.

In Berlin, they were bricking the city in half, but in the city of Harry Angel there was much talk of a new start, of building for the future, of not looking back.

When the letter finally came giving me a chance to leave the mill, offering me a job as a clerical assistant with prospects if I worked hard, my mother slipped out to St

26

Mary's and lit the candle she had promised to, to mark my finding my way in the world and said a small prayer in Polish to some saint she cherished.

Somewhere in all of this, the voices in my head stopped. They had been sometimes strident and sometimes soft. Women's voices around me. Insistent. Aching. Like it was my fault or something.

What they were saying I could not know. They used words that hovered out of reach. Sometimes they pleaded, other times they were hard and scolding. Mostly they seemed to sing of how it was, like they could have plucked any old set of words from a Woolworth pad.

The voices had unnerved me in the same way that my mother's devotions unnerved me. Touching a well that was deeper than me. All I could hear were the returning echoes. I had learned to ignore them. I thought of myself as deceived by the range and the perspective of these echoes. Then one day, as with all childhood preoccupations, they were gone and Harry Angel was free to enter a new world where progress could be written and history concluded on clean white walls, a world of city renovation and housing revenue accounts and elevators.

9

My boss at City Hall was Vernon Smitts. Poor Vernon Smitts. He was forty-one when I started there fresh from the Technical College and a short stay in Galbraith's mill. He seemed old to me, and wise. Now he would be seven years my junior and he would seem to me to be lacking and doleful.

As a boy, Vernon Smitts, too, had dreamed of being a footballer. A midfield artist controlling the play with an elegant passing game. His idol in the Twenties had been Syd Puddefoot. When Syd Puddefoot came to the city with the Blackburn Rovers team which would go on to win the FA Cup the following year in 1928, Vernon Smitts was passed over the heads of the crowd to the children's benches down at the bottom by the pitch and cheered as Puddefoot rallied the midfield for Blackburn.

For Vernon Smitts, football was always to be his salvation, his victory. One day he would mount a subway tram and leave the city for a richer seam of life and its living. I think maybe he entrusted his soul to this pledge. I think maybe he believed this like he believed the sun would rise in the morning. He would make something of his life in this way. How else? And people's hearts would leap like salmon at the sight of him as he, too, dominated the midfield play like Syd Puddefoot.

Oh yes, Vernon Smitts dreamed fiercely of playing professional football. He came close, two trials and a short apprenticeship that disappointed unexpectedly. Close, but what good is close, and he was consigned to pass his days away from the applause of the crowds, at City Hall. Wondering who had cursed him. Listening to the subway trams like they were messengers from another promised world, crying shuckety puck, shuckety puck.

Even though Vernon Smitts had been turned down four times for promotion, I sought to learn everything I could from this man. Out of rejection and rebuff he had come to fashion his own City Hall wisdoms, and these he was happy to pass on to me. For my part, I was a good listener and he seemed to appreciate this. We were a good team. In me he found an audience. Sure, I was no stamping crowd with electric hearts but I was, you might say, better than nothing.

In fact I continued to take in his every pronouncement on the foibles of city government until one day in 1964.

Heat is a stranger to the city. People overdress. There is no air conditioning in the basement offices where I am based with Vernon Smitts. This is a damp and windy city, unaccustomed to the stony stagnant air that clings to people's throats in this summer of 1964.

The pavements bake. Subway lines have buckled. It is airless in the basement where we municipal housing clerks wheeze and grind through interviews with tenants complaining of sewage overflows or window rot or rats in the cistern. Vernon Smitts, the supervisor, is two clerks down. One has bronchitis, the other is skiving off – gone fishing on the reservoir up in the hills. Smitts knows this.

In the basement it is ninety-four degrees. The animal that is the restless queue of people stinks with sweat. One scraggy woman with heavy shopping and a sleeveless sackcloth dress is evading the queue and making a beeline for Vernon Smitts at his desk. He is not attending to members of the public.

His desk is set back and he is filling in the week's overtime and sickness forms for his depleted team of clerks. She stands there, wanting him to raise his head before she speaks. She waits, unhurried, knowing that she has him cornered. He looks up. She opens her mouth to speak, hair blackened at the angry roots.

'Look,' Vernon Smitts says. He has had enough. She is the third queue jumper that afternoon. He looks her in the eye.

'You might think,' he says, 'that you deserve special treatment for being scrawnier and uglier than the rest of that lot, but I'm in charge of this hellhole and I'm telling you to get to the back of the queue.'

The woman opens her mouth to speak again but seems to think better of it. She picks up her groceries and turns away. She leaves the building, but Vernon Smitts and I don't see that. Our heads are back down at our desks filling in our respective forms in the baking heat of the afternoon.

At closing time she returns.

It is ten past five. Vernon Smitts is handing over his overtime and sickness forms to the Head of Section. Several other junior officers are in the room packing up for the day. I am busy behind the screens filing the day's complaints now that we are closed to the public. She still carries her shopping. One or two heads turn round to see who has come down to the basement office at such a late hour in the day.

The woman says, 'Out. Everyone.'

Vernon Smitts looks across to the Head of Section who is bundling up his files and leaving the room. The others follow.

'Not you,' the woman says to Vernon Smitts.

The woman is Councillor Nan Lintock, Chairman of Finance and City Resources, Member of the Municipal Housing Committee, Deputy Leader of the City Council. She has said of the Leader of the City Council, the venerable George Steen, 'That heap of pisspot shit couldn't fart and suck sweets at the same time or he'd choke to death.'

She speaks quietly to Vernon Smitts. She says that she has just formulated a new Council policy. She says that from now on, whenever she enters a room containing the unfortunate Mr Smitts, he is to get up silently and leave the said room. At once. And not return until she has departed.

She asks if this is clear.

She says that he might think he deserves special treatment for being stupider and slimier than the rest in here,

31

but that she's in charge of this hellhole of a city give or take a sixpence or two and she was telling him that he'd be down at the Social Security the first day he wasn't out of a room and the door shut behind him before she'd parked her bum.

For the next five years, until Vernon Smitts goes over the barrier and collides with an oncoming Ford Popular on the A6, he gathers up his things each time Councillor Nan Lintock enters a room, stands up, and leaves the room for the duration. It will happen on average about three times a week. There are to be a lot of exits and entrances.

I learned a valuable lesson that day.

After that, poor Vernon Smitts kind of drifted sideways at City Hall, first into Supplies, later into Security and Cleaning, and I got his job.

Lucky, eh.

When they read Vernon Smitts's will after he failed to avoid the Ford Popular on the A6, they discovered that he had left his pocket watch to me. On the back was an engraving. He must have had it ready, unless he'd had a premonition about death. It said, 'To Harry Angel, The Only Real Friend I Ever Had'. I never knew this.

What lesson did I learn?

Some years later there was a minor scandal in the city. The great names of pre-war city politics had begun to disappear. Jack 'Torpedo' Tomlinson, and Nan Lintock, and

George Steen, whose Ford Popular was tragically hit in a head-on collision on the A6 with a car driven by city employee Vernon Smitts. All gone from the fray.

In their place rose a new breed of City Councillor. Men like Nan Lintock's son, Corwen, still young and green as salad, but keen to make an impact on the life and times of the city.

Corwen Lintock's first major civic role was to be as a junior member of the Mayor's Office and Twin Towns Sub-Committee, travelling to Oostenbruik in northern Bavaria to attend a twin-town reception.

There was to be much conjecture about the incident in question. There were primarily only German guests left in the banqueting hall when the alleged slanders and defamations took place.

The German version of these events suggested that the three English Councillors still remaining at the reception continued to drink copious amounts of lager. The youngest of them, a Mr Corwen Lintock, began to make certain remarks to the remaining German contingent. He then stood on the table, they said, and began goose-stepping up and down and offering Nazi salutes to the host party, making derogatory remarks about German mothers and German sons.

There was speculation in the city that Corwen Lintock's promising career as a City Councillor was to be a short-lived one.

But when the official English report into the incident was revealed to the Sub-Committee, it made clear that the

English version of events was far less dramatic, accusing Councillor Corwen Lintock of nothing more than youthful high spirits.

The one soon-to-be-promoted City Council official still present at that late hour in the Oostenbruik banqueting hall confirmed this version of events. No slanders had been uttered. No goose-steps were seen. No damage to the city's reputation could possibly be inferred from the incident.

Harry Angel, the official in question, had signed the statement which was duly attached to the Sub-Committee report.

Someone is knocking at the door.

When they pulled Vernon Smitts from the wreckage of his car his only words to the ambulance crew were 'Tell me if Nan Lintock comes in.'

Fitsimmons's head appears round the door. Drucker is due to speak.

10

We sit as wise men high above the city. From here we can see the moors lapping the edge of town all around us, marking out the clean edges of our authority. The start of the barbarian other. From here we give shape to the skyscraper dreams of men like the much troubled Leader of the City Council. Much troubled because the way he's started to turn the city's fortunes round was bound to attract enemies. Much troubled because he is about to begin fending off prosecution for conspiracy and fraud and some such sorry things.

It will pass.

There are three apologies, one illness and a traffic accident. This cuts the numbers at the meeting to nine including Drucker as the Director. Liam Fitsimmons and I are also present. Fitsimmons is a new boy rising. Bright as a button. Sharp edged. Red hair. Slim ochre beard, not knitted but scraped across the 'V' of his jaw.

This city, like others, breeds two sorts of officials. Those, like Drucker, like Fitsimmons will no doubt become, who will leave no trace in the sand. Others, who see the clean edges of town as a magical sea which threatens to dash all rafts of ambition on the shores of other foreign things; local men who never dared, with histories and with caged resentments burning. They will leave this place through the oak doors of the chapel planted on the cemetery hill.

We meet like this each week under Drucker's stewardship to see what's worrying the city. See how best we can progress.

What's worrying the city? Some small explosions; impeachment threatening the Council Leader; someone mutilating animals one by one at the zoo. This city is not at ease with itself.

Sat next to Drucker is Daulman, his number two in the Department. The Department is Corporate and Community Affairs, a result of the most recent authority-wide restructuring. I work for Daulman. Daulman with the peasant grin and the uncurious eyes. I am one of his little team. He shades us carefully from Drucker who after five years here remains an outsider. Daulman didn't get the job. He figures lack of dress sense.

Across from us sit Drucker's men marshalled by Fitsimmons. Stankill, the workhorse, cratered complexion, waxy hair, juggles papers on his lap and smokes, waiting for Drucker to begin the meeting. He is picking his teeth with the clean white fingers of an accountant. He has the hands of an accountant. Me, I'm with Daulman. Fitsimmons would say, has said, that Daulman has the brains of a pisspot. Who knows what Stankill thinks. Where he comes from each morning. Whether his heart beats blood.

There are others around the room. You know how it is. Faces. Names. Writers all of progress on the blank white city walls. Then we go home and watch TV and so on.

And so on.

I find myself fingering the pocket watch, the one left to me in the will of Vernon Smitts, the one with the inscription on the back. Then Drucker cu-calls us to order.

Drucker has a small gavel, a present from his wife I believe. The use of it causes Fitsimmons to smile broadly. Drucker hits the wooden platter twice, Bfff Bfff, with a child's intense satisfaction.

Drucker calls these meetings of his 'top twelve' departmental officials once a week. It is part of the action-cen-
tred approach which won him favour at his interview. He
listens with his practised patrician air. His staff talk. Silence
is the safest of all states for a city official wishing to move
forward lightly on the shifting sands of government.

I have calculated that of Drucker's top team of twelve, I
am ninth in line for succession if Drucker hits a bus. This
is assuming there are no external candidates.

In the general scheme of things, I tend to have dealings only
with those officials ranking three up and three down from me.
That's how the system makes use of each of the different
gradings of people. Stankill, who has studied the theorems of
F. W. Taylor and the Scientific School of Management, has
planned it thus for Drucker who is more of a PR man himself.

Stankill has the application of a stakhanovite.

Daulman would say, has said, that Stankill is a pisspot full
of college-boy theories.

The truth is that Stankill is unsound. Sure, Daulman has
conceded, Stankill has plenty of credentials. Plenty of graft.
Just don't turn your back on him in the bathroom.

You think maybe that's why Stankill carries his money
round in his socks?

I will confess to a certain surprise when Drucker asked
specially for me to accompany him to Sam Pound's resurrection this morning, though you will recall that in doing

this he was under the impression that I personally was familiar with the mechanics of dredging every body we have ever dug from the ground. Which I am not. Heck, I only sign the papers.

Until this morning I swear Drucker has only ever said three words to me directly. They are the same three words he uses each time we pass in a corridor or are trapped together for the duration of an elevator ride. On such occasions Drucker will suck his pipe and say, 'How goes it?'

He has never waited for the answer.

Sometimes I have felt that Drucker lies in wait around corners deliberately waiting for me so that he can practise his favourite greeting on me.

'How goes it?'

Maybe I'm wrong.

In Stankill's scheme of things, memos zoom in and out of my sphere like lift floors in an elevator shaft. Some I file, some I sign and pass on, some I use as the basis of reports which I then submit to the offices of Daulman. My office is full of copies of such reports.

My office used to be the sixth-floor storeroom. There seemed nowhere else to put me. When the time and motion man came to do his study of the sixth floor, he mistook the door to my office as an entrance to the elevator shaft. When he finally submitted his report to Drucker, it recommended that everyone's space below the level of Deputy, omitting the name Harry Angel from the list, should be amalgamated into an open plan office.

On the strength of this implied importance of my space and need for privacy I was promoted by Daulman. Thus did I earn the right by virtue of my new grade to attend Drucker's weekly meetings and sit amongst my senior colleagues in Corporate and Community Affairs, measuring the city's progress towards a comfortable full stop in the story of things. Towards a happy ending.

In my new post I have continued to produce reports and consultation documents sketching out the future for that small piece of city for which I am deemed responsible. I never learn how these are received, or whether they are adopted.

Stankill thinks it demotivational to respond to undermanagers on matters of policy analysis. Daulman dislikes memos and avoids reading them whenever possible. Drucker says only, 'How goes it?' when I pass him in a corridor or ride with him in a lift.

No-one says 'Well done, boy,' or 'That last one was way off beam, Angel.' This doesn't worry me, though. When it comes to contact from above I am a firm believer in the motto 'No News Is Good News'. This was the first piece of advice ever given to me by poor Vernon Smitts and I have treasured it like a jewel ever since.

Despite my new-found rapport with Drucker, I have thought it wise to take up my usual position at the bottom of the table nearest to the door and the coffee percolator. I am right to do so. This afternoon, Drucker will pass me in a fourth-floor corridor. He will say, 'How goes it?'

He will not wait for the answer.

I I

Around the table, officials make brief sketch notes. At least that's the conclusion Drucker probably reaches. I never asked. Fitsimmons draws cartoon faces on his pad and writes down verbal goofs from the gathered officials. I find myself doodling, too, usually unconnected shapes, saucers and ovals in rows and the like. It helps me to concentrate.

Daulman doesn't doodle. Fitsimmons says this is because Daulman can't write. This is funny but not true. When Daulman writes, he presses his tongue into his lower lip and clamps his hand over the paper like a schoolboy being examined. Daulman says of himself that he is of the old school, though no-one knows what this means. During the week he can be seen, has been seen by Fitsimmons, writing down words and phrases that catch his ear. Ready for meetings such as these. Ready for smooth men coming up from the rear like the ochre-bearded Liam Fitsimmons.

About Daulman, Fitsimmons is clear:

'Once a boilerman, always a boilerman.'

Daulman has worked his way up from Boiler Foreman at one of the City Gyms. Fitsimmons has not. Fitsimmons is one of Drucker's boys. Come in from the outside and not scared of witches and things.

Fitsimmons has a sharp mind and a clever wit. He is smarter than everyone else in the room. Smarter than me with my carefully constructed reports and good grammar. Smarter than Stankill who, when he runs to catch the lift, jangles from his cotton socks up. Smarter than everyone.

Everyone else knows this except for Daulman. But then, Fitsimmons would say, Daulman is the kind of man who wouldn't know a nuance if it hit him in the face. For his part Daulman thinks the new boy is stupid.

Fitsimmons has been known to encourage Daulman to believe that he is stupid, because he finds this entertaining. Daulman says dumb things. Boilerman things. There has been talk around the table of the troubles last night in the east quarter. Our Department is deemed responsible. Another diversion on the road to the promised land. Daulman had wondered whether last night was the horse that broke the camel's back. There was a pause around the table. The only one moving was Fitsimmons who was writing, frantically, like his life depended upon it.

Fitsimmons never spoke a sentence in his life without it sounding like he'd practised it in the bathroom until it ran on wheels.

12

Drucker is offering a short introduction to the Sam Pound issue for us. Sam Pound who, it's said, had stumbled on a plot to bankrupt his employers Sentex Construction, smear its good name and bring it down. Sam Pound who, it's said, was so paranoid at the end that he carried three sealed envelopes around with him. Naming names. Setting out who was to blame. Now he's dead. Drucker is saying that it's hoped to have the autopsy findings within a couple of weeks. Is explaining that we need to keep a lid on things until then. He means to keep a lid on the east quarter. He means the kurs.

There is another view. Daulman spells it out, slowly for people like Fitsimmons. That some said of Sam Pound that he'd had it coming.

Drucker doesn't elaborate on the debate. Moves on to this morning's dawn events. Departure from the vigilance of vague sentiment is ever brief. It always is.

Myself, I am reaching hesitantly for the report I have prepared on the Sam Pound exhumation, waiting for Drucker to call on me. He looks down to the end of the table. He has said he wanted a report from me. He told me this morning up on the hill to polish it up. My heart bangs blood a little faster. My fingers edge out for the plastic of the folder. But Drucker runs on, calls for more coffee, apologises mildly to 'our colleague with the rolled collar at the end of the table'. Fitsimmons looks across at me, grins, thinks it's funny.

What the hell.

What the hell, I'm only doing my best. Fuck Fitsimmons. My best.

By now Drucker thinks I'm from Supplies. I push back my neatly scripted report with its tidy grammar. Feel at the collar rolled round like rope at my neck. It was a much revised report, not one of my best. But mine. My own singular testament of words wrenched from a silent white page. Mine.

One more shelf-filling affirmation of my optimism in the city. One more small caged resentment burning. I close my eyes and I can see Drucker fleeing naked from the smoking cage of an elevator shaft.

The only person Fitsimmons dislikes more than Daulman is Drucker though this is a big secret since Drucker as Director believes that the new-boy-rising-fast Fitsimmons is batting on his side. Drucker sees him as his protégé. Ha ha. Fitsimmons dislikes him because he doesn't know if Drucker is as dim as he seems to be. Fitsimmons cannot see for sure past the cufflinked exterior. Is there a wheeler-dealer behind the facade lulling us into revealing our sometimes treacherous hands, fooling us all with this surface performance?

Maybe, maybe. The thought eats at him. I know because Fitsimmons confides in me. I'm a good listener.

Fitsimmons early in the game has a good hand but is playing it carefully. The rule is never to show your hand. Like never confessing your ambitions. To ask a man about his ambitions is like asking an inmate about his sentence.

Fitsimmons has told me what he knows, but then I'm no threat. I don't score highly in the scheme of things. I figure he's biding his time. He's an ambitious man. Wants to get on. Get up. To a position where he can shape things. Earn money. Make history.

Everyone wants to make history, Fitsimmons says. You, too, Harry Angel, he alleges. I shrug when he says this. I want to tell him I am history. I carry it with me, inside me. It sometimes talked to me in sweet whispers. In women's voices in my head.

Sometimes I think maybe that's why I never moved on from here. The only reason I'd surely have to move on would be to make history somewhere else. Maybe that's why, even as an outsider, I've become beached here on this tide of green moors. I don't tell him this. I listen. Good listener, you see.

Fitsimmons knows that Drucker's wife is having an affair.

This is useful currency.

With a lesbian nursing assistant. So far, I'm the only one he's told. He is cautious of Drucker's camouflage. He can't risk telling someone who turns out to be one of Drucker's dupes.

Round here this kind of information is nursed like contraband.

The Leader's worried that Sam Pound's contraband was buried with him. It's said it was a kur or two from the east quarter who were responsible for the death of Sentex Construction man Sam Pound. What the Leader wouldn't give for the recovery of old Sam's notes carried in those three sealed envelopes so he could ensure that truth would out. Hey ho.

As a smokescreen, bad people have spread the story that Corwen Lintock, the City Leader himself, has been instrumental in Sam Pound's death, though why this would be remains a mystery. In fact, as if to give lie to these notions, it is the Leader himself who has intervened to determine the truth of the matter and to dig up the body of Sam Pound. The good name of the city, the Leader has said, is being jeopardised by a troublesome and unrepresentative section of the community.

The truth must out. Like a white rabbit from a tall black hat.

Ta-raah!

'Harry Angel meets with them every month out there, don't you? What would you do with them?' They mean the kurs. There are cityfolk and there are kurs. Somewhere in the mind's eye of each citizen is a line, a fine-edged thing. Within it is the us. Beyond it are the others. I figure it's human nature.

'Do they eat out there yet with knives and forks, Angel?'

I smile at the joke.

Drucker smiles his own reflex smile on smooth lips. He

likes party talk. He says it oils the wheels. Never trust a man who smiles too much. One minute later, though, he's finding it hard to smile when the City Council Leader walks unannounced into the room.

13

Before Wiesel, no-one settled free of choice across the river on the land rising to the moors. Men with farming land this way too often had cows giving soured milk, had cows which died mad where no farrier could fix upon the disease which afflicted them; had horses bewitched out of stables after the doors had been safely locked. A wizard was once slain out here. A demoniac born out of wedlock whose fits startled even the clergy was banished to a barn in these parts to beg alms from travellers on the top road. A shepherd who fell down some mine of Wiesel's was discovered four days later having climbed out into sunlight half a furlong further down the hill, delirious, reciting 'I love God, the Lord God, the Hour, Christ, let it be done, let it be done,' the charm gripped in his hand written in cypher with the words *Agla en Tetragrammaton* on the back unable to be prised from his grasp for several hours.

George Wiesel was a German engineer who came to mine for copper and lead in 1654 in the hills to the east of the town. German mining engineering was more advanced than its British counterpart and Wiesel was not alone in coming to England. There were Germans and Scandinavians mining in Cumberland and in the Peaks.

Wiesel's smelting operation at the pitside painted lights on the hills. It made people down below uneasy. It was risking the wrath of the hill witches – setting up camp and living like some pack of kurs under the hills. It was said these men killed sheep for their open-air feasts when they sang songs and got drunk because they missed home. Townsmen saw little of Wiesel's men except when they came down into the town for supplies or to buy prostitutes or to bring their smelted ore through on pack horses. There were occasional feuds between Wiesel's men and locals, fights, and just one time there was a murder. The English-speaking Wiesel was himself happy to wander about the town and drink in the taverns across the river, though he had little but contempt for the townsfolk's concerns about witches.

14

The Council Leader comes to us fresh from court.

Today, the Leader has finally been charged by the magistrate. This day has been a long day coming.

On the steps of the City Courthouse the Leader has given a statement to the hurrying core of pressmen swilling around him. He knows they have smelled blood. His. Emerging from the courthouse building amongst a circle of advisors and legal people in dull suits the Leader has a six-hour shadow of stubble. He has been reprimanded on bail for charges worth twenty years if ever the evidence of the prosecution sticks. If ever the citizens of the jury find him guilty. His back is against the wall and he must hope that his team can build a case to rebut the charges because the Leader knows how closely the city's fortunes are allied to his own, and he wants nothing more than to finish saving this city.

The press are distant and professional and safely routine in their motions around him. He is alert. He has that exhilarated odour of adrenalin upon him.

Like all powerful men, the adrenalin holds him statue-still as he pauses on the steps to speak. Someone has calculated beforehand the optimum position from which to speak in manipulating the backdrop of columns and roofs. No bobbing and weaving. Just a steady flow of energy searing from snake eyes.

The Leader has figured this.

The best form of defence is attack.

He has said this deep into the soul of the whirring cameras:

'Citizens.

'I stand here charged on sixteen counts of extortion, fraud and conspiracy. And I tell you this. If I go down, all the dark forces raged against this city will be singing and dancing in the streets. Think about that.'

He takes a short strong breath.

'I tell you this. If I go down, this city of ours and everything that rides on it in this momentous year will be blown away like dust. Gone! There are people out there, believe me, who want that to happen.'

Wow! That's some assessment. To the Leader, these charges levied against him are the final carefully placed pieces in a jigsaw he himself has identified. Conspiracy, the jigsaw seems to spell.

'I prayed to Jesus, citizens. And he said to me: Have faith in the good men of your city. It will all be alright. It will all be alright. You write that down good and proper in those notebooks of yours, ladies and gentlemen.'

The pressmen glance up as if to say, 'We're writing, we're writing.'

'There are those in this city who would see me fall. But let me say this to every man here: He who is against me is

49

against this city. I ask every man to nail his colours to the mast because I know that I will be acquitted and the city will be saved. This is what Jesus has told me. Thank you.'

And with that, and a smile of aching warmth, he moves on down the steps. Hurried whispers whip amongst his advisors like wind-maddened leaves, this way and that, in the general direction of City Hall.

Let me take a moment to say something about City Housing policy.

As someone who knew the Basement Municipal Housing Offices well for a good while, I was at the cutting edge of things.

It was never down in writing, you understand. Putting all the bad eggs in one basket, I mean. One always had to be wary of the distant City Commissioners. Men who arrive on subway trams to keep an eye on things. To see that all's fair in love and war. A job for the rising Drucker one of these days, wouldn't you say?

It just came as a kind of instinct for us. A nod from the man one rank up from you. Have you ever seen those chains of nodding ducks at the mouths of harbours generating electricity?

One duck stops nodding and all the lights go out.

You see a strange name, recognise a renegade family, spot an odd address, a blood group. And you make connections. The east quarter, you maybe think. Kurs, you maybe think.

There was nothing in it, I promise you, or we'd have been

pulled up for it. Heck, there were enough people standing over us. It's not like we were mavericks or anything. Let me make it clear that down here it's team games all the way.

Quack quack.

There is a raggedy-edged silence as the remains of Drucker's easy words float away and evaporate like thin smoke.

The Leader walks slowly into the room, keeping a distance from Drucker's oak meeting table around which we are gathered.

The Leader is Councillor Corwen Lintock. Older now, of course, than when I first saw him on the public stage on a twinning visit to Oostenbruik, northern Bavaria. Solidly in his forties. Less green. Less prone to goose-stepping. Less damaged by cholesterol these days. But with a handsome cut to his face. Well chiselled. A face set out with purpose and to effect. Good on TV. A face you could trust, would buy washing powder from. But worried none the less. Oh yes, worried.

Lintock smiles an acknowledgement. He smiles beautifully. His face has stilled after this morning. Settled back to the calm of authority. But.

Never trust a man who smiles too much. I said that already.

Drucker smiles also.

A fool's paradise.

You can read the panic. It is, of course, Drucker's instinct to smile, but I can see from even my poor vantage point at the foot of the table the first smear of damp on the forehead of my Director.

Something is clearly wrong or Lintock would not be here, not have personally left his Fourteenth-Floor Leader's Suite. You can sandpaper the edges of the space between Drucker and the Leader.

For the rest of us on the sidelines, there is a breathless stumbling into silences. A stopping of things. Dead. Suddenly hands and necks and pricking chests that we were unaware of until a moment ago are real and heavy in the way they pin us weighed to the chairs. A pause that is sexual in its anticipation. That boiling and turning of the loins as Lintock circles us like we were sitting ducks. Quack quack again.

We are excluded from the central confrontation but not from the situation. We hold in our thickening skins, waiting for the moment's consummation.

Tick, tick, tick.

Daulman clinks his cup and saucer.

Once a boilerman.

Lintock says, 'Ah, coffee. Very civilised.' He makes no attempt to sit down, moving slowly still around the outside of the room. Moving through the room's heavy air. Corwen Lintock is always on his guard against you. Always seemingly ready to pick a fight. A political instinct? Perhaps.

Perhaps.

'Will you take some cu–cuo-coffee with us, Cu-Councillor?' It is Drucker, the conciliator.

Lintock makes no response.

Lintock has one overriding ambition. To take the salute of the good city people on the balcony of City Hall whilst the loudspeakers across the square play 'Happy Days Are Here Again'.

It was worse before Corwen Lintock found Jesus Christ to be his lord and saviour, believe me.

'I need answers, Drucker,' he says. A simple request.

Timing can be everything. Drucker, eager to please, tips headlong into the silence like a Boxing Day swimmer. He says, giddily, that on his instigation his team are asking urgent questions of last night, of the east quarter, of the city. Given the coming election, Drucker is assuring him that answers will inevitably fu-fu-follow.

Answers, answers.

So often it comes down to answers.

15

After the triple bypass operation on his heart, Corwen Lintock had needed answers. He'd had the heart attack in the City Park. It was after dark. His wife, who was with him, was howling like a dog at the time.

After the triple bypass, Corwen Lintock found Jesus in a Gideon Bible left by his bedside. In the hospital.

Jesus is everywhere, Corwen Lintock has concluded. Loving everyone. Loving Corwen Lintock best of all. It was a good message to hear. He cut his hair short to the bony scalp and gave up dairy products. He avoided uttering profanities whenever possible. And he offered prayers to Jesus every night. Jesus had chosen him to save the city.

Corwen Lintock diversified his business interests. He knew that he could help to save the city by investing in it. He bought derelict canalside properties in the knowledge that development grants in the City Hall pipeline might soon allow them to prosper in service to the city.

He bought old mills, wharfs and the like, with a view to developing the city's image in accordance with the will of Jesus who liked him best.

He rescued the ailing community business over in the east quarter which had offered employment to certain local lads to patrol the streets in shifts but which had got out of control; he called it Sentex Security and bought up neat uniforms and got the thing all registered with Aratakis, Police Authority Chairman.

He bought the down-at-heel city football club. The one for which his great hero of the past, the majestic Eddie Melon, had once starred. He said if the city's pride was to be restored, if this city was to be put back on the map again (he used that very phrase), then they needed a football club back in the top flight of which they could be proud also.

At the first home match after Corwen Lintock had bought them out as the 51 per cent majority shareholder, he took to the pitch like some Roman Emperor of old to take the salute of the crowd. The loudspeaker played 'Happy Days Are Here Again'.

There was more. But first.

He stops at Drucker's desk. The desk is neat and precise. Fussily so. Like the man. Something catches Lintock's eye and he picks it up. A small stand holding a presentation paper knife.

'Practical,' he says.

Drucker acknowledges him.

'A present? From your wife perhaps?'

'Yu-yes.'

'Is that her?' Lintock is pointing to a gilt-framed photograph of a tanned woman in her early forties to one side of the desk. A steady gaze. A settled kind of style to her.

'Yu-yes, that's her.'

Smile, smile, is what our man Drucker thinks.

Lintock flicks at the frame of the photograph with the tip of the paper knife. The frame falls flat onto the desk.

Bfff!

Fitsimmons is smiling to himself. Has no need to share the joke. He knows that Drucker's wife is having it off even as we speak with her lesbian nursing assistant. Tuesdays and Thursdays ten till lunch.

Corwen Lintock says, 'Fuck the questions.' He winces at the obscenity, then continues. 'I need to win this election. For the people's sake. You get my drift.' Some days he can look cursed. Bewitched. His lawyers have argued that the case is nothing but a smear, a frame-up so that Lintock can be impeached from his post and denied the chance to put his case to the people. In court his lawyers have provided a litany of Corwen Lintock's contributions to the city in politics and in business. Even the scheme that Dooley Pound's on got a mention – the ball and socket joints, the orphans. I hear the judge made notes.

Drucker nods, making hurried 'yes' noises. Soothing noises. He gets the drift. A master at work. In the back of his mind is a voice telling him that before too long he will be moving on from this place, leaving no trace in the sand. Smiling still.

'I keep telling you, Drucker, I want a strategy. For dealing with these people once the autopsy on that clown shows that they were responsible. Instead I get pretty little reports like the one that landed on my desk yesterday. Twenty years I've put into this town and look at it. Thanks to arty-farty pillocks like you. And you're there greasing your pockets on salaries that hack lumps off my budgets. Earn them, damn you!'

He jabs the paper knife down hard at the desk. There is a crack of splitting glass as the frame breaks under the force of the knife.

Drucker is shallow breathing. Heating up like a faulty valve. Feeling his way from the blind hole he is in, and the instinct that has served him thus far cries 'Buy time, buy time.'

He drags air clean into his lungs, crisscrosses his neat and even fingers, steadies the rocking vessel. Pictures himself in some City Commissioner's chair, confirms to the Councillor that the team have been actively reviewing a number of practical possibilities, some of them this very morning. Ready to hit the decks running is a phrase he produces. Like a rabbit from a hat. Hey presto.

Lintock seems to like that. Hitting the decks running. Or maybe he's just tired. He looks tired these days. Tight under the eyes. There's the saving of the city, the pending election, the trial. Yesterday at the zoo a ring-tailed lemur got slashed.

I reckon Drucker cares for none of this. Drucker senses light above him slanting through the rubble of the encounter. One final push to the surface. Slapping down the windy stutters he says he is obviously disappointed that those in the Department who are responsible have let things come to this. Against his specific instructions. He feels disappointed about this, he feels he can confide to Corwen. And yes, take some share of the responsibility himself as the Director. See some need to intervene at this point personally in the mess.

Across the table, Daulman has long since stiffened. There have been no specific instructions from the Director. Just breezy congratulation and an oiling of the wheels amongst men in suits. Drucker is selling him out, selling all of us out to climb out of the shit he's in with the Leader.

Drucker's hand involuntarily brushes the hair back on his head.

Yes, his specific instructions.

His eyes stay clean away from my own turkey neck and trophy ears, from Stankill, from Daulman, whom he is offering up on the altar of retrenchment.

Tomorrow he will not even remember. He will pass faces in the lift and say 'How goes it?' and warm to his secretary's smile and whistle 'The Dambusters' March' and say that all we boys did weather the storm on that one, didn't we.

Ah me!

With this in mind, Drucker says, he would like to call an early meeting with the Leader and with Aratakis, Police Authority Chairman. A small Task Force, maybe, to focus on the apparent conspiracy seeking to undermine the city's confidence – an incendiary device down by the River Court Hotel, Corwen's impeachment, the zoo animals. The loop in his brain is running, 'Buying time, buying time.'

There will be no Task Force, of course. It is an emblem of the morning's panic. To blow away in the setting of the sun. Then he stops. Remembers the rule. Talking is dangerous. Exposing. Talking is for maniacal Councillors and expendable juniors. Lintock twists the knife and pulls it clear of the broken frame. He says fine. He says Thursday's just fine. Make it Thursday when the police report is in on last night's disturbances in the city.

To blow away like dust in the setting of the sun.

Am I mad? Sure, sure I'm mad.

I am kind of mad about it. You have to be. Next time we all meet like this, Drucker will laugh about it with us and say that we officials must all stick together. And we will think he is a bastard maybe but we know which side our bread is buttered on.

And then you think, well, what about me? Would I have done it to others, sell them downstream to the Leader if I had the well-being of a Department to think about? Maybe he thought it was right. You know. Useful.

And now the moment has gone and we have moved effortlessly into another. And in this other moment, just a touch along in this odd corridor of time and events in which we shuffle, Corwen Lintock is asking again. Less insistent. Sheepish. A peace offering, maybe. I doubt it. There is this something else he wishes to ask. He is asking for pukka berries.

For what?

Pukka berries. Small, sweet, red, growing on pot plant pukka bushes. Difficult to get hold of in this country, of course. Corwen Lintock wants a quarter pound of pukka berries if someone can lay their hands on some locally. If anyone can supply his office he will be grateful. He seems to have put behind him the violence of last night, of this morning.

He says he needs the pukka berries urgently.

In the looping reel of memory I'm busy making connections. I am winning the moment.

Daulman is asking what the hell are pukka berries?

And what of Harry Angel? I'm wondering if the lesbian nursing assistant who Fitsimmons knows is having it off with the Director's wife has a matching paper knife to Drucker's.

16

I drive out from the city in the afternoon dusk that is being drawn into night without an evening pause. A four o'clock dusk turns the skyline of roofs grainy. I'm on the ring road climbing gently. In the sky ahead of me, where the buildings don't reach, there are streaks and strokes of light, like someone's just painted them with a clumsy brush. Like Corwen Lintock's Jesus just painted them with a clumsy brush. At one time it was thought that Corwen Lintock's Jesus had stopped short of these hills, had somehow forgotten, abandoned them. It was a suspicion that long remained. It was recorded, for example, that the last wolf in England had lived in Cartmel Forest and had been shot on Humphrey Head on the northern shore of Morecambe. It was well documented, but eighteen years later three separate sightings of a lone wolf were made here on the St Mary Moors to the east of the city, sworn statements that testified this was a true English wolf.

The last wolf in England was not alone in inhabiting the high ground above the city. There were the dogs, mongrels, in packs on the moors, tamed once but thrown out when food was scarce or illness was afoot or witchcraft involving animals was feared. They could be heard from down in the town, howling to Old Nick, bartering for allegiance.

When this place was busy burning witches, before we got wise to stuff like that, any woman who didn't sink in the river on the ducking stool and thereby proved her skill in the art of witchcraft was called a kur and so she was burned tied to a stake of wood. A gaggle of such women, the Salmsbury Witches for example, the Pendle Witches, were called a kuri.

After we finished burning women for not drowning on the ducking stool and stopped hanging men for stealing meat and started to reform them instead, the City Assizes used a trick of branding the inner palms of plotters, of thieves, of criminals with a red hot poker. Ingenious. The branded mark was generally a single 'K' for Kur. When a man appeared before the court the judge would ask him to show a clean pair of hands. If the tissue of palm was already scarred then the inveterate wrongdoer would be sent off on the next prison ship out of Liverpool.

The name found itself exported and survives today in various forms. Prisoners with a 'K' branded into the base of their thumb used the expression themselves to describe the Maori Indians who hovered around the edge of the penal camps; in turn, the Maoris used it to describe the half-wild dogs which lived uneasily on the edge of their settlements and more often than not brought bad luck and stillborn children.

From the sanitarium most of the city is set out below. It was built in the early nineteenth century as a lunatic asylum. Crazy people are back here today. In between it has been a prison, a workhouse, a fever hospital, an infirmary. It was bought up by a benefactor who wanted a sanitarium to aid his own recovery and who was anxious to offer this same provision to others.

On the hills behind the sanitarium George Wiesel and his men scrabbled for their seams of copper, hacked and clawed at the earth and the townsfolk thought them crazy.

Wiesel lined his trenches with peat and bracken and then set them alight until the rocks glowed with the heat. On his signal, pitchers of water were thrown onto the rocks which would hiss and crack with fury. When the steam had died the men would rive out the rock with hammers and gavelocks.

To get at the seams well enough they dug shafts going down a thousand feet which they descended on rickety ladders. Sheep and dogs were sometimes lost down them. The biggest mine Wiesel called 'The Three Kings' (after Caspar, Melchior and Balthazar). They called the seams of metal they hit upon 'Gottesgab' – God's Gift, although whenever the locals found Wiesel drinking in the taverns down by the river and complained of losing sheep down his shafts which seemed to them to descend all the way to

Hell Wiesel said that it was the Devil indeed who was his partner and laughed all the way back to the hills.

The sanitarium is built of the same crumbling brick as the old quarters of the city. Blackstone polished leather brown by the wet winds that dries to cake in the short summer.

But inside, the high walls are cool and green.

The people in here now are crazy alright. They no longer live in the city. But here on the hill, in the sanitarium, they are safe enough. We don't burn witches any more.

The asylum had been built to keep the lunatics away from cityfolk. Now it keeps the city away from the residents of the sanitarium.

Progress.

Asylum means place of safety.

I am sat with my father by the big window overlooking the poplar-lined garden. Here and there is an occasional lime. The trees are just silken shapes now, dusted onto a blue-ink sky.

Bronislaw Angel has sought asylum here. He has lived in this place for two years. Amongst other things he struggles walking. If I were to describe him now in one word it would be 'undisturbed'. Despite everything. Perhaps because of it. Who knows.

My mother died six years ago. Like all deaths, the pain came from an ending that left things unsaid. There are always things unsaid, it's just that death renders them permanent. Living breathing silences turned to pillars of salt.

I come up to see him irregularly on this hill above the city's east side. Sometimes my conscience is pricked about my not seeing him enough. Sometimes I am just passing this way. I could do more, but no-one in the city seems to believe me when I tell them.

The nurses wear thick stockings and pumps, and blue cardigans over white aprons. They carry keys but only to the medicine cupboards and the outer doors that are locked tight at night against infiltrators and assassins, most of whom are imaginary. Some of the residents think people are out to get them.

These are crazy people, remember.

17

The nurses smile often. Sometimes at the residents. One, with hair that smells like cedarwood and apples, has been known to smile at me. Wowee, Harry Angel!

No-one minds that the residents here are crazy. Here they can be anything they like provided that they don't wreak violence, and provided they don't frighten the other residents and provided they don't go round trying to burn the sanitarium to the ground.

These are the three rules.

One man, with no known name, does little except make chuffa train noises.

Bronislaw Angel's only friend here, Stanley Kubrick, is crazy. Sometimes he thinks he is Anton Chekhov. Exiled from Moscow. From the centre of things. Like he thinks he should have wound up at the centre of the Universe and has found himself somewhere out by the Milky Way. And his real name is not Stanley Kubrick. No-one knows his real name.

Bronislaw Angel, my father, knows he is not Anton Chekhov, though sometimes he thinks he is General Sikorsky, and sometimes Maximilian Kolbe, and sometimes Brogdan Zelenewycz. All of these are, were, real people, which is something. I cling to the consolation that there are degress of craziness. What could I do if he believed himself to be a walnut or a colander?

Bronislaw Angel. Funny name.

One time, my father really did used to be Brogdan Zelenewycz. That much is true.

My father passes much of his time here playing five-card brag. He plays with his friend Stanley Kubrick and with the unreliable Aaron Wold. The fourth player had been Father Keam of course. Now dead. But still getting a hand laid down for him each round. As if it keeps alive a wish. Or a promise. What it would be to live without hope,

Stanley Kubrick has said to me about this smallest of foibles.

Aaron Wold is a former Hebridean milkman with a heavy beard and dandruff who had given up his milk round after a particularly public nervous breakdown. He is given to wandering for days but always returns eventually to the sanitarium. Like everyone else, Aaron Wold is free to come and go as he pleases provided he keeps to the three rules.

One more thing. He doesn't speak. Aaron Wold has not uttered a word to anyone here, resident or nurse, in the six years he has been here. He plays brag in sign, and sits reading this red leather-bound book he keeps on his lap most of the time. He seems to think it's important. Heck, I don't know whether it is or not. He's crazy.

When Bronislaw Angel lists only one name in the column headed 'friends', he is concluding only that it would be difficult to include a man who has not spoken to him for six years. I myself could name two friendships on such a list although one, Vernon Smitts, was prematurely cut short. The other you have yet to meet and I have yet to betray even more grievously than I betrayed poor Vernon Smitts.

Now there are only three players of brag amid the litter of these small winter afternoons in the high-walled lounge of the sanitarium. The fourth player had been Father Keam. Glaswegian, runny nose, dead now.

The priest's excuse for the latterly five times weekly visits had been the need to see his parishioner Bronislaw

Angel, despite Bronislaw's conversion to atheism in his cut-short youth. It was, Father Keam said, a promise he had made to my mother, Bronislaw's wife, shortly before her death that he would keep an eye on him.

That the priest was able both to do this and to cheat at cards simultaneously seemed to make him a more proficient human being than the venerable George Steen, former Leader of the City Council. He, you might remember, allegedly couldn't fart and suck sweets at the same time.

Father Keam's cheating had gotten so bad that Stanley Kubrick had threatened to call in the Bishop. The strange thing was that when they stopped playing for money, when the proprietor discovered that cash was being laid on the table, the priest still carried on cheating every week. He kept spare cards in the stained handkerchief which he kept closeted in the top pocket of his cleric's jacket. It was said he could make his nose run to order.

When he finally went of pneumonia last year, Stanley Kubrick took it as divine intervention.

'That's it,' my father said. It was the first time I had heard a note of awe or majesty in the voice of either of my parents. I was nine years old. This was Caspar's Gorge. Twenty minutes from our home on Beaker Street on the lip of the moors that swam round the edges of town. Sometimes I came, sometimes I didn't, when he muttered that he was 'going up top' for an hour. Heck, I was more interested in volleying marbles through the necks of milk bottles in preparation for a career of goalscoring and wing wizardry like my hero Tom Finney.

I think he was pleased when I went up with him. I never knew. Still don't.

We were standing high up in the moorland plain above the city. My father was looking across a tear in the biscuit of rock, a great scar that exposed fifty feet of stone to the elements in the sweep of quarry face where elsewhere a rough carpet of grass ran over the ground. Here the stone that built the city had been hacked from the earth over three hundred years or so. Before then, of course, wieselmen had clawed at the earth for copper ore.

Around us the breeze filled to a wind in quickening gusts. Whu-u-u-ooosh, then a falling lull, then whu-u-ooosh again rushing past my ears. I had never realised that wind could sound like accelerating city traffic. Some days just seemed made for learning.

I remember my father said little else. Just bade me look. The gist of his bringing me I had to piece together myself. He came out here two or three times a week in the summer. Sometimes to walk. Sometimes to climb in his clumsy fashion on the little-known rock faces of twenty, thirty feet of snapped stone.

He needed it up here, I figured out. A long time afterwards. You see he never liked himself too much. Lonely places were his lovers. Some dumb lost part of his soul. The mountains that he looked at, he became.

I guess, I guess.

He didn't speak much to me. Not ever. Not that he was cruel or uncaring. Not that. Never that. I think maybe he figured he didn't have much to pass on to me or something. We were good at waiting-room silences around the house. To escape, he huddled in the shed in winter over his chunks of wood, and in the summer he came up here. This, I figured eventually, was his favourite spot.

'This is Caspar Gorge,' was all he said to me about it. It was the one massive fissure in the rock around these hills he had not climbed. Too steep, too crumbly, too fucking out of reach. But he would come often in the short summer months to look at it whilst stuff ran through his head and the wind blew his hair flat to his scalp.

I don't know what stuff. He never said. You just saw it flicking like cartoon frames behind his eyes. Plick Plick Plick Plick. You could see the movie running in there, but my father only ever went alone to the movies.

18

Tick tick tick. That was a long time ago.

'We will re-form,' my father is saying. 'I am today negotiating with Marshal Stalin for the release from Siberia of the 15,000 men exiled from eastern Poland in 1941.'

It was a pretty big exile. Marshal Stalin was one of life's great dreamers of new movies. Unlike my father, the Marshal wanted everyone to come with him.

'With American assistance I will have these men moved and trained in Palestine before I lead them to join up with Monty's forces ready for the big push.'

As General Sikorsky, my father is pointing expertly to areas on the map laid out in front of him as he sketches out the details for me. It is an old map of the city which the nurse has found for him in a staff-room cupboard. He points, like they do in the old Pathé newsreels.

Looking at the map I can see that he proposes to move his exiled Polish army in stages from the petrol garage on Beaker Street through the site of the city knacker's yard and finally to muster them for Field Marshal Montgomery by the clothes department of Woolworths. I nod.

'Can't you do more?' I say to the nurse who tends to him each day.

My father is away meeting Marshal Stalin to discuss safe passage through the Barents Sea for the US troop carriers bound for Murmansk and the Polish exiles. Deep in negotiation with the Marshal my father, General Sikorsky, doodles absently on the notepad the Russians have provided, setting out rows of saucers, and ovals shaped like rugby balls.

'More than what?' she says.

She is pretty. Hair smelling of cedarwood and apples, remember.

I think she is brave for working with crazy people.

'He is crazy. Make him a bit less crazy or something.'

'You need him to be less crazy?'

I look at her oddly. I can tell she is angry with me.

'Its not . . . dignified. Sometimes he's Maximilian Kolbe, and sometimes he's General Sikorsky. One man he knows in here thinks he's Anton Chekhov.'

She says, 'Only in the evenings, he's afraid of the dark.'

'And his real name isn't even Stanley Kubrick like he says it is. Everyone knows that. Can't you make them just a bit less crazy?'

She says, 'We have three rules here. Provided they're not broken, people get the run of the place. Provided they don't go wreaking violence on the others, provided they don't go frightening anybody else, and provided they don't go trying to burn the sanitarium down.'

I tell her, 'I think you are brave for working with crazy people.'

I return to my father carrying a tray with his late afternoon tea I have brought back out from the kitchens. It looks nice. I wish I could stay a while. Tea and simple biscuits for my father. On the top landing a man goes by whispering 'Shuckety puck, shuckety puck,' like he was a subway tram or something.

'Will you stay?' my father says. 'My friend Stanley Kubrick is coming round, then there will be a game of cards.'

They play five-card brag, Bronislaw, Stanley Kubrick and Aaron Wold the former milkman from Crull, but not for money. The owner of the sanitarium doesn't allow cash on the premises.

There is a ping-ping-ping sounding deftly. It is the pocket watch I carry with me, the one from Vernon Smitts, the one with the inscription on the back about the thing I didn't know. I have pukka berries to feed.

In his later years, as he had drifted first into Supplies and later into Security and Cleaning, I had come to avoid Vernon Smitts where I could. Heck, I had work that needed doing. There was much work to be done still in the city. It wasn't that Vernon Smitts was bitter, more sort of lost. You looked at him and your first thought was 'Room to Let' in there. You know what I mean?

Sometimes we'd pass on some floor or other and I'd always remember to greet him. I'd say 'How goes it?' but I didn't really have time to hang around for the answer.

I bid farewell to Maximilian Kolbe, who is also my father, leave him ministering to the flock he sees before him in the evening corridor of the sanitarium.

For myself, I know that there is no flock there, that they weep and seek comfort from this resolute priest only in the mind of the man Bronislaw Angel.

My world is made of solid shapes. People making things and selling them. Bettering themselves and righting the city. Then they go home and watch other lives on TV. Watch how we used to burn witches and stuff but not any more.

19

It's a nice apartment.

When I first went looking for apartments after my wife left me, for her better life, one or two likely looking places fell through.

Where did you move to when you first came to the city, one woman asked. She wore colour on her cracking cheeks. When she moved, it broke away like dust. She was called Galbraith. Her family going back two generations had owned five of the town's mills and the great ghetto rows of apartments and courtyards to go with them into which the early east quarter weavers moved. The ones who turned their hand to building the City Park for alms monies when the cotton famines turned them into winter navvies.

Now the last of the Galbraith women owned just the one building near to the park. Not the classiest of places now but nice. Gravel track. High privets. It had been the family house, was these days split into apartments. She had the ground-floor rooms. I was going for the attic apartment which she had vacant.

She talked a lot to me, as widows do given an audience. Made me tea in bone china. I said I'd grown up on Beaker Street in the east quarter, but that now I worked for City Hall. That's nice, she said. That I'd got on. I wondered if she pictured my predecessors digging ditches in the park. She'd be wrong of course. I thought of my mother lighting the candle in the vestry at St Mary's when I was first taken on under poor Vernon Smitts.

She explained that she was all filled up. The apartments. She said she was sorry I'd wasted my time. The advert reappeared the next week. I reckoned she'd forgotten to take it out.

I ended up here, down by the river.

The neighbourhood kids are playing football in the street. Five, six of them usually. An hour after dusk they play by the dirty light of the sodium lamp overhead. You hear the ball every night against the side wall of the building as it hits the brick and falls back.

Thup thup thup. Pause. Thup thup thup thup. And on.

We never had footballs when I was a boy. I played with marbles against the back wall of the yard. See who could strike one through the neck of a milk bottle.

Progress.

They make no sign to me. No welcome, no warning. I wonder if they even see me in their bubble of concentration. Like always I hope maybe one of them will pass the ball across. That maybe the ball will somehow spill over. It would be some kind of comradeship, one or other of the kids laying the ball off just once as I make my tracks around from the garages at the rear of the building.

Some chance.

Ever since I moved here I've hoped this.

It's a different generation of players now. The originals are elsewhere looking carefully older, chasing girls and doing other stuff. Younger brothers have taken their place, thwacking the ball around out here till they get fed up or fancy the TV.

As I near them, stiff from the day, from the drive back from the sanitarium, shifting past their lazy glances, the ball ricochets from the nick of the wall's end and bounces at my feet. I trap it, flick it up, juggle it on my left foot two, three, four times. Feeling the grace of simple movement, and in so small a thing.

Heck, I could have been good. I could have boarded that subway tram with a one-way ticket to somewhere. If only the rest of my dumb life was lived from the mountain-top like this. One eye scans out, puzzling what the boys are making of the suited adult flicking their ball in the air with easy licks, wondering if they're thinking 'Comrade'.

Perhaps.

I clip the ball up higher, flex my tired turkey neck and tap the ball twice on my forehead before banging a volley against the apartment block wall.

Psh-thck.

It rebounds, bounces amongst the group of five who have stood watching, leaning, leering, left out. Who cares?

Who cares!

I shrug. They look gloomy, make no response, whisper things I can't catch. I decide that they picture me as someone who has stepped across the line. Intruded. Sure, why not. Turkey neck, trophy ears, butting in on their private rituals. I figure maybe they're thinking who the hell's this screwing up their party. I figure maybe they'd like to burn me. They just sneak their ten-, eleven-year-old glances across dipped shoulders at me. Waiting for me to go. Waiting for the all clear.

Inside the apartment I hear nothing for five, ten minutes. I mess around sorting something for tea. Put the TV on. Then: thup thup thup thup. It starts up again.

I have lived in my fourth-floor apartment over by the East River, across the water from the east quarter proper, for pretty much the whole of the five years since my wife left me. To her better life. That's what she said. Since I failed my interview with the mourning Mrs Galbraith and with others.

This block was built at the turn of the century, at the height of our turn for glory. These blocks were inhabited by overmanagers and the like from the cotton trade. Local solicitors. Assistant bank managers. Men of that ilk, of a certain standing. Now here are we. More progress, although it is true to say that anything in the city which still remains of the original quarried blackstone is down at heel now. Less well kept. It's the geography of respectability. So what, I say. I like the old brick.

So much of the old blackbrick has gone now, anyhow. The old clocktower that banged out the hours to dusk for the millworkers in the weaving sheds. And the old Technical College, where the once young Harry Angel and Coleman Seer studied just how the world gets better and better each day in Elementary History. Corwen Lintock plans a fibreglass and steel revolution through his Sentex Construction firm. Sometimes we forget that we were the once proud kings of cotton.

Like all cities, this one in the two centuries after the signing of its charter grew big on a geographical fluke. Damp winds, long rains, high moors down which the water ran to power the early mills, quarryable stone. The fragile cotton threads loved it here. Otherwise it might have stayed a market town on the way to nowhere in the hills, but it grew to the clatter of a thousand mills and the singing of 'Jerusalem' chorused by an army of weavers come from the land and the hamlets all around, wanting to get on, get on, like they could hear some clock ticking.

Where I live is fine. Fine, really. There are just two drawbacks.

One is the subway track that slams out of the rock just across the way there. Every eight and a half minutes a subway tram comes slooping overland out of that hole in the side of the black city rock and goes, 'Shuckety puck, shuckety puck, shuckety puck.'

For five years, my life in the apartment has been punctuated with the commas and colons of overground subway trams going 'Shuckety puck, shuckety puck.' It has driven me mad and it's kept me sane. Waiting for that same pattern of noise every eight and a half minutes.

The other drawback is the proximity of the east quarter. Sometimes you hear things. Like tonight. I can hear things tonight, except for every eight and a half minutes when a subway tram comes slooping past overland.

'Shuckety puck, shuckety puck.'

20

When my wife left me it seemed touch and go for a while. I had to tell myself I was too strong for this. That's what I said. Forgetting to change the sheets. Running out of milk or bread. Growing a blue stubble at weekends and having to hack it off on a Monday morning with a blunted

Superblue and cursing the bastard woman with every stroke.

She left a note. Did I say? It said this: 'The man came. I've paid up the milk. Harry, I need more than this. I need a better life.'

Just that. What was I supposed to make of that?

I've not seen her much since. I know she's doing fine out of town somewhere.

I kind of knew it was coming apart, but you hope. I'd had it down as small things. Like we were dancing just that beat out of step. Not much, you know?

Those waiting-room silences. I liked TV. Her, it drove mad. There were other things. She said toe-may-toes, I said toe-maah-toes. You know how it goes.

I never thought we were so much on the slide. It just goes to show. I never thought she had it in her. To leave I mean. I figured we'd just go on dancing our little waltz together.

Then the note.

I was better than this, I thought. I pulled through. To my credit I didn't turn to drink or to drugs while the balance of my life hung on this thread around me. Or to Jesus.

I took up growing pukka berries.

My pukka berry plants stand on numerous flat surfaces around the apartment. On window sills and tables and bookcase ledges. Curious short shrubby plants with shiny red berries which, according to the books, are edible but a bit of an acquired taste. Also, you have to be a bit careful. The other two similar-looking varieties contain a slow-acting poison. It's like some of the mushroom varieties. You have to know one from another.

They've been a kind of therapy for me. I grow the pukka berry plants from seed. They're difficult to grow in this country and require precise feeding times and careful transplanting from seed tubs to peat-lined pots at dead on four weeks. And so on.

You have to be so patient with them. This is what I've discovered. And after all that they only bear fruit the once. I have it all set out in charts in the kitchen for the various small batches I'm cultivating at any one time. Also they seem to be helped by the vibrations from the passing overland subway trams across the river.

Shuckety puck.

The plants pick up the vibrations as the trams go past. It seems to reassure them. When the subway men went on strike for the summer last year over redundancies and such things, the pukka berry plants hardly grew at all in the apartment during the six-week lay-off. When the subway trams started off again, the pukka berries picked up.

Like I said, this strain are edible, but I don't like them. That's life I guess. I take them up to my father at the sanitarium. He seems grateful for them so I drop them in when I'm passing and start work on the next batch.

Since my wife left me I've also had my teeth for company.

She used to nag me to go to the dentist. I used to simmer, aggrieved that she should think me such a child as to need her chidings.

'I was going, I was going,' I would say in my defence. Since she went, I've not gone near the place. More and more I seem to suck my food through softening sediments. Sure, I could go. I could. When it's cold, the air catches this one particular molar. Each morning when I see Fitsimmons, my first thought is usually to cuss over his perfect straight white teeth.

21

Days pass. Pukka berries ripen. I sent some to Corwen Lintock through City Hall's internal mail. You recall he had need of them. And now he has sent for me.

These days the boys outside the apartment block clear a wide berth, hang on the fence while I pass. The East Quarter Community Forum want to meet with me to air their concerns. I'm going out there later on. Mary Pound has asked again can I get her out from the east quarter. I've said sure, I'll see what I can do. You're a good man, she has said again.

The memo in my tray from the Leader's Suite on the Fourteenth Floor said nine o'clock. You see I sent a little note along with the packet, so he'd know who they were from.

The morning papers are spread like maps on Corwen Lintock's desk. Lintock himself, holding a thick red pen, is leaning over the desk alongside two other men circling and lining, circling and lining, checking the truth of nearby days before it sets. One is Aratakis. I've heard of him, seen his face in the evening paper. The other I've seen around on the floors of City Hall, in lifts and things, though I don't know his name. He's one of the dull suits from Planning.

Their strategy for the day ahead is set out in lists and charts in the same red ink on large sheets of paper. Truth will out, even with a slide rule.

It's a week or more since I saw the Leader at Drucker's Departmental Meeting. These are difficult days. You can read about them in his eyes.

His trial is up and running and has not been going well, I hear. The pause before the Sam Pound autopsy results hangs over us all. Corwen Lintock like all of us wants to know who the culprits were. The waiting has been hard on the Leader who has been anxious to clear up the controversy, to put the city right before the election which looms closer with each passing day.

Corwen Lintock's troubles began with an anonymous note sent to Aratakis, Chairman of the Police Authority. It could have lain there safely gathering dust but for the additional copies sent out to others. In the end Aratakis had to investigate.

What's the Leader accused of? He's accused of having a thriving business empire which thrives a little more each time the city thrives a little. His detractors can't see that he's leading the recovery, not leeching off it. Oh sure, there's other stuff. The way planning regulations were bent, the way a development grant was awarded to Sentex Construction, the way the insurances were handled on old mills his people bought up. Corwen says that he's been framed by dangerous men. Like I say, he has recent days etched on his face. Fear not, he has help.

Jesus Christ no longer appears to him in dreams.

Jesus has called on Corwen Lintock in person since I watched the Leader last from the Officials Gallery of City Hall.

Lintock had been in the bathroom of his Southside maisonette. He had been masturbating over a copy of *Hot Girls Extra* when Jesus Christ came knocking to offer answers to a man in turmoil.

The bathroom of his southside maisonette is a familiar retreat to Corwen Lintock in troubled times. His wife is the daughter of Councillor George Steen, once a colleague of Corwen's mother.

The daughter was badly affected by Councillor George Steen's car crash on the A6 when an oncoming vehicle ploughed through the central reservation and hit his Ford Popular head on. She is afraid of the roof falling in on her. She can only do it out of doors. And after dark.

In the summer he takes her at sundown to the City Park. They make love and she howls like a dog. But triple bypasses do not take kindly to winter sojourns in the park.

In the house, Corwen Lintock keeps a collection of *Hot Girls Extra* under the floorboards of the airing cupboard. In the dead of winter the bathroom offers precious relief.

I have knocked on the open door, hovered on the edge of the room waiting to be bid enter. I knock again, louder. All three men at the desk look up quickly.

'Are you Harry Angel?' the Leader asks. He seems suspicious of me. And Oostenbruik was a long time ago. Twenty years. A once green Corwen Lintock has forgotten it was me who saved his bacon.

I nod. I say, 'You sent for me.'

'The pukka berries?' he says, seeming to query himself. He doesn't smile, but instead grunts an appreciative noise. He is still looking at me, apparently trying to place who precisely I am.

I help out. 'I'm with Corporate and Community Affairs,' I say. 'Harry Angel, C and CA.' It sounds like a political slogan. Like I should wear it on a lapel badge. Like it's something I should swank about, the way my mother once did to Father Keam. Like it was a commission in the Polish Cavalry or something.

'Oh Drucker! You're with Drucker!' He makes it sound pretty basic.

'Yes, I'm with Drucker.'

He nods, then signals to the two men standing close to him. The younger man collects his diary from the jumble of newsprint and markers and leaves. The older man stays a moment longer. This is Aratakis, Police Authority Chairman. A bullish man slowed in the transacting of his business by heavy grammar. He chews his words and seems to spit them out in whispers. He shares with Corwen Lintock the gift of creating unease in those around him. He plays golf with the Leader. Many a city's future has been set out on the rising greens of a southside golf course.

There is a pause.

I ask, 'Is something wrong?' Corwen Lintock is giving me this butcher's look.

'They bring it on,' he says as though he just figured something out, holding up the newspaper nearest to hand. It is underscored with red felt-tip here and there. 'They provoke it. How did they think I could keep the people off them after the Sam Pound thing? Can't you see, Harry? The kurs – they only need shut of me now. I'm the last bastion. If I'm out of the way then what's happened so far will seem like nothing to what will come after.'

I say, 'I'm sure, only I only sent you the pukka berries. If you need me to go . . . '

What's happened so far. He means his impeachment, some small explosions, the mutilations at the zoo. Yesterday it was a female marmoset. They had to put it down. Lintock waves a dismissive hand, as if to say that things are alright now. Aratakis is making slowly for the door, having set his own agenda for leaving. He makes no passing reference to my standing there as he walks by me. The door closes. I have this urge to feel my flesh, just to check.

They're lucky, I am saying. My parents had the paraphernalia of an Aliens Act to contend with when they arrived in the city. I tell him this and it soothes his concern about last night. Other nights. I sense he'd like to hear it.

Another comfortable ending.

'How's Drucker doing with the Department?'

We are seated. Corwen Lintock has produced the pukka berries which I sent him a day or so back from a drawer in his desk, a quarter pound of them, and is counting them out in front of me one by one as if they were pounds sterling.

'I don't . . . I can't . . .'

'Harry Angel, let me tell you a secret.' He leans back in his heavy leather chair and whispers across the table to me.

'They don't believe me. I told them this morning but they don't, you know. Drucker, Daulman, even Aratakis there. They nod but I see the jeering in their eyes. Will you believe me, Harry Angel?'

Lintock is watching me carefully, looking for a reaction. I give him none. Does he mean the plotters who vanish into nothing when Aratakis's men go hunting them in the east quarter?

'I really did see him, Harry Angel. He did come to see me yesterday.'

'Who?'

'Jesus Christ.'

'Jesus Christ?'

I feel this man warming to me, like other men do when they realise they have found a listener. I'm a good listener.

My face makes earnest arrangements of itself that draw the spit and bile from any man's heart.

'He has been to see me, Harry. Not just in my prayers. In flesh and blood. He came to my home and blessed me and spoke to me about the city. He's going to come again. You believe me, Harry, don't you? He's going to get me off the charges. He says anyone with faith can be saved. He wants this city to be raised up in his eyes. He has said, in so many words, that I must win the election. I could tell, Harry, I could read the signs. That this is our only hope, that I am the only hope.'

I smile my beatific smile to him. I know that for any man his name, his story, is just the sweetest sound.

'He wants us to be his chosen people. Us!'

He has finished counting out the pukka berries now. He seems satisfied with the final tally and is tipping them back into the bag several at a time with the minute concentration of a young boy.

'You're a good man, Harry Angel.'

All I did was bring him pukka berries. I don't even like them to eat. I tried once. I got indigestion too, and this saccharine aftertaste like pricks of salt on my tongue.

He asks how I got them.

I say I grow them, that it's a hobby of mine.

'Hobby?'

'I grow them at home.'

'You know, Harry Angel, that hobbies are for failed men. For those who've wrecked their lives into cul-de-sacs and can only dream alone.' True men, he says, are those who look with a restless spirit always to build in the world of real things.

I admit to having wrecked my life into a cul-de-sac in which the pukka berry plants have been a kind of therapy for me.

'You eat them?' he asks me a little later. He means the pukka berries.

'No, I don't like them. They're too bitter for my taste. I give them to my father.'

'What does he do?' Corwen Lintock asks. I hesitate, then decide I'm no match for any games he might be playing and settle on the truth.

'He lives in a sanitarium on a hill over the city. He plays five-card brag in the long afternoons with the other residents there.'

I tell him that my father loses a lot, that he's a bad player of brag. Apart from that he reads. The proprietor has a big library of books from all across the world.

Corwen Lintock says he knows of the proprietor.

I say that when he's not doing that, my father believes himself to be General Sikorsky and other such people. I shrug, as if in surrender to the facts.

He says, 'What sort of things do you do, Harry Angel, that we pay you money for when you are not visiting your crazy father?'

For a minute I think that he is going to sack me. I tell him, give him a list.

'The east quarter,' he says, alighting on one sentence. 'That's good, that's good! Some time soon I shall give you a job to do, Harry Angel, in the east quarter. You want a job to do?'

'My boss, Mr Daulman . . . '

'Don't worry about that lot. I'll speak to Drucker, the gutless shit. When the time comes, you do this job for me, Harry Angel, and I might even have you promoted.'

It sounds like a child's pledge to rid the world of hunger.

By the way, he says, before I leave for the east quarter to meet with the Community Forum, there is one more thing. Have I any more pukka berries he can have? Perhaps before the weekend?

I say yes, maybe, if there's enough of the plants in fruit at my apartment. I grow them there, I say. What does he need them for, I say.

He says that they will buy him answers. He says he is going to save the city. To win the election. To be found not guilty by his peers. To lead us to a promised land. He says Jesus Christ is coming to see him again, but only if Corwen Lintock pays him in pukka berries.

22

The east quarter was once an elegant part of the old city across the East River. It had music hall theatres and narrow streets and elegant blackstone buildings four storeys high with cold cellars.

Now it has the broken face of an old woman. Its people cling together. In business. In love. In lies of silence.

People know stories about those who live there. Bogey-man stories.

If you're not back till when it's dark you'll get snatched by the ratcatchers from over the river. Don't you hit your brother or you'll be sent to live over there.

They live twelve to a house and up in the attics and in tunnels going down into the earth, and belch in the street and go hunting little boys.

They eat dog food and kill goats in the home and run secret societies and write backwards. They put spokes in wheels and bring bad luck and fix the evil eye on you.

They stalk the City Park at night and howl like dogs at the moon. Watch out or they'll get you.

Or so it's said. Who knows.

There were witches once in these small hills, when there were only hills. Then there were hamlets, crowded in on themselves against the witchy hills. Then there were far-mers, then there were tinkers, then there were miners, chipping at that black slabby rock for lead and copper on the belly of the wet witchy earth.

Then came the market town down in the valley, then came the waterwheels turned by the streams, then came the city and the poundings of mills and the singing of sweet 'Jerusalem'. You know the rest.

In my Elementary History class at the blackstone Tech-nical College where I studied with Coleman Seer they explained that such was progress. That history was a way of getting to the end through the vision of good men.

And so the city made things better. Bread and bones and bowling alleys and so on. And now here we are at the end of history, and we don't burn witches any more. There are so few pages left to write, then all will be well. All will be well.

Long after copper mining and dreams of finding wafers of silver had gone from the moors and the remaining settle-ments there had merged with the still-young city beyond the river to become its eastern quarter, it remained some-how still separate. It became a place where black markets flourished. Where travellers and itinerants settled. Where moneylenders thrived during the frequent cotton famines. Old women said that kurs maintained a pact with the Devil in the east quarter because of the uncanny way none in their community seemed ever to go hungry during the hard times, because of the way they huddled together like keepers of secrets.

Shards of glass crunch underfoot, biscuit-thin snaps on my shoes. Two or three of the shops and a house or two got turned over last night. Stray cats flew. Sometimes I wonder how men like Coleman Seer have survived intact in such a place as this after all these years. Don't get me wrong, it wasn't just looting. It was a selective thing. They were marked out with white lime mulch on the doors, the single word 'Kur' tattooed on each building like it was the Passover or something.

This stuff cleanses the living as well as the dead.

Young men earn their spurs by raiding the east quarter boulevards, raising hell and sinking back into the safe side of the city. There are rules, kind of. Jesus couldn't make it last night for the Passover so the people of the city deputised.

It rained a lot last night. Most of the lime pitch has been washed away. The gutters are bleeding dirty white. They say only one man died last night, a taxi driver caught up in the melée on Beaker Street whose heart gave out.

They say he was a good man. Maybe Jesus was busy taking him home.

23

No-one has touched the church, not from outside the quarter anyway. The lead stripped from the roof has been allocated internally. The building is otherwise as it was when my mother first brought us here, friendless, into the city in the aftermath of war. As it was when I was baptised here before being tossed high into the air on the way home by women giddy with the news of peace and the promise of new lives and different ways.

Once, it had been a village church. A barricade against the witchy hills. But in days when the community was widening and deepening, when England's bread hung by a cotton thread, when the Galbraith mills pumped prosperity like blood into the body of the town, then the building of St Mary's had been extended and newly consecrated.

The huge church, the biggest in the city, catered for the weavers crowded into the map of streets round about. It was a signal of the city's pride in itself, of its place in God's gently evolving Kingdom. We knew this to be true. The good guys had just won the war. Some folk had televisions. Everyone had 'Much Binding' on the frying bacon wireless airwaves. No-one would have to pay the doctor. No-one would get sick. All we had left was the victory lap.

Looking back, that seems the gist of what the priest said to me. To us. To the children of Beaker Street Primary. That's what a young Father Keam said through the spit and slavver of his Easterhouse prose in this very church.

Picture this:

Everything as cold stone and shadow. Boys. Seven or eight was truly boyhood then. Boys in short pants. They follow the angry-vowelled Father Keam as he does his tour. His party piece, the Bishop has called it. Too gleefully, the Scot has thought in uncertain moments.

They walk around the side aisle, scuffing their feet on the hard floor behind the cleric who is as magisterial to them as Abraham and Moses. What do they know? They are barely beginning. They confide in whispers that hum like organ notes under the high ceiling.

At the end of the procession is a slim boy with fair hair and wide rabbit ears. He holds out his arms, trails the cold edge of the wall, feels the pale grain of the plaster against his fingertips.

Harry Angel, you cry. Harry Angel!

I think not, as I remember this. I think Harni Zelenewycz. It was a long time ago.

'No straggling at the back, keep in your pairs.' The teacher cranes her neck, pivots against the tension in her shoulders as she seeks to keep the imagined rebellion in check.

She is shapeless, tall, hairy. Unloved. It's her last year. Reservist teachers are no longer needed now the war is ended and forgotten. She retires at the end of term. How old is she? A hundred and eight. Harni Zelenewycz knows this. Sam Pound has told him so. Joe Mole told him. Coleman Seer told him. Also she's a witch. Howls like a dog at the moon from the night-time City Park.

The voice again: 'I want no-one wandering off under a bus.'

Harni Zelenewycz seems not to hear. His fingers still trace the shape of the wall. The wall sighs with him, has a heart that breathes through its bleak skin.

She moves back through the group, aggravated beyond reason by the fair-haired boy's reluctance to stay in line. He looks up, notices her suddenly, surprise in his open face like he's just come back. He hears voices in his private hinterland. Women's voices. The teacher ushers him forward with a flap of her hand.

It is a battle she wages in the classroom. Ask her. She will say she is a straightforward woman. No fuss or frills. No room for it in these parts. Will leave the town like most through the double oak doors of the chapel rooted on the cemetery hill. She has no time for the boy's mooning.

Once she, like others, had wanted to leave. She had wanted to teach from the off but it was a pipe dream in a city married to its great manufacturing adventure. She went into the mill while her brothers learned a seven-year trade. Her teacher cried the day she signed on at Galbraith's India Mill, had wanted her sent to the Technical College, wanted her to grow into a teacher, a reporter on the city's evening paper. A writer. Anything but shrinking into what so clearly awaited her.

In her forties she developed emphysema. It happened a lot. It was a price to be paid by the kings of cotton. She did a nightschool course. Became a reservist teacher when war broke out. Was offered a glimpse of what might have been.

Too late. Too late.

She kept a tight order and begrudged those in her charge the last remnants of faith she saw them clinging to. The last remnants of hope. In anything. Small things. Childish worthless things.

At the back of the church, down the centre aisle, Father Keam tells them 'Stop!' and turns round. High up on the wall a sinewy figure stretches out his arms against the background of a wide cross. The figure seems a dozen feet high, a towering sickening height.

Father Keam says it is a working Christ. Designed for their working town. The boys stare up into the flat shape of the wall, the darker texture of the carving leaning out frozen into space. The hands of the figure are large, calloused, as though the Christ were a millworker himself.

The priest bids them sit. They shuffle into pews and Father Keam speaks. The gist is this: most of the boys, he knows, will go on to work with their hands in the town. It's the will of Jesus, the need of the city. And here was proof for them that Our Lord thought of them, was amongst them. They had much to live up to, he said. They had a fine past. End of speech.

24

Inside the house of the priest young men turn round sharply from their seats around the TV when I enter. They are refugees from the troubles. Each of their houses, I learn, has been marked with the sign of white lime mulch. One of them is the whippet-like Jason Pound. He has ripe bruising down one side of his face. Also, there is Dooley the Cowboy and others, familiar figures in the east quarter role call. The new priest, called Daniel (he prefers first names), wants to tell me things. He says I am a good man who will listen. I say I am happy to help. His surname is also Daniel. It's a long story.

The young men sit close in a semi-circle away from us, smoking, eyes low, swapping short words I can't make out. I am reminded of Drucker in the lift, but Drucker is not like them because he has a wife who gives him presents for the office and because he has dreams at night.

The priest called Daniel Daniel says that each of these young men has white lime mulch spattered on their doors.

Gotcha, was the message.

The priest speaks shyly and he isn't sure what to do with his hands, with his flapping arms. Liam Fitsimmons would be amused. Also he has this crude and ugly jaw half-hidden by hair. Square and bolted to his neck. Everything sounds like the fourth scotch and soda.

When Daniel the priest had first moved here six months ago on the death of his predecessor, these youths had shadowed him down Beaker Street, mimicking his slurry words and chanting like scabby gibbons three steps behind him.

One time he turned on them and said, 'Why?'

They looked hard. Testing. Just wondering.

They said, 'Why not?' They made gibbon noises again, but more half-heartedly this time. Maybe their powers were waning. For sure, they don't go out of the east quarter so much these days.

Maybe their powers don't stretch that far. Who knows.

They never bothered the Glaswegian Father Keam, impervious as he was to gibbons and the evil eye. He could work miracles with bread and wine and stuff, but no-one came to his sideshow any more. He was not bad. He was tired. In the east quarter they knew he cheated at brag and they knew he drank. It helped him to drink, otherwise he found that he saw things.

Once, when he had forgotten to drink, Keam saw the city guardians come down from the south side to impose some discipline on the east quarter. Young men and eager, knowing right from wrong like a pickaxe from a cheese-cake. Knowing who to blame for the failed cotton city, the crumpled lives they had got saddled with.

They cornered two youths who'd been known to slaughter goats or some such thing, and their guilty as hell father, and knelt them on the rutted verge and walked them on their knees from one end of Beaker Street to the other. Eating the grass. Until they puked in great gobbing lurches over the road from the church of St Mary's.

Just games with rules.

Then once he saw a house being firebombed by eager guardians, and children tossed high in the air from windows to escape the flames. After that he remembered to drink early and increased his brag-playing at the sanitarium on the hill outside the city to five times a week. Then he died.

Daniel the priest doesn't cheat at five-card brag or get drunk early. He runs a youth club in the community centre. He does other things. As a consequence he hears much.

He says the east quarter is a friendless place abandoned by the city, that here good men are bullied and bad ones are beaten and worse simply for belonging in this place as a curse on the good people, and that after all the fine speeches I should be sure of any guilt to be apportioned before I go making pronouncements to men like Corwen Lintock.

'Sure,' I say, 'sure.'

He says they're not animals here, despite the gibbon noises. He stares, his penguin arms flapping uselessly at me, and I wonder if he's putting the evil eye on me.

25

I recognised the look that Daniel Daniel the priest gave me.

It was the look my wife offered me on the day that she left me, to her better life, the look that said, 'Harry Angel, you're a fool.'

Yes, she gave me that self-same stare, a very English kind of look I always thought, which pleased me even in my distress.

I had determined, of course, to marry the most English girl I could find. Anybody in my circumstances would have done the same.

After the disgracing of my father, events which we have yet to touch on, which I'm coming to, it seemed I had no option but to seek a kind of Englishness which would protect me from such things. There seemed no respite, you see, because my mother was herself developing her own excessive devotions to Our Lady of Kocjelska.

My mother was by this time taking refuge in a past which she understood scarcely more than the present. When I came to leave home, to be married to my very English wife, she was even then increasingly seeing herself as eighteen and back in Warsaw, humming to herself in our blackstone cellar to some morose polonaise on a wind-up gramophone and preserving her virginity against her nightly predator, my fahter. She saw statues cry.

Towards the end of her life she retreated almost wholly into speaking Polish, even to her English friends. Father Keam thought her a goofball but she brought him whisky and polished his church and so he made nothing of it.

She saw stigmata on her hands. She saw Our Lady of Kocjelska walking towards her on Beaker Street, but eventually the priest persuaded her otherwise.

During all of this she continued to hate my father for secret humiliations wreaked on her which I could then only guess at. I thought at the time these were merely sexual. The follies of youth, you see.

They would circle each other in some complex dance I didn't know the steps to. There were rules you see, but I was excluded. My preference was for good guys and bad guys which dispensed with the need for rules.

So hard did they work to avoid the other's darting glance. The sly incidental look. Only later did I learn things about them.

There are more things in Heaven and Earth than sex, it's just they take time to come out. Vernon Smitts found that out. Of the other things my father did to my mother, the least worst was to lead her to England and promise her a new life, only for her to find when she arrived that the old one had seemed to follow her here.

For myself, I married the daughter of Vernon Smitts.

I loved Elisa Smitts dearly but she taught me this: sex tinges the world with sadness and surrender.

I thought my wife was brave for living with a man as handicapped as I. I was, you see, addicted to games of chance, notably the roulette that was my procreative need. Each time we locked our limbs in sexual congress I carried hope in my heart that all would be well but it was a vain and wilful wish.

I used to believe that sex was the ultimate loneliness, but now I see it as one of many routes to a single terminus. With my wife I felt that we learned about sex together but in different rooms. Do you understand what I mean?

At first I couldn't get it up.

I prayed. Oh yes, I prayed to any God who would listen. To Whom It May Concern, I began, and beamed my little story skywards to the blinking stars above the town.

Did it help? It felt like praying to an empty car park and I cursed my limp member for mocking the rest of my OK body.

Then when I did get it up, I seemed to spill my careless seed always at the wrong moment. During this torment of mine my wife seemed as a silent observer. Patient, of course. An English virtue.

I got what I paid for, don't you think?

Later, practice, familiarity and an absence of fear allowed me the rhythm of intercourse to my heart's content, but to no obvious advantage for my still patient wife. Our infrequent copulations seemed, henceforth, to end in a kind of truce which sounded like nothing so much as the cries of grief.

26

We had been introduced, Elisa and I, through Vernon Smitts, her father, my comrade in the City Hall basement. In those days he was still my boss and the benefactor of wisdoms fashioned from his failure to gain promotion.

'Harry,' he'd say, 'the cream might rise to the top but it's always the first to curdle.'

In those days poor Vernon's head didn't shoot round each time the door opened. In those days when you looked in his eyes there was still someone there. Also, he was a hell of a careful driver.

One day he said he had this daughter who'd given up college and who didn't get out much. He said she was very pretty and very English and still untouched. He actually used the word.

He was right about the untouched bit but not about her looks, much as I loved her. Of everyone I ever worked with she most resembled Daulman. This would have amused Liam Fitsimmons which is why I never told him I was married. It turned out I'd met her before, as a ghostly student at the Technical College who never spoke much but smiled sweetly and who Coleman Seer and I had both secretly lusted after.

Small world.

She wore flat shoes and didn't know there'd been a war on and that some people had died. She thought everyone in the world spoke English, just that they all watched *Take Your Pick* presented in different accents.

I thought these were the most English virtues I could imagine and I fell in love with her on the spot.

She was twenty by now but still, as Vernon Smitts kept saying, still untouched in the way it was once possible to be, and it was only when she'd grown up and found things out and come to dislike me that I realised that I'd married someone's childhood. When she grew up it took me by surprise as for years I'd watched both my parents seem to grow back down into childhoods that they'd reinvented for themselves. It didn't seem such an uncommon pastime, but my wife would have none of it.

We're back in the church of St Mary's. Father Keam is preaching to the class of boys who itch like salmon to go run or something in the clean air. He does too, but he can't. He's going through the motions. He had wanted to be a clerical scholar, had seen himself walking under shaded Vatican archways and researching twelfth-century sainthoods in dusty rooms. The Bishop had laughed, sent him here for the good of his soul, thought it a huge joke.

At receptions he tells of his earthy little priest from the north and the party piece tours he does around the huge blackbrick city church of St Mary's.

Wordlessly, the young Sam Pound offers a liquorish to Harni Zelenewycz and to Coleman Seer, then returns to his intricate carvings on the varnished pew knee high. He engraves an elaborate 'S' with the penknife hot in his pink fist. In the end he decides he doesn't like it, but his efforts to cross it out only scar the varnish without obliterating the shape of the letter.

Instead, head bowed in concentration, the mumble of the priest's words in the distance, he shifts along a little and carves 'Hitler Was Ear' in thinner cleaner letters. And on the last curve of the 'r' his hand is ripped back from the surface of the bench by the priest. Father Keam has caught sight of him and sneaked up while still talking.

'Surely not,' Father Keam says, 'in the Lord's own house?'

'I was . . . '

The priest, blunted by the effort of the morning, failing to turn the labour into an act of worship, is speechless, breathless, looks to the teacher for a sharing of outrage, looks back at the boy Sam Pound. He brings the boy to the front, stands him in front of his peers, waits for the slivers of noise to die. Anger is much the sweeter after some cold pause.

Finally the priest says this: 'Our Lord holds out great hopes for everyone, child. Great hopes. That each child will grow to fill their appointed place in His kingdom.'

Everyone knows there is a 'but' coming. Here it comes.

The moral is this. It comes out in the terse torn Scottish words that fall from his mouth like stones. Boys bow their heads, confused, curious, empty.

The words falling like stones say this: Individuals and communities strive to get better. In God's world, everyone gets what they deserve. In this God-fearing, hard-working city everyone gets what they deserve. Hitler got what he deserved from the British bulldog. This child standing at the front will get what he deserves. One day he will get his just deserts for this small outrage to God.

It was said like one day fate would creep up onto his shoulder and yank him round like Father Keam had yanked him round. Like for Sam Pound there was no hope now that the varnished bench was scarred for life with the inscription, 'Hitler Was Ear'.

It was said like for Sam Pound the end of the road was being signposted right here and now.

Spooky.

What I remember most from that day, though, was that as the priest looked across to the teacher for affirmation of this teaching she was laughing to herself. A small reedy noise almost as though it were caught in her throat. She was laughing at what the priest had said, at this private joke she had heard him tell which we had somehow missed.

I thought he would be angry. Surely. But the noise seemed somehow to break him, like a simple thread had broken. He just turned slowly, watched her for a moment.

Said, 'They're all yours.' Then left us. Like he'd been defeated or something. Left twenty boys pooled in silence and an old woman who was making noises over and over like something was caught in her throat, making noises that bounced tinny echoes around the church rafters.

Why did my wife finally leave me?

I think because she learned how to cry. Funny, that. One night she went to the City Park and howled like a dog through her tears. Have you noticed how only grown-ups cry properly? Children are always half-listening for the reaction. My wife Elisa, though, cried oblivious to all, blindly and happily, confessing her pain to the world.

She came back home, those five years ago, packed and went, saying, just as the stony face of the priest Daniel Daniel has said this morning on my errand for Corwen Lintock, 'Harry Angel, you're a fool.'

When people ask me why she left, I say, 'She grew up.'

When they ask me how that happened I say, 'It's a mystery to me.'

27

Around the Recorder's table in the City Hall Chamber there is a flurrying of papers and not a little confusion and the sifting smoke of a hundred filter-tips and cigars and sucking pipes.

Rising above the arena of the chamber are the two public galleries. Such galleries they said were 'in the gods' in the old theatres that once were spread across the artistic east quarter of the city.

No more.

The people had no use for them in a new century interested in other things, in TV game shows and in the production of human bonemeal, and so the gods had been vanquished.

One of the galleries is reserved for the city officials who are compelled to attend but to watch the proceedings dumb as mutes. It is the elected Councillors who do the talking. Drucker, silent as he should be, sits two rows up from me, sucking and puffing, sucking and puffing. Silence being his natural state.

Others like Daulman fidget. Stankill sits stiff as card holding his clean white accountant's fingers. I am the least senior official required under the city's rules to attend. My silence is coloured with respect. Here is the future of our community being chiselled from the friction of debate, from the steady rub of policies and the lubricating oil of reports stapled under heavy agendas.

What of Fitsimmons? I figure maybe he's thinking about sex.

I met Fitsimmons's wife once, by accident. It was nothing planned. It's not how we are, Drucker's team. She is some lady, Fitsimmons's wife. Once or twice, lying in my so-alone bed, I've imagined what it would be like. With her. Sex and stuff. But when I close my eyes and picture her naked, she just stands there saying 'Yes? Yes?' in this little crescendo of impatience.

The other gallery holds the general public. This is the people's show but here, unlike the game shows of TV Land, the public like the officials must remain dumb as mutes as they watch from up here in the gods. For reasons of procedure. Maybe that's why TV is more popular. TV is real life with the sound turned up.

Two sword lengths apart across the Recorder's table, the two sets of councillors review the city's steady march. Councillors on the far side allege incompetence and profligacy. Jobs are down, investment is down, morale is low. Something is amiss. What of the flesh wound of the recently assaulted tigress at the city zoo? Someone else throws in corruption but Corwen Lintock, dark suit, lowered head, makes no move, bowed over his papers. One or two ask about progress on the Sam Pound affair.

Councillors to the near side counter with the facts and figures of office. Three hundred more here and two per cent there and the climax which is promised this centenary year. There are some yah boohs and sucks but no bloodshed. We don't burn witches any more this far down the road.

Someone offers an update on the Sam Pound affair. Mention is made of the proposed special event to mark the three hundredth anniversary of the City Charter. If ever the tide runs gently against them, Councillors to the near side cry out not to sell this fine and crumbling city short to those who would decry the faint pains of steady progress.

28

At length Lintock rises. He has said nothing. Not for Drucker's reasons. For his own. The chuntering stops. This is why. He can seem to rise much higher than he should when he stands. Sometimes, when you look into his face, you wonder how any man can bear the singular burden he carries. The lines on his pale face are driven in like divots.

He carries no notes, but then he has no need. He has told me why. He has met Jesus. Good News! Corwen Lintock's Jesus has spoken words of guidance and compassion to him. All this time we thought we'd been abandoned, but now Corwen Lintock has found the route to salvation.

The Leader brings these words to the City Chamber to explain their relevance to our community. He speaks simply. It carries high and wide to the galleries dumb as mutes. He begins, 'Good cityfolk.'

In everything he will say and do from hereon in, remember this: that when he was small, in days when he was willing on the great Eddie Melon to do demon things on the turf of the city football ground, his mother Councillor Nan Lintock locked him in the airing cupboard for days. Days at a time, feeding him through a small airlock. You see, he wet the bed. He had to be punished. Had to be. If only he'd been Eddie Melon. If only he'd been able to volley marbles through the necks of milk bottles. Boy, he'd have shown them, if only.

He knew stories about bogeymen, too, who'd get him if it didn't cease. His mother said.

Corwen Lintock is still afraid of the dark but he doesn't pee in his bed any more. Also, he's out to get the bogeymen.

I recall I was once out walking on the moors above the city. Bear with me. This tale has a point to it. We will return to Corwen Lintock's fine rallying call to the good folk of the city, his chosen people.

It was part of my self-imposed programme of recuperation after my wife had left me. Despite my father's love of the solitude up there, I had not been much attracted to the empty places. I wanted filling to the brim.

But in the face of questions which a half-shipwrecked life throws up I found the high moorland places which my father had once shown to me reassuring.

Whilst I grew up they seemed in my remembrance to be ugly things and aimless. But their bulk had lasted and so there was hope, it seemed, for me, Harry Angel with the turkey neck and the ears like trophy handles and the wife gone to her better life.

The copse of pines I was in on the side of the moorland hill had canopied out much of the sky. It was a place where the silence had a smell to it. Dung-earth covered the slabby rock that soaked up the noise in its layers and bewitched the thin trees into falling horizontally in the unseen night so that they lay around me like the matchstick debris of some storm I'd somehow missed.

And then, imperceptibly, there was a hum, a buzz. An engine in the far sky. Aeroplanes use the moorland expanse for fighter training. For low level passes.

It got closer, and louder. I couldn't see it. Finally it got so close and so loud that it seemed to swamp the sky although I still couldn't see it against the blue smudged out by pine branches. My stomach lurched against the vibration of bilious noises from the thing overhead. I thought the sky was falling in. The beast was so close, howling and screaming. Screaming blue murder.

And then it got louder. Just turned up the volume. I couldn't see it. Where was it? I couldn't see it oh God help me help me it was falling in on me thirty feet high and spewing blindly into the trees and my pink fleshy body. I threw myself to the ground, shaking, curled foetus-small on the earth floor. I let out, I recall with distaste, some useless animal noise. And the sky was black with my predator.

The jet screamed overhead, unseen. Casually. Fifty, maybe a hundred feet. Laughing at my antics, roaring over the head of the valley in the blink of an eye and onto another green sea of land in the island kingdom. Behind it, a vacuum of silence fell like a hammer and my skin went from aching warm to shrill cold before I was stood on my feet.

Only once elsewhere has that same stinking animal fear ever come over me.

29

As the Miscellaneous Developments Officer, I go out to the east quarter for the monthly evening meetings of the East Quarter Community Forum on behalf of Drucker's Department. People seem pleased that I have a worthwhile job. I say sure, sure, it's good to make a contribution to the bettering of things.

This one time the meeting had overrun. I had to get back, I forget why. Some pukka berry errand I expect. I left early, made my excuses courteously to the Chairman.

Walking. I was walking. I'd left the car outside the quarter's mean streets. I'd figured to walk the half a mile having found a safer place to park. Somehow I got caught up at the tail end of a group of young men, on the aimless brink of adulthood. The kind who were at home among the dark places, picking clean the bones of a decaying quarter.

From the top of Beaker Street came a hum, a buzz. As it came closer the sound of footsteps came clumping ahead of the buzz that became a mumble of voices and a rumble of yelping and yawping.

City boys come from across the river to go hunting the renegades. Only last week Aratakis set up a raid on a meeting of the secret council of kurs which is rumoured to be co-ordinating the campaign of action against Corwen Lintock. What action? Some small explosions. Mutilated mammals and the like. The Leader's impeachment once his guilt is proved. New members were being sworn in. Aratakis's men found only an empty warehouse, old newsprint blowing, a single light-fitting swaying lazily this way and that. It seemed to prove to Corwen Lintock that even City Hall had been infiltrated by them for word of Aratakis's swoop to have leaked out thus.

City boys come to beat the blood drum.

'Kurs! Kurs! Kurs!' so the chanting went.

When I took the most recent batch of pukka berries to Corwen Lintock, he gave me a job to do out in the east quarter, a part of the city I of course know well. I figure he was impressed by my local knowledge. Was keen to reward me with a challenge.

What does he want of me? He wants me to root out the killers of Sam Pound. You see, he knows they reside in the

114

east quarter somewhere. He has seen a preview of the Sam Pound autopsy report with its sequence of clues and hints as to the bad men who did the deed one dark city night. Root them out, Harry Angel, he has said. Someone will talk. You know what they're like over the river. Use the connections you have there. Do your city a service.

30

Corwen Lintock's speech to the City Council when he rises is, in its own way, a speech of forgiveness.

It is also a speech of explanation.

Has it occurred to you before now how life goes on from day to day ravelled in a series of crossword clues that always seem just that touch out of reach. Then suddenly, 'bam!', someone like Corwen Lintock comes along and explains it to you and it all falls into place.

You've spent half your life walking round with this sneaking feeling that you're not to blame for the mishaps and the mayhem of the city, not responsible in the way your churning guts say you are. You can't seem to put into words this niggling belief that misfortune got your name by mistake.

Boy, has this guy hit the nail on the head. Corwen Lintock

speaks like he finally got himself some answers, and just in time with the election looming.

All these late years, he says, we've been borne down by misfortune, by duff wages and shabby streets, by lousy luck and friendless nights, by bad lies about Corwen Lintock and the rest of us, and by howls like a dog coming from out of the City Park. But no longer, brother!

What do we do with misfortune?

Return to sender.

Corwen Lintock is forgiving us because we know that we have done our best. He knows that, when the shackles are off, we will prosper again. All we have to do is to re-elect this man, support him through the ordeal of his trial.

Bless you, Corwen Lintock.

We go to work, we earn our pay, we deserve better than we've got, just like the man says.

So what's been holding us back? Corwen Lintock is looking up around the Chamber into the eyes of every one of us, in the galleries, along the Councillors' benches, because he knows that we know the answer. Why are we not up there with the greats in this final furlong of history? Sitting at the top table? Walking safely in the City Park of a night?

Who put the evil eye on us?

And we all want to jump up from our seats and shout, 'We know, we know.' But we sit, dumb as mutes, while Corwen Lintock, the man loved by the pukka-berry-eating Jesus, speaks further to us. And we are gleeful now that we understand because Corwen Lintock has spelled things out for us.

Corwen Lintock, face chiselled by misfortune and concern, outlines the litany of misfortune to have befallen us and pins the blame where it rightly belongs. Over there in the east quarter which hangs round our necks like an albatross. Except that this albatross can't up and fly away. Heck, we even built them a community centre in the days when the city ran a surplus.

In the east quarter they have ruined the city's great manufacturing adventure and left our blackbrick city crumbling like cake. In the east quarter they live like bogeymen twenty to a house and in their attic dens. They dig tunnels under the city. They put spokes in wheels and eat dog food and howl like dogs in the park after dark, picking the bones of the city clean. They killed Sam Pound because he was onto them, because Sam was allied to Corwen Lintock by virtue of the fact that he worked for Sentex Construction which Corwen ran, building bowling alleys and the like. An honest enough profession, he maybe thought, to keep any man safe. They keep themselves to themselves, they write backwards and they are plotting things. They framed Corwen Lintock.

They put the evil eye on us alright.

Lintock holds up a piece of paper. This is the proof that he's been hunting half a lifetime to account for things. To show that kurs won't rest until they've undermined the city like they've undermined its cotton, broken the back of

Sentex Construction, put the Leader in the dock. Won't rest until they've slung Corwen Lintock headfirst from authority since he's the only man strong enough to stand in their way.

Lintock's minutes detail how the kurs are organised; times, dates, places underground, cellars and warehouses where they meet; rules. Stuff never seen on paper except for new members to study and then destroy. I think Fitsimmons's men tracked it down – confirming things till now just rumour; giving details of an oath to subvert everything precious in the city, to bring it down and take its place with kurish things. A sad and crumpled document as he holds it up to the crowd. Appearing like something some damned fool wrote up one night in pencil in a hurry. Appearing like some white rabbit from a tall black hat. No matter. Corwen Lintock's heart beats fast at the touch of it.

Well at least it's all out in the open now.

Elect me, he says, and I'll protect you with my life. Count on it. And Lintock's proof flaps in his fingers for all the city to see. And first one and then another claps and claps him, slowly at first, people like the taciturn Stankill squinting sideways at Drucker to see what he will do, people like Drucker watching the city councillors on both sides to see which way they will jump, until the applause ripples round the hall like thunder.

And Harry Angel? Hell, sure, I'm in there clapping in the middle of this noise that rolls like thunder.

My grandfather, I was told, went a-hunting rats for sport in the open Poznan sewers at the turn of the century. When

I heard that, my little English brain thought: Thank God I'm in England now where history is all but done.

They came closer, closer, that night that still runs in loops in my dull brain as I sought to get out of the east quarter after my meeting with the Community Forum. I ran this way and that down blackstone alleys. Ran with them, but the hunters followed, penning us in one of the dripping courtyards, stamping, stamping their feet. Hunting kurs like rats for sport.

The blows and the beatings began and, before I was dragged clear through the remnants of a bricked-up window by the strong fists of Joe Mole or of Sloopy Den Barton, I remember that same single wet animal fear on me.

Screaming blue murder.

Shuckety puck, shuckety puck, shuckety puck.

Beating the blood drum. Who knows, tonight the hunt could be on again.

31

My father Bronislaw is seated at the card table in the drawing room of the sanitarium. A fire crackles in the hearth. The steady hiss of steaming coals is muffled and soaked up by the carpet. A clock ticks.

His opponents, Stanley Kubrick and Aaron Wold, study their cards. The fourth chair stands empty. The empty chair is left partly as a mark of respect for the deceased Glaswegian card-cheating priest whose chair it had once regularly been, and partly because no-one else in this place will admit to understanding the rules except for the proprietor who refuses to gamble.

The man with no name knows how to play, but he does nothing except make chuffa train noises. He used to be a tram driver on the city subway but people kept throwing themselves off the blackstone rock in front of him as he came slooping out of the tunnel.

Shuckety puck, shuckety puck.

I am here to try to claw back a measure of the pukka berries I have recently delivered to my father. There are no ripe batches in my apartment at present. I'm at the wrong end of a carefully patterned cycle of growth and I need to keep Corwen Lintock's channel to Jesus open.

These games can run for hours.

This is why I am colluding in deceit. If my father does not soon wind up this game he is embroiled in and attend to me – no pukka berries, no more Second Comings, no return to Eden.

Is this the great man theory of history or has it to do with Cleopatra's nose? Heck, it's a mystery to me. Do you think if someone had actually bought Hitler's paintings I wouldn't now be reduced to cheating for my father during a five-card brag session in a sanitarium?

I am signalling to my father Bronislaw over the turned shoulders of Aaron Wold and Stanley Kubrick about the hands held by his two opponents.

Strictly speaking, I needn't be bothering with all this cheating, although it does calm my nerves, makes me feel like I'm accomplishing something whilst the game runs its course. You see for one thing Aaron Wold is losing hands down as usual.

They didn't play brag on the Hebridean island of Crull, and Aaron Wold doesn't understand the rules. Without speaking words, however, this is a difficult fact to get across. And anyway, he seems happy enough simply to accept the silent companionship which this baffling game offers to him.

Usually Aaron Wold bids three or four rounds in each game, puffing on the filter tip which hangs incessantly from his mouth and drips ash onto his soft beard, then loses his nerve and pulls out, sacrificing what he has staked so far but confirming again his stature as a serious brag player. Some people are easy to please.

Sometimes he goes walkabout for a day or two. He's used to the wide open spaces of the Scottish islands. But he's always back for the next game.

Stanley Kubrick on the other hand is a good player, but note this. My father will not wear his spectacles outside the privacy of his own room along the corridor there. He says they make him look like Herbert Morrison which for some reason of his own invention he regards as intolerable. As a result, Bronislaw can recognise that a kaleidoscope of shapes at the back of the room is moving in synchronicity with the turning and pitching of cards, but not that this pattern of shapes is me, or that I am signalling to him in explanatory semaphore just what cards Stanley Kubrick is holding.

But none the less I am here signalling truths to my father on both hands, just like Corwen Lintock is signalling truths to this community of ours from his mountaintop.

32

The deceit is failing badly. Understandably. It is perhaps fortunate, therefore, that my father is winning, albeit against limited opposition. So why do I carry on waving even though it's having no effect on the game?

Heck, I don't know. Ask yourself the same question.

Stanley Kubrick is a good player but he prefers the drama of the event to the climax of victory, especially in view of the attendant audience today. Me. And so my father seems set to force an early victory. Stanley Kubrick's is a performer's instinct, you see. This is Stanley Kubrick's stage.

Stanley Kubrick arrived as a refugee from the real life flowing beneath them in the basin of the city streets some years ago. Down in the city the now septuagenarian Stanley Kubrick was once a theatrical turn, playing the music halls of the east quarter and of other lesser towns further afield in the hills. Once a week he writes to his old friend Stavros Kouros, impresario and theatre owner, at the Grand Theatre. He writes that it's alright here in the sanitarium. That the nurses are good, the food is eatable. Basic stuff between friends.

Now, no-one much will pay to enter a theatre since they can see all of this and more on TV, in the game shows and so on, and so the theatres are all closed down and levelled to make car parks. For the cars most people can afford now that we've progressed some more.

Stanley Kubrick, the man who lived for theatre, was left beached and forgotten by this changing tide. So now he has to pay to be someone else. Each month he signs a cheque, and the nurses with white pumps and thick stockings let him sometimes be Wee Willie Washington, 'The

Chocolate Coloured Coon' (his former act on stage) and sometimes Anton Chekhov. Most of the time he is just Stanley Kubrick, whose name he once saw on a picture credit when he was watching TV, seeker now of simpler drama in the afternoon brag sessions with Bronislaw Angel and Aaron Wold in the sanitarium on the hill.

Stavros Kouros never writes back.

During his long correspondence with theatre impresario Stavros Kouros, Stanley Kurbrick has not had a reply for the last twenty-three years. This is the amount of time that Stavros Kouros has maybe been dead and buried in the ground and that the Grand Theatre perhaps has been flattened to make way for a car park. It is difficult to tell.

Stanley Kubrick's letters, which carry no return address, have mounted steadily over the years I guess in a cardboard detergent box in some car-park attendant's lavatory.

It gets me when I come up here to the sanitarium, the seriousness with which these games seem to be invested, when out in the city there is so much that remains to be done. In the card games they have to start on time and finish on time and bet all the right amounts and deal and cut in turn and all that stuff.

It pains me that Bronislaw Angel – a soldier, a man of four languages and two names, a weaver of dhootie cloth and a husband and father – should be reduced to surrendering his talents on a game of cards. Before that, of course, surrender had been played out over his woodcarvings, which no-one but me had even seen.

After Bronislaw had finished each one of these carvings, which took him anything up to six months and stood anything up to six feet tall, he carried it up the hill, over to Caspar's Gorge, and set fire to it. Then he sat some, came back to the house, and the next day started work on the next carving on a virgin piece of wood picked up from the riverside timber yard.

This he did for thirty-eight years until he moved up here a few years after my mother died, and took up playing five-card brag each afternoon.

33

Corwen Lintock has given me a present. All these pukka berry supplies which are feeding the city with absolution and stuff are much treasured by the City Leader. That's good! Mind you, it's taking some co-ordinating, keeping him supplied to order. These are temperamental plants at the best of times.

I was sat in my now customary chair in the Fourteenth Floor Leader's Suite when he handed over the Weetabix box. I slit the sellotape along the top and opened it. Inside

I found a stack of magazines held together by two fat elastic bands. On the front of each magazine was emblazoned 'Hot Girls Extra'.

'Oh,' I said.

'They're for you.'

'Yes?'

'Go fuck yourself,' he said, grinning broadly.

Joke, joke.

Corwen Lintock can't get it up any more since Jesus Christ first came to see him. Each time he sits on the toilet seat in his maisonette bathroom and unfolds a copy from his library of *Hot Girls Extra* he feels the cold hand of Jesus on his shoulder. His member has remained completely shrunken in fear of the Lord, and now Corwen Lintock has determined on a vow of no self-abuse to go with his winter-long celibacy. Harry Angel is the lucky benefactor.

Corwen Lintock has told me about his abstinence. He says that Jesus Christ feels an affinity for this city, has taken the Council Leader to the hilltop over by Caspar's Gorge so that Corwen Lintock can see things clearly.

Corwen Lintock has told me, 'I want you to plan the denouement to my work in this centenary year, Harry Angel. I want you to orchestrate the tercentenary fireworks. Bring a circus to town. Things like that.'

He says he trusts me. This is important. In the court case which is proceeding presently some people have testified against Corwen Lintock, saying he has been corrupt and untrustworthy and guilty of torching buildings to claim the insurance and fiddling development grants and planning permissions in favour of Sentex Construction and awarding contracts unfairly in favour of Sentex Catering and so on.

Fortunately, the principal prosecution witness at the outset of the case has kind of withdrawn his testimony, but things are still tough for the Leader. I sense that to have someone he can trust means a lot to him.

Corwen Lintock has developed a taste for the pukka berries. He is due to take another quarter of a pound from me as soon as they are ripe. Some he will eat himself. He eats them in lieu of the sex he is now denied. They have a sedative quality, possessing the same hydrobromic acid compound as bromide does. Half a dozen a day relax him, so to speak.

The remaining pukka berries he will save in a brown paper bag. You see, according to Corwen Lintock, Jesus Christ is coming again on Sunday night to the City Park to offer more advice to a beleaguered city and, as ever, he wants payment on receipt.

'Jesus said for you to have a circus and some fireworks?' I ask.

'He said it's okay for us to have some fun to keep the people happy,' Corwen says. 'I forget his exact words. He seemed okay with the circus thing.'

Corwen Lintock has also said this to me: 'I have told

Daulman and that wanker Drucker to let you have a crack at organising the big display. Did I tell you, when I mentioned your name, Daulman thought you were the man who empties the ashtrays? But Drucker; I don't think Drucker's ever seen a circus, Harry. Still, he seems happy enough with the idea. He smiled a lot anyway.'

'Why not do something with the remainder of your life?' I ask my father in the break between rounds of five-card brag. 'Something constructive. Something that might leave your mark on the world, instead of just playing cards.'

'It gives me pleasure,' he says to me. 'Playing cards. That is my mark on the world.'

The card games, he says, didn't seem to frighten the other residents, and didn't end up in violence, and the sanitarium wasn't in danger of getting burned down as a result of their playing. This seems to be the clinching argument for him, but remember he is living in a crazy palace.

They resume playing, and my father says this, that playing five-card brag with his compatriots, Aaron Wold and Stanley Kubrick and the now dead Father Keam here in this high room has been the happiest, most satisfied, he can remember being, apart from when he has stood on the hill above Caspar's Gorge watching his carvings burn stubbornly to ash in front of him.

Then he leans over his cards and he bets another five pukka berries to raise the taciturn Aaron Wold.

Pukka berries?

Didn't I mention it? In the absence of legal tender up here, which has been banned absolutely by the proprietor for reasons best known to himself, the card school runs each afternoon on pukka berries which are the only acceptable brag-currency here in the sanitarium.

No pukka berries, no play. Just like Corwen Lintock on his mission to Jesus Christ. Ironic, really.

The silent Aaron Wold scratches his dandruffed, ash-littered beard and elects to fold a potentially winning hand once more.

34

He flips up the latch on the shed door, steals in while hinges creak, is met by the stale, sawdusted air.

He is Harni. Flesh and blood. A boy with a boy's perspective. Centred upon himself. Each day he grows a little more. Each day he wakes needing to add to the sum of his flimsy knowledge. Each day he voyages with charts that are insufficient for his seas, sailing to the edge of what he knows, until he loses his nerve and returns to the safety of what is solid and forever. His mother's prayers, his father standing stiffly posed in a borrowed uniform in Warsaw, 1938, in the photograph above the mantelpiece. The house on Beaker Street. The shed. Physical things. Borders.

He sits on the upturned tea chest, his thin metronome legs swinging above the ground. There are splashes of light from the kitchen bulb across the yard. He is light. Weightless. Children are unaware of the boundaries of their physical selves. Harni Zelenewycz can drift between people, his unbordered self slipping noiselessly through the flow around him. He is all promise and dreams.

Promise and dreams.

Along the shelves are racks of tools, stiff stained brown card boxes with screws and nails and such things bundled inside. The workbench is gouged deep with scrapes and chisel runs. An oil lamp hangs from a bent nail in the roof.

Tick tick tick. The boy Harni plays at being the father Brogdan, imagines himself working the wood. A row of carving chisels, Brogdan Zelenewycz's only souvenir from the war, lie spaced in their wooden tray. Harni picks one up. The floor has been swept clean the previous evening. It had been the boy's job. Patches of sawdust lie in the corners where the broom had been too clumsy to reach.

The boy Harni pushes the door fast shut, blocking out the kitchen's light. He sits back on the tea chest, fingering the chisel's cold length, sawdust smells rippling through him like some secret, warming code. A cotton cloth, dhootie cloth, drapes the carving which stands on the centre of the table.

The boy reaches for the cloth, drags it clear. The figure, a cherub with hands clasped together, stands three feet high and bruised with the first blunt strokes of the knife, hinting at a crisper shape to come. The boy sometimes fancies it is him. A prayer. A hope expressed. Maybe, maybe, maybe.

But surely the magic of creation.

This is a boy's perspective.

Too engrossed in his thoughts, in his unbordered self, the boy doesn't hear footsteps in the yard. There is a clunk and the latch on the shed door flicks up from the outside. Clumsy light breaks in. The boy spins round as his father's shape fills the door.

They stand facing each other. Watching, waiting for the other to make a first move.

'What is you doing?' Brogdan Zelenewycz asks.

'Just looking.' The boy leans to make space between them. His father edges in, grateful to respond. He takes the cloth from the boy, scrunches it like a duster in one hand.

'I say not to touch. Not ever to touch anything.' He is stilted, unsure of his ground. His words come out hard, sudden.

'I didn't. I just wanted a look at him.' The boy swallows. His father has been back with them for two years now. Not long enough, maybe. There is much to make up. To forgive.

Brogdan Zelenewycz looks across from the boy to the wood. Runs his fingers down one of the chiselled sides. Breaking the contact between the two of them in here who feel and breathe. Still in his work clothes, his cloth rucksack gripped under one arm, he takes the chisel from the boy's grip, looks at it, twists it around in his one available hand, grips the handle, begins to slice the thinnest strip of wood from the flank he has stroked with his index finger.

'Go see's when tea ready,' he says softly in his still breaking English. He can speak now he is freed from the glare of direct contact with the boy. He looks across. Harni waits, then nods, wedges himself off the chest, slips out into the yard. They have made a kind of peace.

Zelenewycz steps back, clutching the blade. In the early stages he has learned to feel his way in. Not to rely on sight to gauge where to strip away at the wood but on touch, on texture.

He lets the knife follow the sweep of his thumb, nipping lightly at the wood. He only ever takes off the wood in sixteenths, maybe eighths of an inch at most. It is a perversely slow way of working but he sticks always to the same ritual. Learning of the soul of the wood, layer by layer, his eyes alive, his fingers pressing, pushing, meeting the grains at the border crossing of his senses.

When this last winter had first descended on them, the boy had blunted one of his father's special blades. He had been trying to scratch his name on the shed wall in copying some stunt of the young Pound boy along the street. Zelenewycz had banned him from the shed, banging his fist down on the kitchen table with an anger that had alarmed them both.

It had been weeks before the boy had dared approach the

shed again. Finally he had crept in one night, stood at the door waiting for his father to react. Zelenewycz had looked up and let him be. The boy had moved slowly to the tea chest and heaved himself onto it, and Brogdan Zelenewycz had forgotten that he was there, lost in the tensing of his jaw and the flaring of his nostrils as he had worked on the wood.

Sure, sure, that was me. Going back some. These days I carry concerns more for the living than the inanimate dead. Carry out small tasks that build like blocks in the steady progress of things.

On my way to the sanitarium today I completed one such small task. Another burial as it happens, but not one which will require lime to mask the smell.

This time I buried a parcel wrapped in brown paper. A report on the autopsy of Sam Pound. This autopsy contained information which would surely not have helped the situation in the city. Not at all. I agreed with the Leader that action would be helpful. To the city. I switched reports.

I collected the official version from the city morgue on behalf of the Leader and I buried it, alone, on the hills above the east quarter near to the rock face my father knew as Caspar's Gorge. No-one much goes up there these days. Just me. Then I replaced it with a more constructive report provided by Corwen Lintock. This I delivered to the offices of Aratakis, the Chairman of the Police Authority.

Both reports contain genetic fingerprint read-outs and

such things, but on the version I have passed to Aratakis some lines have been left blank. Why? Heck, I don't know. The report I have passed on to Aratakis points to culprits from the east quarter. That's plausible. It would fit. It would tie in for sure. The buried document unhelpfully named other names, Corwen Lintock assured me.

'You're a good man, Harry Angel,' Corwen Lintock confirmed as I left for my small task.

And I smiled my beatific smile for him.

My father once asked me this: when I came to look back on my life, at what moment did I think I would have been happiest? That was when he was being Bronislaw Angel nearly all the time.

What a terrible question to ask a man. How does it leave you, I thought, if you figure your happiest, most fulfilling moment has already gone and you're down off the peak? What if you think it was when you were seven years of age and watching your father expertly crafting, chiselling some sublime cherub you took to be a representation of yourself in the draughty backyard shed by the light of a hanging oil lamp?

What if you say that?

Back to today. My father has come up trumps, for once trouncing his playing partners with a final jack-high flourish. Now there are enough pukka berries on our team for Corwen Lintock's needs and sufficient left over to see my father through the rest of the week's brag playing.

35

The truth.

Let me tell you what my father Bronislaw Angel told me.

You see, Bronislaw Angel was not just a survivor. He was a war hero. When he was Brogdan Zelenewycz, that was.

Odd, that. The family goes and changes its names to blend in with the new world to which we had pleaded entry and my father, Brogdan, goes and settles on another Polish christian name. My mother told me it was so if ever he was knocked down by a passing subway tram it would be relatively easy for him to remember his name if he were delirious and hurting. I should have told Vernon Smitts that.

Me? I was happy with Harry. Happy as Larry.

It was my father who was driving the lorry. Too hurriedly to stop even for the birth of his son in the back.

This is what he told me.

The whereabouts of the partisan group my father and mother had been with back in 1942 had been betrayed by an informant who had gone to the German troops down in

Rajska and spilled the beans.

In the camp of the partisans, my parents had sung songs with the group at night around the fire.

Quiet songs.

'Kde Domov Muj?' they sang.

It was the song of the partisans.

'Where Is My Home?' was their song in the hills.

It was a good time for them there.

Despite everything, there was hope.

My father helped three of the partisan women and my mother to escape in a stolen goods lorry from under the noses of the Germans. One of the women wore a green ribbon in her hair. Brogdan Zelenewycz drove the lorry for two hundred and fifty miles on dirt tracks and sideroads and through two separate roadblocks to get them to safety. Behind them, all of the other partisans in the group were caught and interrogated. They were told to send letters to their families, each of which said 'Es geht mir gut.' Then they were all killed. The leader they crucified upside down on a tree.

Brogdan Zelenewycz was an eighteen-year-old private in the Polish army which had looked west in the summer of 1939. He fought in defence of his country against the Nazi blitzkrieg, and later joined up with a group of vagabond Poles and Slovaks who called themselves partisans south in the Carpathian foothills near the village of Rajska, taking his new wife with him.

Down in the valley the special boxcars from Vienna were carrying their human cargo to the nearby collection of camps at Auschwitz where the bodies of the people would eventually be starved and gassed and thrown onto heaps and the smell masked by mounds of lime mulch.

The railway track going north ran to Warsaw through the city of Lodz where the ghetto was being beaten and starved into extermination. All in all it was a productive geographic basin for the manufacture of human bonemeal.

It was this betrayed vagabond group from which Brogdan Zelenewycz rescued the lorryload of women in 1942, driving them further south to safety.

He had wanted his wife to reach England where one day, he said, they might share a new life, and so he delivered them to Salonica where, finally, she was smuggled out on a bust-up cargo boat bound for Alicante. The boat was running Turkish hashish and a sideline in human exiles desperate to make for neutral Spain, but the now two-year-old Harni Zelenewycz knew little of this, wrapped in his swaddling clothes of ship's linen.

The boat took only women as human cargo.

The captain perhaps felt safer from mutiny that way. And so my father, Brogdan, stayed on in Central Europe, meeting up with other Poles who were making their way through to Persia and on to Palestine. Here they were to be equipped with American armour and trained into a kind of army by British troops based in Haifa.

Thus would my father eventually exchange, so to speak, the Polish grey he had once worn, for a British brown serge uniform to join up for the remainder of the war with the Polish Second Brigade, formed under General Sikorsky, which had fought first at Monte Cassino and would later take part in the Normandy landings.

He returned to Palestine in 1946 and the following year, through the assistance of a refugee organisation based in Geneva which helped to locate displaced persons, he travelled to England to be reunited with his wife and young son in a now peaceful Europe.

My father talks little of this. In fact he tells me of these things just once a year, on the anniversary of the invasion of Poland. September 1st.

He is sad on that day. Lacking.

My mother called it the day when innocence, his innocence, was lost. In war, of course, it is the innocent who get hurt. War is about clichés. The crueller the war, the more pointless its inception, the simpler the language. This is what my mother wrote one time sitting at her kitchen table with a forty-watt bulb watching over her. How else could you convince people to fight each other, she said. Offer prizes?

Innocence.

Have you wondered what sort of man could be an innocent in such a world as this? In a world where the principal product of Auschwitz, human bonemeal apart, was maybe spoons? Spoons manufactured by the Haftlinge from iron plate within the camp complex. One spoon per living person. It was so they could eat the soup. The whole complex produced a greater tonnage of spoons than the synthetic rubber it was supposedly designed to make.

Spoons were like gold. There was a huge trade in illegally forged spoons. No spoon, no eat. The three watchers at the birth of Harni Zelenewycz still each carried their single spoons sewn to the inside of their clothing in the back of the stolen van that raced south to safety.

When the camp was opened up, the British Tommies discovered a mountain of spoons spread on one side of the Buna works. Waste not want not, they maybe figured.

What is an innocent in such a world as this?

How about: someone who doesn't see it coming.

And then it is out of his system, it seems. He has never to my knowledge gone to any of the reunions of the Ex-Servicemen's Association, and he has always preferred the solitude of his own company, in the backyard shed on Beaker Street, on the hill over by Caspar's Gorge, lately in the sanitarium give or take a card game or two.

Brogdan Zelenewycz didn't see it coming.

One more thing.

He didn't consent to my mother's plea to change our names because of the difficulties of pronunciation. I lied to you. I wanted to shelter him for a while from the discomfiture that truth sometimes brings.

He consented because, when he finally got here to join us, they thought he was a dumb foreigner. And even though they knew that some people had died, they didn't believe my father had fought on the Normandy beaches and they didn't know where the Carpathian Mountains were. They would never go there. Didn't care.

They said only, 'Did you have knives and forks over there and did you eat dog food and put the evil eye on people?'

My father Bronislaw Angel once told me something else.

It was during one of his September 1sts, so you can take it or leave it.

He said that all the men he ever knew seemed to be born in tragedy. He said it was ironic that they all seemed to die in torpor. In between times, their torch songs seem to run like nursery rhymes but, heck, he could never remember which ones.

I took this as much as anything as my father's commentary on his own life. And I believed him, as sons do. I believed he had been born in tragedy and he would die in torpor, until I discovered that he lied a lot, but then that was September 1st for you.

High on the hill the breeze blows Harni's hair flat against his seven-year-old face.

Here he is well out of bounds, well out beyond the border. But heck, he is just curious, has just headed out on the tail of his discontented father who has laboured up here

140

above the city with a pack like a dead dog slung over his shoulder. Sure, Harni thinks, I know what's in that sack, hanging like a dead dog might. And he has come to see his father's cherub which could so easily be him planted in the dull earth to watch over this city of other angels.

This he does not see.

He first smells the sweet, sweet, lapping woodsmoke drifting from where his father stood. Smells like incense rising out of the earth. The carving stands on a pyre of loose wood chippings, smoking and hiccuping like nothing was amiss. But the flames lick higher, and ten feet away the man who is sometimes Brogdan Zelenewycz and sometimes Bronislaw Angel stands and watches, and the boy on the brow of the hill spies too. Turns, runs, falling, falling, down into the bowels of the city's earth. Not looking back, but running and falling down into the bowels of the city's earth.

One more thing. The voices. The ones that once made siren sounds in my head as a child, the ones that were surely women trying to tell me things. You know what! They have come back.

36

The votes have been cast.

The people have stood up and been counted. Said 'yes' to a brighter future. Said 'fine' to a re-vamped Housing Commission. Said 'sure' to a better outlook for the animals in the city zoo, safe from the atrocities now and then visited on them.

It is no more than Corwen Lintock has asked of them.

Even now, as the last stragglers are slotting their voting slips into the boxes, the city is safe in the knowledge that the exit poll carried out by Sentex Information Systems suggests a solid working majority for the Leader and his team.

Now dusk has fallen and the counters are set to begin counting. Corwen Lintock has been campaigning all day. His chest is on fire from heartburn. It is maybe tension. His jaw aches from a thousand smiling interjections. I know. I've watched him. A little help here, a little errand there. He trusts me, you see. As a city official I may not campaign openly for one side or another, but this trust the Leader has placed in me has compelled him to second me to his Unit over the last week or two. Already he's given me a little job to do for him after the election is over, when I'm back with Drucker's Department, working under the direction of Daulman with the uncurious eyes and the questionable dress sense.

'You know what, Harry Angel,' Corwen Lintock says. 'You're a good man.'

I picked a slogan for him. It said this: Feel Good, Real Citizens Have Nothing To Feel Bad About.

Lintock's election headquarters had badges run off. I'm a Real Citizen, they said. Support Your City, they said. Don't Give Me No Evil Eye, they said. It made kind of a talking point, and maybe it picked up votes along the way.

Free football tickets went out to everyone pledging support for the Leader. It's a sort of team-building thing. And you know what, the Corwen Lintock team has sure been pulling together. Even in court the team has pulled together. Only this week a couple of alibis turned up to pull the Leader clear of the legal precipice he was getting near to. Sure. Both Aratakis and Liam Fitsimmons of all people remembered, having rechecked their diaries, that they were with the man on one or two key occasions.

Phew!

The Leader slipped out of the rally held for his election team a little while back. The results are imminent. I think maybe he needed a little peace or something away from the crowd, to let his heartburn settle down out in the night air.

When I followed him it was just that something made me curious. He mentioned heading for a breather over by the City Park. That's how come I finished up following him. That's where he headed. Like I say, I was just curious.

And here I am.

Corwen Lintock has told me about the spot in the City Park where he used to take his wife after dark when she would howl like a dog while they were making love; scene also of the heart attack which precipitated the Leader's triple bypass and threw him back onto the resources of his secret library of *Hot Girls Extra* now, curiously, in my own possession.

It seemed like not a bad guess given the general state of things that if Jesus Christ was going to make an impact on his return, he would pick the scene of his subject's greatest humiliation to put himself one ahead. To steal an advantage. And I've been proved right. This guy Jesus plays it by the book. Except that it isn't Jesus.

What a discovery to make, and on election night too.

The surprise is not that Jesus Christ is, in reality, Aaron Wold. It is, I am to discover before long, that Corwen Lintock already had a hunch about this.

Let me rephrase that. Lintock doesn't know Aaron Wold from, well, Anton Chekhov. He has never been to the sanitarium, never even seen Wold until his recent appearances to the City Leader as Jesus Christ began. But in his heart of hearts he suspects that this is not the same Jesus Christ of Good Book fame. When I am to ask Corwen Lintock later on how he came to suspect it he will say it was the filter-tips the man called Jesus smoked. He will say it had seemed improbable from the off.

From my vantage point by the trees I can see the lone figure of Jesus Christ who is, of course, Aaron Wold. He has arrived first at the clearing which has borne witness to so much of Corwen Lintock's past. The light has all but drained out of the city sky. The night's blue shadows lie strewn and stretched under a cool city moon. A witchy kind of moon. It's the kind of night where once you expected to hear howling coming from in here. But that was before the Leader met up with his Jesus Christ and found us some answers to this failing town of ours.

Aaron Wold, thick-bearded, clad in navy anorak, stands expectantly on a rise in the copse waiting for Corwen Lintock, Leader of the City Council, to arrive. Corwen Lintock is not the only one in the city comfortable in the role of saviour.

It is a part the now taciturn Aaron Wold had learned for the Hebridean Mystery Plays which are performed only once every ten years on his home island of Crull, a role for which Aaron Wold, in accordance with ancient custom, had been selected at the conclusion of the last cycle of plays ten years previously on the island.

'You Bethlehem Ephrathah,' the prophet Micah announces by megaphone to the gathered crowds on Crull, standing above the narrow island streets filled with straining faces, 'though you are small among the clans of Judah, out of you will come for me, one who will rule over Israel, whose origins are from of old, from ancient times.'

The Hebridean Mystery Plays of Crull attract many thousands of visitors to the island for the six weeks they are performed once a decade. They begin with a torchlight procession at midnight through the streets of Crull and a performance of the Old Testament Creation of the World. The Cycle of plays ends six weeks later with the Resurrection of Jesus and his Ascension into Heaven.

It's a good story with a moral and a happy ending. A feelgood ending. The straining faces by the roadside are here for the happy ending. You don't pay out $7,000 a time and pass up the Florida Keys to miss out on a happy ending. For $7,000 you expect to feelgood.

It has always been a deeply spiritual event going back a thousand years and with its roots further back still in St Columba's sixth-century conversion of the Celts to Christianity on nearby Iona, and it is an unbreakable tenet of these Mystery Plays that a local man born and bred on Crull and chosen at the conclusion of the previous Cycle must play the central figure of Jesus Christ.

The format of the Cycle allowed Aaron Wold, the Hebridean milkman chosen for the part, an extensive apprenticeship to the part of saviour and he smiles a fatherly welcome now as a still tense and gassy Corwen Lintock approaches his Jesus Christ in the City Park, a seeker, still, of answers in a night strewn with lazy shadows. Aaron Wold is well versed in fatherly smiles after ten years of adjustment.

Then the next surprise as Jesus Christ holds open his arms.

Aaron Wold speaks!

Aaron Wold has a deep and lilting voice, resonant with his Hebridean roots. It leaves me wondering why has a man with a voice easy like honey and the practised demeanour of Jesus Christ which he perfected over an apprenticeship lasting a full decade chosen to speak to no-one for the past six years? Here, truly, is a man from a crazy palace.

Aaron Wold, who is Jesus Christ in the eyes of Corwen Lintock, speaks to the City Leader, practising the long-learned words of his apprentice years.

He says to him that the day of judgement will separate the godly from the godless. He says that this city must become honourable in the sight of the Lord. He says that Corwen Lintock must favour the good and fear the heathen in building a new Eden here.

And so on. Phew!

Lintock seems to know what's being talked about here. What's needed. Me, I could never get the hang of parables and stuff. Always had a soft spot for the guy who buried his little pot of gold talents. What's wrong with that, I kept thinking as the Glaswegian Father Keam droned on. Safest place, I thought.

These are the things that Aaron Wold learned to speak of during his ten-year apprenticeship to the role of Jesus Christ in between milk-round deliveries in the Scottish dawns.

Corwen Lintock asks no questions. He knows a day of judgement when he sees one. He nods deftly after each sentence. At the end of the audience, Lintock hands over the small bag he has brought with him. Jesus Christ counts out the pukka berries inside, reckoning the total, and sees that this is good. Then he tells Corwen Lintock that he will come again in seven days' time with more observations on the city's ills now that the election for the Corwen Lintock–Jesus Partnership is in the bag. The City Leader acknowledges this.

He says, 'Same deal?'

'Same deal,' says Jesus Christ, who is Aaron Wold, in his lullaby Scottish west coast accent, and he turns and walks softly away, huddled against the winter night in his navy anorak. He is clutching his bag of pukka berries which are his currency for the five-card brag game tomorrow.

Later in the evening, when the election has been formally won and coloured balloons float happily in the sky above the town and there is dancing for the feelgood team and food supplied by Sentex Catering Supplies, I say to Corwen Lintock, 'Do you believe it is Jesus Christ?'

'I have my doubts,' he admits. 'It is the filter-tips he smokes that worry me most.'

He asks me how the preparations are going for the tercentenary city celebrations. They're going fine, I say, just fine. I've worked hard on them. Got some real whizz-bang fireworks. And I tell him I've booked the biggest and best travelling circus I could find, using the Tourism and Development account to meet the costs as the Leader said I should. Dancing bears, the works.

In fact, I say, should the fireworks and stuff go well and should Corwen Lintock want to reward me at some point for this as well as for supplying all those batches of pukka berries to him on a regular basis, I would be delighted if any promotion took me to the Fourteenth-Floor Council Leader's Admin and Support Unit permanently.

Secret ambition, Harry Angel?

Maybe, maybe. I just keep remembering poor Vernon Smitts. Finished up going sideways till he fell right off the edge.

Corwen Lintock doesn't look too sure about my suggestion, so I figure to give it a push. After all, I have no wish to finish up spread across the Al mumbling some weirdo incantations.

I tell him: You remember Oostenbruik? All those years ago? That was me, that was me! Harry Angel. I signed the report. I tell him he can surely rely on me. Just remember Oostenbruik.

Heck, I hope I didn't misjudge this one.

'But you will continue going to see him?' I say later, 'paying him pukka berries and addressing him as though you are sure of who he is in your own mind?'

'Without faith there is nothing,' he says to me. 'And besides, this Jesus hasn't lied to me so far.' That seems like a good basis from which to horsetrade, don't I think?

What can I say?

37

Another morning dawns. Another subway tram goes slooping by.

It is some time since Sam Pound was dug from the earth.

It is also some time since Corwen Lintock claimed his first batch of pukka berries from me.

The election is a done thing, and the time the City Leader met his Jesus Christ in the chill City Park night as I looked on recedes into memory.

Time passes. It is the way we learn things.

My errand. The one set me by a grateful Leader which will help me to show my mettle.

I have tried, and got nothing, from the priest called Daniel, from Mary Pound, from other enquiries. So now it is time to call on the house of Coleman Seer.

I have come with a package and a favour to ask. I need information to find the culprits Corwen Lintock is looking for. In breaking a chain of reticence, look to the weakest link. Coleman Seer, the weakest link, comes to the door in his stockinged feet. Behind me, in the courtyard, stray cats watch from distances that dare. I go in. Behind me at the door Seer raises an arm. Cats flurry, rearrange position, judge distances again from this crazy human.

My package is a box. It says Weetabix on the side but there is no breakfast cereal in here. I have placed it on the table between myself and the awkward, folded shape of Coleman Seer who adjusts his glasses, smiles his little smile, licks his lips.

Coleman Seer is Chairman of the token Residents Forum in the east quarter of the city which I attend once a month. He will tell you that he takes his duties seriously with regard to the Forum. He recognises it has been a genuine attempt by the City Council to consult people there and to involve the east quarter community in the difficult decisions which affect their lives.

Daulman has called it one of Fitsimmons's mickey mouse college-boy schemes straight out of the Kremlin.

Coleman Seer has a little smile when he tells you of his faith in this attempt to work with, not for, the people but his smile, as ever, has sharp edges to it and it leaves you kind of wondering.

Coleman Seer is a bony man with a barber's haircut thinning rapidly on top. He is a stick insect, all angles. His hair is smeared flat on his head and he has the knack of wearing all his clothes half a size small for him so that they restrict his insect movements like a crusty, half-shedding skin.

Weird.

His little eyes follow each movement in the room. He is a man jabbed and prodded by life and its twists and turns. So Coleman Seer, unemployed citizen, community leader, sits in his chair by the TV in his stockinged feet eyeballing everything that moves around him, smiling that funny smile with the edges to it.

He might not stop it, but Coleman Seer will sure as hell see it coming.

The package with Weetabix stamped all over it is full of magazines. Yes, those magazines! The ones presented to me by Corwen Lintock, City Leader.

Hot stuff! The top magazine in the box (I know, I checked), offers Teenage Twins Sex Lust. You should see what they do over forty-eight pages. Hang around and I'll get round to telling you what's inside.

Boy, will I tell you.

For now, my magazines have found a useful purpose and a good home.

Coleman Seer, recipient of my box of goodies, has been out of work since the last textile mill closed down by the East River.

He'd been a union man there at Galbraith's India Mill since our apprenticeship days together, not liked but at least respected for his thoroughness in pursuing cases. Wind him up and set him loose, the union bosses used to say of him. They thought he was funny, like a dog with a bone.

There were a lot of bones to gnaw on in those days. The mill, which had been up since the 1850s, was long past its production peaks when Coleman Seer arrived there.

Seer nitpicked over every batch of redundancies, quibbled and remonstrated that every bout of lay-offs was not the 'final cut', as management would invariably suggest, but was simply the next step in a systematic stripping of assets.

He stood his ground and was railroaded over, and eventually he went too. It broke his nitpicking heart. It was all he had lived for. He got moved from one satellite mill to another in the Galbraith chain as each one got wound down, until the last one was finally sold off to Sentex Industries in some arrangement that had to do with insurance. It burned down not too long after that.

Coleman Seer only ever reached the rank of foreman. You wonder why? A nitpicking man isn't easily favoured for promotion. Also, he'd fiddled the books in the factory. The union got to hear about the fiddling but said nothing to management for fear of a scandal that might weaken still further the union's credibility in fending off future restructurings and thinnings down. Instead, they just hinted that he was unsound.

I, too, was involved in this sad little drama.

I made a list once, you might remember, of people I had truly befriended on the planet. One was Vernon Smitts, poor Vernon Smitts, former council official and father of my now estranged wife. The other was Coleman Seer, ex-union man at the latterly bankrupt Galbraith's India Mill Textile Company down by the East River, now reduced to playing what Fitsimmons calls 'kiddie politics' in an irrelevant Community Forum to keep himself alive.

Know what I mean?

Sure, sure you do. Having something to get up for. Something to believe in. Something to make sense of a seeming wreckage of lives. Heck, a happy ending.

Me? I had the old pukka berries.

38

We go back a long way, Coleman and me. All the way back to the old blackstone Technical College where we both went to study textiles.

We were friends there, Coleman Seer and me. The kind of friends men are in cities. I knew his name, his team, but not his address, his dreams, whether his heart beat blood.

Once or twice while we were there I recall that Coleman said he had fallen in love, but no-one fell back in love with him and so he married the union and now he lives with his TV and with his black dog that doesn't bark any more.

He had wanted to court Elisa Smitts, the girl I would myself eventually marry after it turned out she was the daughter of Vernon Smitts. Coleman Seer knew her when she was just sixteen and half-heartedly doing some obscure part-time course at the Technical College, and she seemed to us both to be very English and very still and seemingly untouched. She was the only female that Coleman Seer ever appeared unfrightened of. I knew this because he never raised his voice to a boom around her.

It's a neat test. Try it.

Like me, though, he didn't know that this was because she was still a child. She smiled sweetly at us both when we passed in a corridor or stood together in a lift but neither of us secured a word of encouragement or interest from her at this time. For Coleman Seer, like a dog with a bone, it drove him mad.

Forget it, I used to tell him. Stick to learning things. But Coleman Seer's mind kept drifting back to that bone until eventually one night he was found howling like a dog under her window and Vernon Smitts came and chased him away with a broom and determined to find a sweet man one day soon for his daughter to wed and thus protect her from such craziness.

Soon after that, of course, I won Elisa Smitts. I offered her a new life with me. In this respect I conned her just like my father Brogdan conned my mother by promising a new life in England for them both — the one that turned out to be the same as before. Any new life that my wife, Elisa, forged was entirely due to her efforts alone. I figured this out after she had left, to her better life.

I asked her once, near the end of our marriage, why she had taken up with me after her father, Vernon Smitts, had introduced us.

You were such a child, she said.

Hmmm.

I conned Coleman Seer too.

He said people would always need cotton, that the know-how of the English artisans would safeguard their position at the head of the textile world for a thousand years to come, that ours was a community which was owed its destiny.

He said the most powerful and most rewarding position on the face of this earth for him was to shepherd the union's flock in a great manufacturing adventure like the weaving of cotton cloth into necessary human commodities.

He said he would always feel privileged to serve the members he represented and he scorned the prospect of promotion up the greasy pole, saying he preferred instead the respect of his peers.

He didn't know about being unsound.

I conned Coleman Seer because I knew he was talking rot when he said all this.

But what can you do?

People said, 'Why does he go on like that?'

'It's a mystery to me,' I'd say.

I strung him along, letting him believe he was smarter and wiser than me. I let him stew in his own juices. It was a kind of betrayal, I admit, but it wasn't the worst thing I ever did to him.

Coleman Seer opens up the sellotaped Weetabix box which is set down on the table between us in his third-floor east quarter flat. The city pays the rent on the flat which is good of them. He collects it fortnightly from the benefits office. He hasn't offered me a cup of coffee yet but then he isn't used to visitors. If that dog of his had a bark, he'd be woofing at me in surprise.

Coleman Seer slips open the top flap and looks inside and takes out the top magazine. You already know what it says, that it's called *Hot Girls Extra* and that it promises Teenage Twins Sex Lust over forty-eight full-colour pages. Breasts, lips, pale skin, young blue eyes. You don't know what's inside, though! What patterns this flesh makes. What little sucking, pressing noises will sound in Coleman Seer's head.

Patience, patience!

Coleman Seer doesn't either, and he licks at his lip nervously. He doesn't get out much these days, and there are twenty-nine more magazines in the box as well, remember.

Nowadays, as I said, Coleman Seer chairs the East Quarter Community Forum, originally set up by the venerable George Steen as a result of a Housing Commission recommendation.

My reports to the committee lay great emphasis on the present-day Forum as a necessary, useful and effective tool of city management. Seer runs it, what there is of it, with the same single-mindedness he once gave to the cause of the Allied Textile Workers at Galbraith's India Mill. I have therefore painted handsome pictures of the Forum in clear blue words.

It's not easy, though. Coleman runs it mostly from his front room. He is not well liked by the newer groups of disparate citizens who have made their homes here, nor by the groups of youths who pick clean the bones of the blackstone courtyards after dark of an evening. There is little support for him and for the Forum, which is seen largely as an empty exercise by the city authorities. Look around us, people say. Is this the result of consulation?

Stones are thrown at Coleman Seer's windows. They fed a cocktail of milk, bleach and turpentine to his black dog out in the yard that stripped out the animal's throat and made it crazy for a week.

Now the dog doesn't go chasing the legion of cats any more round the alleys. In response, the cats have extended their ground. Mounted an assault to get him out. So he believes. They pee daily on his refuge till a smell like sour cheese creeps in the air vents.

Now the dog has no bark and it sits silent at Coleman Seer's stockinged feet in his fortress flat. They don't get out much and they watch a lot of game shows together on the TV in the corner.

I ask Coleman Seer how he thinks the Forum would take the introduction of some kind of protective measure. A curfew, maybe, on the east quarter some nights when trouble's brewing?

Fine, fine, he says, but – I can tell he's a little distracted – what are you going to do about the cats? And will there be more Weetabix boxes?

The worst thing I ever did to Coleman Seer was to get him to sell me two names from out there in the east quarter for the murder of old Sam Pound in return for the offer of thirty magazines in a Weetabix box.

'For old times' sake,' I say. 'For Sam.'

'How much evidence do you need?' Coleman Seer asks me.

'Enough,' I say. 'Just enough.'

And he gives me two names on the back of an envelope underneath half a dozen badly drafted sentences.

39

When my father Bronislaw sat down to eat his first meal in the works canteen at the old India Mill they were astonished to see him eat with a knife and fork. Where did you learn that, they said.

Under the terms of the prevailing Aliens Act as it stood in 1947 he was obliged to answer all questions from Englishmen politely and with deference. That was the interpretation placed on it by the police sergeant to whom the Zelenewycz family were registered, and who was Bronislaw to argue with that?

Among the onlookers at the table that day were the venerable George Steen, union chief at Galbraith's India

Mill and City Councillor, who would in due course rise to become the respected Leader of the City Council, and one Arthur Daulman, father of the man destined to rise to number two in Drucker's Department, nine places above me in rank despite his mediocre taste in suits.

Such people were, not unlike my father Bronislaw, building a new world for themselves after the adventure and privation of the war just gone in which some people had died.

They were keen to make new lives for themselves as brothers in arms with a new free universal health service and with Football League fixtures back in full swing.

Naturally, my father made every effort to accommodate them, starting by agreeing with my mother to change our name.

And so Brogdan Zelenewycz became Bronislaw Angel.

He rose in the mill to a position of undermanager. He was punctual and clever and courteous, mindful of the advice of the police sergeant long after the Act fell into abeyance. But he was always a little suspect, a little un-sound with his clipped sentences that he converted from the liquid Polish in his head.

The union, under the leadership of the venerable George Steen, was immensely suspicious of him when he assumed a management position, even after his change of name. They worried that he might be a communist plant or a fascist spy or eat dog food or howl at the moon or something, but they were stuck with him because the

Government said that men like him could only be employed in specified industries with work that was suitable for them as Aliens. This work consisted of coalmining and agriculture and textiles.

The nearest coal mines were maybe fifty miles away, and it was well known that cows didn't like foreigners with their hot salty hands, and so men like Bronislaw Angel né Brogdan Zelenewycz were drawn here by the manufacturing adventure which had made this a once great city which would surely prosper again. At least cotton manufacture would last here a thousand years and offer everybody a new life.

Promises, promises.

What follows I learned from the Woolworth exercise pad my mother wrote in now and then. She wrote in such precise English words that it seemed as though she were simply producing reportage, as if these weren't events which happened around her, touched her life, put the cap on things.

For an undermanager, Bronislaw Angel (sometimes he forgot to turn round when people called his name) went surprisingly early in the rounds of redundancies when the peoples of the world learned how to make their own dhootie cloth.

At least, though, they shook his hand and said thanks and told him he had time to start over again.

He got a job as caretaker at the Southside Grammar School and, like Aaron Wold on his Hebridean milk round, he discovered the joys of the early morning and the sweetness of his own company as he swept and hoovered and cleaned and cleared.

He had his own big storeroom which doubled as his office and brew station. He had a chair, a kettle and a home-made shelf, and instead of going back home between his split shifts of 7 till 10 in the morning and 3 till 5 in the afternoon he stayed put in his cubbyhole office and drank hot tea and read books that he borrowed from the school library while the din of the school day went on all about him beyond his four sweet walls.

In the eight years he was there as school caretaker he read the entire collection of stories of Richmal Crompton's William. He read Arthur Ransome's *Swallows and Amazons*, and Billy Bunter's adventures, and *The Wind in the Willows* which was his favourite and which he read and re-read each term, and in all of these he found the England to which he had sent his young wife and son on a busted boat out of Salonica with its cargo of mute female refugees and Turkish hashish.

At this time I had just been taken on by City Hall, my mother's candle lit at the church of St Mary's in honour of my having made my way in the world.

One time I went into the school to see my father. I forget why, some errand or family business. The day after that, my father Bronislaw was out clearing the school grounds of rubbish when he came across a big chalk drawing on the side wall of the school facing the main entrance. It was a good drawing, the kid had talent, of a face with a turkey neck and ears like the handles of a football trophy, and underneath it said 'Kur!'

At that point he gave up trying to join the club, I think. It was easier in the books. And he sought compensations. No, no, not drink, not that old chestnut. Anyway, when he drank he saw faces and heard noises. No, not drink.

He had a secret, from me, from the school, from his wife who was increasingly taking refuge in music down in the cold cellar of the house and in weeping statues and other such things.

His secret was four inches wide and went through from the back of his cubbyhole brew shop to the girls' changing rooms on the other side where the Fourth Form sang the school song as they stripped down to their pink flesh and showered.

It had a ventilator grille over it which, once he had changed the style of grille from a strip to a mesh, he could see through and watch nearly everything beyond.

Right into the clubhouse, so to speak.

When they finally sussed it and fired him, they hired in his place a twenty-year-old boy from the estate with a broken-comb moustache and tattoos of 'love' and 'hate' on his knuckles who did no work and spent his time chatting up the girls, but at least that didn't make the papers.

Across the city, on the same day that my father is being fired, a young Corwen Lintock has wet his bed again. He is saying to his mother, 'Why the cupboard under the stairs? It's dark in there, I don't like it.'

His mother is saying, 'If you don't go in, the bogeymen will find you for peeing on your sheets.'

Even now, she is saying, they are laughing at him over the river. They know, they know!

The young Corwen says, 'Why do they come for me when I pee in the bed, Mam?'

It's a mystery to me, she shrugs.

Slam!

In there it's cold and dark. He holds on to his *Charlie Buchan Football Annual*, golden men like Eddie Melon clutched to his heart whilst beyond the panel leading to the outside coal store is the scratching of whiskered rats burrowing to get in to him. Sent from the kurs across the river to get him for peeing on the sheets. Sometimes he can see them through the nick in the plaster pointing, gnawing day and night to get closer, closer to his heart.

40

Aaron Wold is sitting by the fire in the lounge of the sanitarium.

'I'm glad I found you here,' I say, 'because I wanted to talk to you.'

'I know,' I say. 'That you can talk, I mean.'

Aaron Wold sits with his large red leather-bound note-book resting on his knee. His pencil hovers over the page. I tell him I doodle too. It passes the time, I say.

Stanley Kubrick is in the library, writing with sweet eloquence to Stavros Kouros at the Grand Theatre.

It is a pleasant room. High green walls, a log fire, book-shelves. The proprietor is interested in reading, and the shelves are lined with all kinds of volumes from his own library which the residents may read if they wish.

Aaron Wold greets me kindly with a nod and rests the wandering pencil on his notepad. Upside down, his efforts look like miniature radio waves bobbing along the lined paper.

He will tell me a little later on in the conversation that these are not his own doodles but those of his grandfather which are contained in a total of eighteen volumes, be-queathed to Aaron in Grandfather Wold's will.

The collected handwritten works of Kegan Laurie Wold were completed in the old man's declining years, long after he too was abandoned by the family, to the Carnegie Institute for the Criminally Insane.

After a lifetime of travel and adventure as a soldier and later as a journalist and diarist, Kegan Laurie Wold was locked up in 1917 for trying to burn down the Dundee Assizes (there was no-one in at the time).

The act was a protest which followed hard on the heels of the trial and execution of his youngest brother William and the seventeen men under him from the local Dundee-based regiment who had been arrested after eight months in Flanders following their refusal to bombard a Belgian village in which everyone knew there were only civilians living.

The fire started by Kegan Laurie Wold although it injured no-one burned down seven-eighths of the Assizes. It was never reported under wartime reporting restrictions. Neither was the trial and execution of William Wold and his men charged with insubordination. Nor the committing of Kegan to the Carnegie Institute for the Criminally Insane, an institution established through charitable donation for the 'care and upkeep of those poor wretches whose sense of the real has been swamped by the demons of the unreal and the imagined'.

That was telling them.

Aaron Wold has come to believe that all the wisdoms of the world are held in these volumes of his grandfather's. Maybe he feels safe in believing this now that the Carnegie Institute for the Criminally Insane is a multi-storey car park.

His difficulty, he tells me, is that his grandfather wrote everything in code for fear that his colleagues and ultimately his gaolers would steal his revelations, kill him, and make their fortunes by claiming these wisdoms as their own.

Some chance. When his gaolers heard that he was writing his memoirs, they asked, 'Are there some really ingenious things to do to people in your books so that they die horribly?' Wold's reply made them laugh and proved to them once and for all the lack of sanity and commercial nous of their captive.

He said, 'Not really, but there are some really ingenious ways to ensure that people stay alive.' He must have been crazy to think people would kill him for that, but it didn't stop him putting everything down in his homemade code in the eighteen volumes; as it happened, one for each year of his incarceration.

Aaron Wold's doodling as he sits by the fire of the sanitarium is, in fact, his attempt to decipher the words of his grandfather's eighteen volumes. If only he can break the mysteries of these works of Woldian history which have been left to him, he would know everything he would need to know.

This is the belief which has sustained him through six years of silence around the high rooms and long corridors of the sanitarium on the edge of the city. Each day he painstakingly translates another sentence or two, like he was chipping away at the past with a toothpick.

So far, after six years in the sanitarium, Aaron Wold is up to page forty-six of Volume Three. Kegan Laurie Wold had unwittingly stumbled upon a previously unsuspected talent as a codist.

My own doodles have progressed from rows of ovals and saucer-shaped circles, and now I make simple cartoon faces using these shapes. I use the ovals as the shape of the head and I use the saucers for wide round eyes.

I line them up alongside each other on the page in face-chains. The faces look out from the paper but they never say anything to me. You know what I mean?

I tell Aaron Wold that one time I saw him playing Jesus Christ in the park for the benefit of the City Leader, Corwen Lintock. I say I know that for many weeks since the election he had been meeting with the City Leader, offering him what seems to Corwen Lintock a light in the dark, and also suggesting remedies for the Leader's gassy stomach, indigestion and chest pains. He's been told he's working too hard.

In return, Aaron Wold tells me in his lullaby Scots vernacular about the Medieval Mystery Plays of his home island of Crull where he had once worked as the island's milkman in the lonely, exhilarating Hebridean dawn.

It had been a good job, milkman. He enjoyed it, he says. He took the milk round on a horse and cart in the early days, and everybody on the island knew him with his neat black beard and his navy anorak fastened against the cold or the wind or the rain or whatever, and his clinking pints and his horse that left steaming piles of coddy muck on the cold ironstone roads.

In the winter, he says, you got used to the cold and in the summer there was the gold and grey of the dawndays when his heart sang and he was happy and that was enough.

I say to him, 'Why did they choose you to play Jesus Christ?'

'It's a mystery to me,' he says.

Perhaps, I say, it was because of his likeness to the popularly held image of the man Jesus. Or maybe it was that Aaron Wold, like Jesus, followed a simple, practical, honourable and public trade for the community. One was a carpenter, I say, the other a milkman.

He says that he thinks they got his name from the phone book.

It transpires that, after ten years' apprenticeship to the part, Aaron Wold didn't see through to the end his role of Jesus Christ in the Medieval Mystery Plays of Crull.

I ask him why and he says this:

'They were going to crucify me.'

I ask Aaron Wold why for six years, during the whole of his time here in the sanitarium, he has not spoken a word.

He smiles at me with that practised gentleness and says, 'Because they're all crazy in here.'

He goes to the City Park a lot. All life is there, he assures me. I ask him if this includes Corwen Lintock having sex with his wife who howls like a dog at the dead of night.

Sure, he says. It beats TV, especially when all the best game shows are off during the summer.

You should be careful, I say, going wandering like that after dark. The city's Housing Commission now under Stankill's control has been known of late to relocate people into the east quarter for stuff like that so as to keep an eye on them.

Aaron Wold says that when he goes walkabout, when people out in the city decide that maybe he is a goofball, or a wino or the Son of Man, he doesn't mean any harm by it. It just keeps him in pukka berries for the next game.

41

Reconstituting old legislation didn't seem like such a bad move. Heck, the team just dusted off the bye-laws from the old Aliens Act to help us zone the city, restore some order. How else to combat the plot against the city uncovered by brave Sam Pound before his death and by Corwen Lintock brandishing his proof which we now know, shorthand, as the Beaker Street Oath.

I have a game-show question for you. No conferring. The question is this: How do you eat an elephant?

Answer: In small chunks.

Bit by bit.

Corwen Lintock's had this thing for a while about the final straw. You know — the one that, unbeknown to Daulman, broke the camel's back.

He's had a bee in his bonnet you might say. A stone in

his shoe on the oh-so-long walk with the rest of us to Damascus.

'One more act of defiance,' he's always saying, 'and that will be the last straw.'

Well now he's got it.

There's this one old man lives with his wife down by the East River, not too far from my own apartment as it happens. Now and then he's been burgled, had his fence broken, his shed set smouldering. A couple of times they've had jewelry stolen. But now the old man is pictured in the papers boarding up the windows. Bang bang bang. His wife is in hospital. It's her skull. Her spleen. Three pounds ten they got. Bang bang bang. He's an old man. Christ he looks so old. He fought at Normandy he thinks. He's crying as he hammers.

'Do you think it'll stop 'em, old timer?'

It gets a quote.

The TV men want to know what else these people have done to him. A list is always much better when you're going for human interest. But the man is old and forgetful. It's a while since he was forced out under some redundancy package and worked his last shift at Galbraith's India Mill. He has had an operation on his ears and he forgets things. One time on the phone he forgot his name and the surgery put the receiver down on him, thinking he was trying to put the evil eye on them.

He says that they kill goats.

The TV men say, 'Have you seen this?'

He says he knows about the Beaker Street Oath. About the kurs. He says, 'They live twenty to a room and eat dog food and put the evil eye on me and shut all the mills down.' He looks like a breaking man.

When I see this on the evening news in my apartment I can at least console myself with this thought: if the two culprits who did for my buddy Sam Pound have been involved in any of this latest mischief, it'll be the last spit in the wind for them. See, by now the two names given to me by Coleman Seer will be on the desk of the City Leader.

It was inevitable that people would respond. This was the last straw after all. One or two kurs went missing on raids on the east quarter, and part of Beaker Street got torched in the middle of the night, and the old man just kept on hammering in between visits to the hospital. And in the middle of all this raiding and burning and hammering on the TV and in the papers and out in the city down by the river my front door bell rings and I find that my daughter has come calling on me.

You didn't know I have a daughter?

Sometimes I forget this myself.

Like the other women in this tale, my daughter makes only a fleeting impact on the chronicle of events.

This is for two reasons. One is that virtually all the main characters herein are afraid of women. They avoid them, seek the company of other men where the rules are simpler. Women's friendships are built upon questions. Men's are built on statements. Heck, I should know.

Men are happiest when they are away from the company of women, when they are heading off to kill things or to make history. Someone said that. Probably a woman. Fitsimmons is all for making history. Fitsimmons rising. Fitsimmons who pounds through every new day like the old one was another pebble out of his shoe.

The other reason is that women lack the ingenuity of men, and I figure if this tale is about anything it's about the ingenuity of men.

What sort of ingenuity, you ask?

Ingenuity in making history. History is when things happen to people. And when things happen, usually you need plenty of lime mulch afterwards to guard against the smell.

Ingenuity in the manufacture of human bonemeal and the production of TV game shows.

But what about love? Where is the love?

Well, if I were to count up, I'd say there are four people in these proceedings who have been truly in love. Difficult to define, I know. Especially looking in from the outside. But worth a shot. Two twos I make it, as it happens. And of the four, only one of them ends up nailed to a tree. Percentage-wise it could have been worse.

My daughter Sonja and her lover are two of the four. My daughter is a nursing assistant and she is in love with the wife of Drucker, who is the Director of the Department for which I work at City Hall.

I say to her, 'You should bring your . . . her round once in a while.'

She says, 'You'd stare and make her uncomfortable.'

I can't help the way I am.

She says, 'She's ordinary, like me. An ordinary girl. I love her.'

And I say, 'But what do you do with her? I don't get it.'

She has come to say that Drucker has beaten up his wife and now she's leaving him and my daughter needs a month's downpayment and some cash for furnishings. Just basics. Furniture, carpets. A bed.

Where? I say, where?

In the east quarter. The Housing Commission, which rubber stamps all applications to move around the city, says it must be the east quarter for Drucker's estranged wife.

I think they knew who she was see, my daughter's . . . the other woman. Knew what she'd done to the soul of the shiny Drucker.

Oh shit.

Furniture, carpets, a bed. Sure, sure, I can pick up a bed.

But what do you think they'll do in it?

Heck, I know what Fitsimmons would say.

42

When his apprenticeship of ten years was over on the island of Crull in the Inner Hebrides and it was time for the bearded Aaron Wold to cast aside his navy anorak and take up the role of Jesus Christ for the assembled multitudes and the gathered tourists, they measured him for a white robe and the best tailor on the island cut the cloth and tacked it and sewed it until it was ready to wear.

Aaron Wold put on his white cloth robe and all the people smiled and said he was their man and he sure looked like Jesus to them and he presided over the Creation and the sequence of Bible stories which followed.

He was due to ride into the town on the night depicting Palm Sunday on the horse that pulled his milk-cart. It seemed like a nice touch. Dusk finally came and the route was lined with people holding slim burning torches of wax to welcome the man in the white robe who was playing Jesus for this Palm Sunday procession.

It had been a bumper harvest of tourists who had arrived on Crull over the previous weeks, clattering off the ferries and peering out at the sky while the coaches backed up.

Many of them had been booked in on the island for the

full run of the Festival. The Americans especially loved it. They said that the whole thing was truly moving. They cheered louder than the English and threw coins to enter into the spirit of the thing.

The Scots and the islanders threw nothing, recognising it as an ancient and sacred rite. This is what they called it in the programme. But they smiled all the same for their island neighbour Aaron Wold.

For Aaron Wold it was real.

For ten years Aaron Wold had waited for this moment, and in he rode to town on his plodding horse in the re-enactment of the Palm Sunday procession. He acknowledged the cheers of the crowd along the road. He steered his horse into the town. He looked warmly into the faces of the people who had turned out to pay homage to his Jesus. And then he went crazy.

He doesn't remember too much about it these days. Some said he began to rip off his white cloth robe and gibber like an idiot. Someone else remembered him curling up like a foetus and making little animal sounds of distress which the Americans in particular found upsetting. What everyone agreed upon was that it had been a terrible sacrilege.

The Americans paid up and went, and spent all their remaining travellers' cheques in Edinburgh and York and other classy places where public figures didn't salivate or make animal noises in the street.

The English made other excuses and left on the next batch of ferries.

The islanders counted the cost of Aaron Wold's outburst in terms of lost money and in the lost credibility of the festival in the eyes of the outside world, and they decided he would have to go. The cost came to six figures and a franchised TV documentary which had been in the pipeline. Not to mention the embarrassment.

All this was ten years ago.

As Aaron Wold speaks to me now in the high-walled lounge of the sanitarium, the Medieval Mystery Plays of Crull are again being re-enacted on the Hebridean island which was once home to Aaron Wold.

They bundled him onto a ferry once they thought him cured enough to look after himself and told him not to return. Now, of course, they have hired a professional actor for the leading role who is paid not to salivate or to howl like a dog during the proceedings and everyone seems a lot happier with the whole thing.

So I say to him, 'Why did you go crazy and spoil those good people's fun?'

'You think they came for a holiday?' he says. 'You think they came to sing a few psalms and be friends with me?'

I don't know what to say to him. He looks old and sad, and the magic of the heavy red leather book on his lap seems not to help him too much any more.

'All those people,' he keeps saying. 'All those people created in my image. Acknowledging me as though I was really somebody after a lifetime of delivering silvertop.'

'Yes? Yes?' I say.

'I kept looking into their eyes as I rode down the road on my horse. I kept looking and thinking.'

He stops.

'What? What?' I say.

'I kept thinking that in six days or so, after all I had done for them, they were going to crucify me.'

'Yes, but why did you go crazy like that?' I ask.

'Under the circumstances,' Aaron Wold says, 'it seemed like the only useful thing to do.'

43

'Sure, sure,' Daulman says, 'just burn the whole fucking place down.'

Once a boilerman.

The memo from Lintock's Fourteenth-Floor office lies square on Drucker's desk. It asks how we propose to have the east quarter taken out of the equation, he uses that very phrase, by the time the city comes to celebrate the tercentenary of its charter. When there will be fireworks and things. A circus, even. Something to remember Corwen by.

Parallel Habitation, Fitsimmons suggests we call it, this package of ours that divides the city into zones, districts really, just to quieten things down, to re-establish the sense of order once brought to the city by the Aliens Act, and Drucker smiles at that. He thinks the Leader would like the idea, especially the new oath of loyalty to the city which has been proposed and which Stankill's Housing Commission will oversee, and merrily we roll along through the morning's chores having got a handle on the issue of the day, having set down the germ of the response document to Corwen Lintock.

Mind you, it's a shame about Beaker Street.

At the end of the session, Fitsimmons and I get the job of setting out the report for the Leader's inspection.

Can we have a first draft by the morning, Drucker asks in that pussycat-smooth way he has when he's on top of things.

Sure, I say, sure. Fitsimmons just smiles. It'll mean staying on late tonight and maybe grabbing a bite to eat together afterwards while we proof it. I'm just grateful it's not Stankill I'm paired off with. Stankill sucks his food like he was sauté-ing it. Have you heard steak sucked?

It was the venerable George Steen, City Councillor, who first established a Housing Commission in the city. It was set up as the council's response to the first wave of street clearances.

I bet he never reckoned on Stankill running it. Stankill

who sure as hell can chair a committee and suck steak at the same time without choking.

Stankill, of course, is responsible for beefing up the Commission. Making sure people are where they should be. Some fine democrat wanted the greatest good of the greatest number, did he not? Well that's what Stankill wants. Like a dog with a bone.

With the draft committed to paper, we go out to eat at eight, eight-thirty. City Hall is dead by then. At first I think we are the last two out. Just the commissionaire left on the steps of the George Steen Porch. He touches the peak of his cap, and for a minute in catching his profile I think it is poor Vernon Smitts saluting me. No, no, the A6. I remember! When I glance up I see that there are still men in dull suits, five, six floors up, passing windows, moving papers, looking down on the city. More of Corwen's men building Corwen's world.

'What you having, Harry?' Fitsimmons wants to know.

I've always had this thing that I look like a man who probably eats alone in restaurants. Some men do. Look that way, I mean. Also I have this urge to apologise to waiters.

'Your fish has been delayed, sir.'

'Oh, I'm sorry.'

You know.

Fitsimmons, well Fitsimmons has a handle on it. He's good in restaurants. Like he's owed it. To me, he goes through most days like he has a bankroll stashed away in secret.

Don't worry, Harry, he says. Christ, Harry, why do you always look like you're hugging a bomb? I tell him I don't know. Voices sometimes. Just a bad feeling.

Like heartburn? he asks.

I tell him it's like I'm off balance at the moment. Maybe it's the car not firing right. Maybe it's the pukka berries.

Fitsimmons collects my order and relays it with his own to the waiter who appears beside him.

A good day, he says. Good business, Harry. The draft report sits on the table between us, ready for Corwen Lintock tomorrow. It took us maybe two, two and a half hours. It surely looks well presented. You should see Fitsimmons's dinky fingers whizz around that keyboard. I figure Fitsimmons will go home happy tonight. Fitsimmons's wife has dreams, you see, of what he might achieve. It kind of turns her on. Lucky Liam!

We laugh some about Stankill, running his little committee down in the City Hall Basement. Fitsimmons laughs, I follow. It's not respect, it's more a natural order. Like he's better at firing into each new moment than I am; I come tip-toeing in just that fraction later. Come in more warily for fear the moment should strike me back. I tell him about poor Vernon Smitts and the Basement years I knew.

'In a Ford Popular?' he says. 'What a peach!'

The food arrives.

'You got some mustard back there?' Fitsimmons asks.

The waiter leans across me to get my plate down onto the table.

'Sorry,' I say, shuffling.

Corwen Lintock's best move of late, Fitsimmons believes, has been the rescuing of Sentex Security, the community business in the east quarter whose books got defrauded by its chairman Coleman Seer and nearly went under. The way Lintock bought it out, changed its name, kept it running. Local lads in the east quarter patrolling the vacant apartment buildings to curb vandalism and the pilfering of roof lead and so on until places can be re-let. Fitsimmons thinks this will prove a useful investment. These lads will possible be handy in the new scheme of things. Who knows, he might be right.

Me? I'm just a little out of this particular conversation. I'm having this private wager with one renegade tooth that the first iced beer has set on fire again and won't be calmed.

Fitsimmons always did like the way Corwen Lintock thinks. Two, three moves ahead. Riding the advantage of media concerns. He keeps asking what do I think. What do I think, he wants to know. Am I behind Corwen? What do I think?

I tell him I'm worried about the elephants.

I tell him maybe I'll have the sticky toffee pudding.

I tell him I've got this bastard of a tweaking tooth.

Finally I tell him what I think. Tell him while this slinky little pain is knocking me off balance. I think all this

Parallel Habitation stuff is a distraction from the business of the tercentenary. What are people going to remember in twenty years' time? The Harry Angel circus, that's what. The circus of dreams. Providing it's done right.

Damn it, this thing is important to me. To the city. There's where to put the fireworks stations and whether the whole caboodle is going to arrive on time, and ticket sale franchises and safety certificates for the ferris wheel and whether Corwen Lintock will be well enough to have a speech programmed for him and where all the grandstands will go in the City Park. Heck, all sorts.

And you know what. Fitsimmons just watches me with a sidelong glance that I think I've seen before and just at that moment there's a rattle and a plop and out through a sluice of sticky toffee pudding comes this cold as steel molar filling sucked from its jacket of tooth, leaving some cave that my tongue can't stay out of for the rest of the evening, pushing and licking and probing this new anatomy, this gentler, personal, duller ache up high by my right cheek.

On the way home I come to a conclusion. All night I've watched Fitsimmons waiting in expectation. For the waiter. For the next course. The next drink. The next idea that he's busy squeezing out like water from a damp towel.

Fitsimmons is forever waiting, booked in for the next stop down the line. You know what; it wouldn't matter what the circumstances, he'd always have lived his unregretted life in this one straight enviable line.

No time for Harry Angel's panic-stricken glances up and back down the line. For regret. Shit, I never meant to say that.

One time I heard someone spill out the secret of a good life. What was it:

Never play cards with a man called Doc;

Never sleep with a woman who has more problems than you;

And keep the hell away from an animal called regret.

Good advice, like driving slowly in fog and keeping your secrets locked tight in a biscuit tin.

These things go rolling around in my head, along with a little Spanish wine from the meal and the knowledge that Fitsimmons has the finished draft on Parallel Habitation and the necessary zoning it embodies safely bundled up for tomorrow.

So it comes as a real shock to get back home across the city to find that my apartment has been ransacked and all my pukka berry plants stolen and the walls smeared with shit and graffiti and the graffiti saying 'Eat Shit, Kur' and me shouting into the empty room 'I'm not, I'm fucking not.' I find myself checking for the biscuit tin that I keep under the floorboards. Its contents have lain safely un-abused under the floor through the apparently desperate search above, and despite the loss of the pukka berries I get this small seepage of relief.

But who would do all this? Break in for the pukka berries. Leave the mess. And then I remember that outside

the building there were no boys nursing a football, no rhythm of 'Pthuck, pthuck, pthuck' against the side wall as I washed around the debris of my home. And I think this:
  Bastards!

44

Fat Mary Pound, who sometimes smells, is grateful that I'm getting her out. Out across the only access road into the city from here, the charred bones of Beaker Street. Okay, so it took a couple of months. So sometimes things move slowly.

New regulations mean that all residents of the east quarter now carry yellow stamps on all public items of identification. Small circular circumspect marks punched on with an indented stamp.
  The yellow marks carry with them implied restrictions. They indicate that this person or that person might just go howling at the moon or come slooping across the Beaker Street pyre to put the evil eye on you. Yellow badges identify non-citizen guests of the city with a guest's responsibility to behave. An administrative nicety. Myself, I carry blue. Phew!

Because of all this, because of some popular misconceptions about what these changes mean for the east quarter, Fat Mary Pound has fussed and fadded gratefully around me all morning like Drucker does around the Council Leader, and I am doing my best to lap up the gratitude being offered my way. Sometimes she overdoes it. Fat Mary, like her son Sam used to do, can talk too much.

I will have two advantages at the imminent monthly meeting of the East Quarter Community Forum at which I must address the misconceptions, apply a little balm to the general situation.

Firstly, the meeting is generally poorly attended. No-one has faith in the Forum and without faith there is nothing. And secondly, it is chaired by our ally Coleman Seer who is beholden to us to the tune of thirty full-colour magazines handed over in a Weetabix box.

The van, parked at the courtyard entrance to their scorched Beaker Street apartment, is slowly filling up with the family's possessions to the beat of Dooley's ghetto-blaster which is jammed under one of the youth's huge arms. Around the fringes of the courtyard, others watch us in silence, curious. They themselves are going no-where.

I stand sucking the holes in my mouth, the newly settled crater at the back whose texture I am familiar with by now; my mind draws pictures of its splintered rock formation while I'm doing it. It helps that I'm off the aspirin for the time being.

The Pounds in Fat Mary's day had worked long and hard in the mills, aiming for a promised land. They thought that they were investing their sweated labour in a bank. Their bank had its windows whited to blot out the sun. To save the threads. They thought maybe Jesus or the City Council would repay with interest. One day, one day, some day. They invested in the dream like it was a promissory note. Heck, someone's to blame because they surely deserved better than this.

Mary Pound reappears in the doorway carrying Sam Pound's old cowboy hat and smiles as she shows it to me.

'He always wanted to go and see them places,' she says to me. 'Cowboy places. You remember, Harry. But he never got anywhere really. It all stayed in his head, like he could escape there. He thought it was great, the Wild West, General Custer, John Wayne. He never did go. He never had the money, see.'

She shrugs, as if to say 'Excuse the reminiscence', and I nod. The others are watching me. Mary Pound's offspring, it should be said, are less impressed by my intervention on their behalf than their mother.

'He'd to make do with the fillums, see. Cowboy fillums and ranchers and Indians. And the music. Loved his country music did Sam. Hate it myself. Bloody racket. All those crying guitars.'

In truth, there is little for me to take the credit for. The transfer out of the Pounds is all Corwen Lintock's doing. I'm just the bearer of glad tidings, the booker of the van, the overlooker of the Pounds' move.

The Council Leader has agreed to the Pounds' request to be reclassified, not to have to carry yellow passbooks around the city. This will, in fact, be the last time a family moves thus from yellow to blue, from the east quarter across the no-man's land of rubble that once was Beaker Street and now marks the line where Corwen Lintock's neat wall will run, elegantly that's for sure, separating city lives from our guests in the east quarter.

Stankill is to make use of his Housing Commission to judge these things from now on, to zone the city so as to bring peace to people's lives. The trusted Harry Angel will do much of the background administration and write up the reports.

When the Commission's work has been done the community will surely be restored to health. This seems likely. Also, Stankill sees it as a useful vehicle to push for promotion. He doesn't know yet about being unsound.

For this reason, you can be sure the Commission's work will be thorough and effective. Thorough is what Corwen Lintock wants. Effective.

But that is a little ahead of us. For now, as the Pounds load their luggage onto the van, I am able to put into practice another of the lessons learned long ago from the Vernon Smitts Book of Life.

This one says: Take credit for whatever goes.

Smitts said it was like accruing interest at the bank. Look after the pennies and the pounds will take care of themselves. I wonder if maybe it pays better interest than investing in dreams.

I smile at Fat Mary Pound as she lugs the next load from the apartment and down the stone steps, acknowledging her gratitude to me for finally getting her out of the east quarter. It's alright Mrs Pound, my nod says, I just wanted to be here to see it through. For Fat Mary Pound the dream has come true. Her investment was well placed. The investment where she remembered seeing Sam's notes one time on how some kurs had tried to burn down a Sentex factory and to frame Corwen Lintock on some insurance scam whilst his night porter burned to ash.

'You're a good man, Harry Angel,' she says, 'getting us out from this place.' Her words are spoken against the racket of music from Dooley's machine. 'My Girl In Wyoming Is So Far Away', the voice on the tape sings on the machine under Dooley's arm.

Dooley Pound is nineteen and he has a mental age of maybe eight. He feeds the army of stray cats who catch the rats who own the crushed alleys round Beaker Street.

Dooley is heavy and lumbering, he has one dull leg in a calliper and he wears a cowboy hat, a copy of his father's which Mary Pound has just carried from the apartment.

Dooley has this weird collection of annuals and books on cowboys and cattle ranching and country and western singers. Also he has this *Encyclopaedia of the American West* which he keeps by his bed. It had been his father's until Sam Pound's violent death when he fell from Caspar's Gorge.

Dooley especially likes the pictures. Most times it stays close by his side when he's in the apartment. When he's out with his ghettoblaster listening to 'My Girl In Wyoming Is So Far Away', he hides it under the floorboards in his room, reasoning that it's too precious to leave lying around.

The Encyclopaedia of the American West 1830–1980 contains all the wisdoms of the world Dooley Pound will ever need to know, and every so often through the morning he has brought it out into the courtyard for me to look at. He will show me a picture and point and say, 'Get that.'

I think I'm supposed to nod and agree or something. It's difficult to tell.

If you ask Dooley who he is, he doesn't say 'Dooley Pound', he says 'Jesse James'. Maybe it's a joke. He has holsters and posters of cowboys and picture books of cattle drives across the Mid-West. One poster in his room, the big one that has hung until now over his bed, shows the huge landscape of Oklahoma with cowboys beating their hats against their thighs as they ride on horseback, urging their epic herd of steers forward across the turn-of-the-century plain. The word dustbowl had yet to be manufactured from the great farming adventure of the Mid-West.

The American West is Dooley's world. I see it as the sense of freedom it offers to someone cruelly restricted in the real world of the blackstone city. It was the same for old Sam Pound as well, perhaps. It seems like a good thing to dream of.

In the city, Dooley doesn't always know what day it is, and he doesn't know how best to look after himself. But he knows that Custer was known as Hard Backsides, and that after the Battle of Washita General Sheridan ordered the Cheyenne and the Arapahos to surrender at Fort Cobb or face extinction, and he knows that his Encyclopaedia is safe under the floorboards and this is enough for him to cling on to. As long as he has enough to believe in, enough to know about, I figure he'll make it.

Maybe Dooley Pound's in a state of grace. He has his Encyclopaedia and his music and his hat.

You think he should need more?

On the machine under Dooley's arm, a voice sings out to him of blue skies in Tennessee. In Tennessee, Dooley Pound knows, blue skies reign.

The two girls are seventeen and sixteen. Like the others they have dark hair, but these two are pretty in a sly and unexpected way, with small noses and pale skins and short, sour mouths. They move to and fro across the courtyard from the apartment to the van carrying their bits and pieces. They do not speak. Their eyes have ignored my glances across at them through the last half hour as the van has been loaded up.

When I do catch the eye of one of them I say to her, 'You must be glad you're moving on from here?' And she gives me that look, the one that says, 'Harry Angel, you're a fool', and she carries on briskly going to and fro from the apartment to the van.

Jason Pound is the eldest of the four at twenty-two or three. Who's counting? He has done none of the work. Skinny like a fast dog, where Dooley is slow and wide, he sits perched on the nearby courtyard wall wearing a Che Guevara tee shirt. He watches me. He has the measure of me and I am uncomfortable around him.

'Hey, turkeyneck,' he has said. 'You think you're a big man? All this?' He gestures around him at the van, at the move.

'No. No of course not.'

But he's got my number alright. He says, 'You think I couldn't have got us out if I'd wanted?'

I shrug aimiably. I say, 'Your brother is interested in America. Like your father was.'

He says, 'Sure he likes cowboys. What of it?'

I say, 'Why cowboys?'

He says, 'Cause they get to fuck up the Indians.'

Some dream.

45

Jason Pound is eyeing me again, paying no deference. He's never paid deference to anybody. He's never had to. Never worked for Drucker's Department.

'You're no big man,' he says when Fat Mary has retreated again into the apartment. 'You didn't fix this up. Lintock fixed this up.'

His words pull me up sharp. He has no right to know this.

I say, 'Who told you that?'

'People told me that. It's true.'

I say, 'No, it's not true.'

He says, 'People who know Lintock told me that.'

'You know Corwen Lintock?' I ask.

'I said people, turkeyneck. You don't listen or something?'

I tell him, look, I'm an important man who is choosing to help them out. I don't tell him any more than this. It wouldn't be right. Maybe he's guessing. I am trying to keep Corwen Lintock out of the equation.

Jason Pound says, 'So you're the good man come to rescue us, like one of Dooley's cowboys on a white horse, eh?'

'Sure,' I say, 'that's me.' Come to rescue the Pounds on a white horse. I'm a good man, you know.

'Sure,' he says, chewing. But he sniggers like he knows things. 'Me,' he says, 'I can do anything. Free spirit, me. Come and go. East quarter, southside, wherever. You, you can't go toss yourself without putting your hand up and asking,' and he throws me a pukka berry from the handful he has been eating and he looks at me.

After they've loaded up and locked up, he sizes me up again.

'You're just a big brain on legs,' he says languidly. 'You can't toss yourself without someone else saying: Go ahead, turkeyneck, fuck!'

And while he's speaking, Dooley slouches past with his player under his arm, thinking he's Jesse James.

Cowboys these days have this neat trick with the cattle they ranch.

Dooley Pound knows it. It's in the rancher picture book he showed me this morning. 'Look at its dick,' he said and showed me the picture. He's slow.

All good ranchers need to know when the herd is in season. The ones who can tell them best are the bulls. Stands to reason. The bulls know things. They're clever that way. So the bull is let loose to suss out what's what amongst the herd. You know, physically.

But here's the neat trick. The bull's penis has been re-routed sideways by surgery so that when it stands erect it signals the message to the cowboy rancher that the herd is on heat, but at the same time the bull can't interfere with the artificial insemination programme which keeps the meat farm on track. He can't consummate his passion. He could go humping all day but he's unlikely to make much progress, don't you agree? Dooley's picture shows the bull with this bent hard-on going just nowhere.

Ingenious, eh? The things we've learned to do.

The bull can point up what's going down and who's on heat, and what needs doing – all with his dick sticking out sideways from under his belly like semaphore, but he can do bugger all else without a nod and a wink from the rancher.

That's why this bull is called a sidewinder.

Before long I will be reminded of all this and I will tell Fitsimmons about the sidewinder of the American Mid-West, and he will fall about laughing, saying, 'That's rich, that's rich.'

I got this memo the other day from Corwen Lintock's office saying it had been fixed for the Pounds to get out of the east quarter before, as the memo put it, the doors close. It is an atonement for the death of Sam Pound and for the guy's growing place in the city's mythology.

The memo said that a new apartment had been set up for them. It said also that employment in a newly expanded Sentex Security was being considered for Jason Pound, in a firm which I know like the others in the Sentex Holdings group is headed up by Corwen Lintock. Jason Pound was turned down twice by the original community business for having the wrong attitude, but it helps to have friends.

The two Pound girls are to be taken on in a part-time capacity by the Secretarial and Administrative Support Unit to the Council Leader's Office and a place will be made available for Dooley, the Cowboy, at some special school.

Dooley only wanted to know if the stray cats would die after he'd gone away. I said they'd probably all go to cat heaven. He just looked at me sideways on. Just another day out, maybe?

All this charity for the Pounds has made the Council Leader feel good about things. It's nice to be able to make things happen.

The memo said I was to book transport and see them off from out of the east quarter, and make sure there was no trouble and that no-one put the evil eye on them or anything. If they did I was under no circumstances to act then for fear of inflaming the situation, of upsetting the Leader's plans. I was merely to let Corwen Lintock's office know and he'd take care of it. He's very thorough when he takes care of things.

If anyone asked, I was to say nothing about their flight from the quarter, or why or how come it was happening. As from now people need to understand that there is a gulf between cityfolk and the east quarter that cannot readily be bridged.

Coleman Seer has come snooping round like he was some stray tom looking for chicken bones or a leg over, wanting to know how come the Pounds are moving out, but I've fobbed him off with some story or other.

When we lived on Beaker Street I used to have to go chasing rats out of the yard. Sonja used to have this storyline in her head that I was the Pied Piper with a kind of power over them. That they had to go when I said or they'd die.

One time we got a rat in the cistern and I got poor Vernon Smitts, who was in Cleansing by then, to send up the Council ratcatcher. Sonja found it dead, poisoned, in the bin. Just lying there glassy-eyed. She just hugged me and hugged me. She wanted to believe it was me had done it, had made it die because I was the Pied Piper, so I just hugged her right back and said everything was fine now. Everything was just fine.

46

Fitsimmons says, 'And he showed you the picture . . . of its thing going sideways? Priceless, priceless.'

He is still laughing about the sidewinder's useless sideways erection semaphoring to the rancher when Drucker calls us to order.

In Drucker's office for the weekly meetings there is more smiling and less stuttering than before.

But, as Corwen Lintock would remind us, we are not out of the woods yet and, in these trying times, our collective semaphoring penises are still on the line. So to speak.

Drucker has worked hard to build up the Department in trying times.

In the shifting sands of City Administration it is important to have a clear ethos to convey to the elected members of the City Council, an approach to city government to help you stand out from the rest. One that helps you to defend your Department and safeguard the employee futures entrusted to your care.

Drucker's ethos is this:

Drucker is a chameleon.

Drucker wears crisp white shirts with knife-thin creases.

His just greying hair is swept back behind his ears. His suits have the faintest of pinstripes. But underneath he is a chameleon. He is all things to all men. He is a damp sticky pussycat to Corwen Lintock, and he is an enigma to his immediate lieutenants.

A recipe for success, wouldn't you say?

In this job, as Drucker knows, as even a man halfway down the pecking order like me knows, you need always to maintain a balance between those making the rules and those seeking to put them into practice. If you're like Drucker and you can do this without seeming to apportion blame then you get to be Director and have time off for golf and to marry a smiling girl who can have all the physiotherapy and nursing she needs twice a week on her knee to make her perfect again after the ski-ing accident.

So. Sam Pound is dead.

We have two names and plenty of evidence from the autopsy which followed Sam Pound's wrenching from the earth.

We know the names of Sam Pound's killers who also had the dog drink a bleach cocktail that made it go mad and burned out its throat.

Which names?

The names supplied to me by Coleman Seer in his stockinged feet against the background of his barking TV and his silent dog.

47

Through the meeting I have this same eerie feeling I've had for a week now. Boy, is it weird. It's like as the city slowly picks itself up off the floor so I'm increasingly weighed down by this feeling of . . . something. Maybe I'm working too hard.

I had a hangover like this once, when my wife left me for her better life, but without the voices.

Those damned voices, like when I was a kid. Women's voices. Slow and heavy like I remember them down in the City Hall Basement as they queued to see me and Vernon Smitts and the rest about rats in the cistern and damp in the walls.

I mentioned this to the proprietor when I was up at the sanitarium the other week. This was in the aftermath of the raid on my apartment. I had gone up to see if my father, Bronislaw, had any spare pukka berries I might be able to cadge so I could keep some kind of supply going to Corwen Lintock. I'd had to tell the Leader even before the raid to think about cutting down, that there wasn't just a bottomless pit of the things. I just hope he didn't take it the wrong way, that I was somehow threatening to cut off his supply of pukka berries or use them as a lever against him. Heck, I was just giving him the pukka berry facts of life.

Of course since the raid and the loss of all the bushes in bloom it's been a nightmare and I've all but used up the stock of ripened and picked berries I'd had stashed about the apartment.

I thought the proprietor of the sanitarium, who lives just as one of the residents (except he doesn't play cards or gamble), might have known something similar but he said no, he didn't get voices.

Lucky Eddie Melon. A slice of real estate and no voices.

Whilst I was there we got talking about fathers, being as how I'd come to visit mine. Just talking in general, you know.

'Eddie,' I said, 'did your father ever lie to you?'

'Sure,' he said, 'why do you ask?'

I told him that after my mother died I discovered my father had been lying to me all his life.

'That's tough,' he said. So, I asked him, how come his father lied to him.

He thought about it, then he said, 'My father worked in the mills all his life. Went to work in the dark, came home in the dark, spent his days inside the mill where the windows were blacked out to keep the sunshine from drying out the weaving threads.

'He told me life was going to be tough. He said there'd

be no crowds out there waiting to cheer me and no money or women or power falling into my lap like I seemed to think there would be. He said I'd have to make do with a tuppence ha'penny job in the mill and suck up to my boss. He said there'd be sleepless nights and difficult decisions and maybe the rent would be hard to come by and there'd be rats in the cistern and stuff.

'But he was wrong. He lied to me.'

48

I've not slept well since the night of the break-in at my apartment.

I've been seeing less of Corwen Lintock. The pukka berries I'd had bagged up before the raid are now all used up. I tried and failed to grow some more from seed – but it's the wrong time of year. Now I see trouble ahead. The next set of pukka berries is owing and I'm cleaned out of the damned things. I've been using the excuse that I've been busy with the city's tercentenary show; the circus and things.

What has helped buy time for sure has been the Leader's willingness to keep a distance from me. I wonder if maybe it's to protect us both after our subterfuge over the Sam

Pound autopsy report. Also he's vomiting regularly. He's got some bug. It's true as well, though, that he trusts me to get on with the circus and the fireworks, doesn't feel the need to keep looking over my shoulder despite the importance of the thing. Fitsimmons has told me this.

Life is hard without the punctuation marks of watering and feeding and tending to the pukka berries in my apartment. In their place, these damned female voices in my head flood in everywhere in all the nooks and crannies of silence.

The lift slides smoothly to the Fourteenth Floor of City Hall. It stops with a whir and I step out into the lobby, to be greeted by three young men in well-made dark suits. Small world. One of them is Jason Pound, shaved and neat. He wears a badge on his lapel saying 'Sentex Security'.

He says, 'Hey, it's turkeyneck.'

Sentex Security, the firm bailed out by Corwen Lintock after Coleman Seer cooked the books, keeps an eye on things in the east quarter. They watch for pilfering and vandalism. They check IDs. Stuff like that. Ask why someone needs to come across into the city if what they want can be got right there behind the Beaker Street line. Some people, it's known, only come in to cause trouble.

I know how far it is up Beaker Street, one end to the other, from the India Mill on the edge of the city up the hill into the heart of the east quarter. I walked it often enough. Walked it with Sonja on my back, lying still as a dead dog on me, asleep.

Some nights, if we'd been out for the day somewhere, I'd carry little Sonja out from the subway tram right up the length of Beaker Street. Then she'd always time it so's she'd wake as we got to the top and were turning into our apartment block.

You fell asleep, I'd tell her, Sure, she'd say, I know. I knew you'd carry me, Daddy. You always do.

Of course the subway tram doesn't stop round here any more. Nothing much to stop for. Everything's moved on, I guess. There's progress for you.

'What you want, turkeyneck? You come to see the chief?'

I say, 'I've come to see Councillor Lintock.'

Jason Pound says, 'The chief is busy.'

I say, 'The chief? You're working for Corwen Lintock?'

'Sure! We are his personal security.'

It is known that for some time Corwen Lintock has been worried about his own security. He thinks someone is plotting to kill him, plotting to move on from the animals. The polar bear lost its head. Someone sent it to Corwen in a box. He thinks someone's put the evil eye on him. A graffiti campaign right in the heart of the city is being carried out against the Leader by someone or other. Everyone has their suspicions.

The graffiti says, 'You piss on us brother Corwen, we lock you in the cupboard.'

After that, Councillor Lintock expanded Sentex Security into personal bodyguard work.

I smile at Jason Pound. I say, 'Will you tell the Leader that Harry Angel of C and CA is here to see him.'

'I told you. He's busy.'

I say, 'I need to see him. I'm a senior Council Officer on Council business.'

Jason Pound says, 'There's no callers to the office today. Why you need to see him?'

I tell him I was robbed a while back and my apartment was turned over. Corwen Lintock will be interested in this, I say. It affects things.

'Sure,' Jason Pound says, and he smiles that smile at me, the one that his luscious sister smiled at me when I was moving them out of the east quarter that said 'Harry Angel, you're a fool.'

'So if you'll excuse me,' I say, but as I try to walk past them towards the Council Leader's office I am restrained, gently, by the three of them. They hold me, barring the way, but without losing control.

'See, turkeyneck, we get on-the-job training too, Mr Lintock's boys. Before, I'd have kicked your balls in for that. Now you just get shown to the lift.' He is pleased with himself. I agree it's an improvement. As I do so, the door to the office suite opens and Corwen Lintock appears, pulling on a topcoat. He is similarly dark suited and his hair has been cropped close, I notice. He looks pretty poorly. Yellow skin that seems dry and flaky in sunlight.

Heck, maybe it's the evil eye. Maybe kurs have poisoned him.

'Ah,' he says, 'Harry Angel the Believer. You have come to see me?'

Yes, I say, gesturing at the human barrier between us represented by Jason Pound and his two companions.

'It's okay,' he says. They part to let me through.

'I'm on my way out,' the Councillor says. 'How can we help you?'

I look across at the three young men, then back to Corwen Lintock.

'It's alright,' he says. 'These are my boys. I trust them, don't I boys? Just like I trust you, Harry Angel. Isn't that right, boys?'

'Sure, chief.'

'So, what's new?'

I tell him my news. I tell him I am finally cleaned out of pukka berries, what with the burglary and all. I tell him I have none to supply him with in order that he can continue his discourse with Jesus Christ (who is Aaron Wold from the sanitarium). Whilst I explain, the whippet-like Jason Pound is smiling.

He thinks I can't see.

Corwen Lintock is listening intently. 'Come,' he says, gesturing to the lift. 'I'm late, get in.' And so we ride down together.

In the lift he says, 'I know about the break-in.'

Corwen Lintock knows about the break-in. It was carried

out by three young men in suits. One of them was Jason Pound. Their errand was to safeguard the supply of pukka berries for the Councillor. They made it look like a raid by kurs, like someone put the evil eye on the place, to throw a little smokescreen. Crude but necessary.

Hence the shit everywhere.

I say, 'Why?'

Corwen Lintock says his boys were safeguarding their Leader's best interests. There was concern after I had asked for reward for my troubles in delivering the berries. It was felt that the Leader's supply was at risk. That he might be held to ransom by me as the city's only supplier of pukka berries.

Corwen Lintock says he needs to feel as though he can learn to trust me all over again. Says that for a moment, before Fitsimmons had convinced him of my integrity, he had felt his trust in me wavering. What with my mention of possible pukka berry supply difficulties and of Oosten-bruik which was a long time ago and best forgotten.

Sure, I say. I understand. I'm sure I'd feel the same if it was me. Heck, he might have lost his connecting line to God, and Corwen Lintock just couldn't afford for that to happen with the city's prospects so finely balanced.

I soothe him with little details of the fireworks I am planning, the circus of dreams, ideas I have for laser lights above the city, but it's hard to feel that he's taking it all in.

Corwen Lintock's meeting is at the River Court Hotel, with the Pound twins Sarah, seventeen, and Hannah, sixteen. In the Coral Suite.

He asks me one more thing. You and Sam Pound, he says. You went to school together? You were good friends, yes? Could turn to each other in times of trouble? You were someone he might have confided in if ever he was in a tight spot?

Sure, I say, sure. It's how I'd like to have it seen. Me and Sam went back some way.

Corwen Lintock is due in committee in an hour's time. The girls are going to have to work quickly today. One up top and one down below, as Fitsimmons would say, no doubt has said now that he's pretty much living up there on the Fourteenth Floor following his recent promotion.

49

It is surprisingly full in the community centre. There is some concern about recent developments and my task tonight is to quell those concerns. The quarter must be kept manageable whilst other steps are taken and the city is exorcised of its sickness. I got some instructions from Corwen Lintock's office. Do nothing to upset the Leader's plan. Just signal developments to him on my return.

It is a familiar venue to me.

This building now called the community centre was just about the first I can remember on arriving here with my mother on Beaker Street. It was in here that they ran the Depression soup runs, here the evacuees were sorted in 1940 and '41, here the VE Dance was held in the week after our arrival in the city, although my mother didn't attend. Already, people felt there was a sadness about her. Others said that in her position she ought to show more willing.

It was the venerable George Steen who formally re-opened the building as a community centre. It had seemed like a good idea at the time, and there was money spare in the kitty. Cotton threads were still spinning. It seemed to prove that things were on the up, even for those on Beaker Street.

I can see Daniel Daniel the priest from the Church of St Mary's at the back of the hall. Sloopy Den Barton who supplies most of the speed consumed in the east quarter is here. Also, Joe Mole the rip-off merchant and pedlar of unsound goods who hangs around on the end of the broken-boned Beaker Street is here. Both of these speak well and will need watching, but I have their number.

The meeting is led by Coleman Seer in his capacity as Chairman of the East Quarter Community Forum. This evening he will be an ally of, and an apologist for, the new policy being fashioned by the City Council to help the situation. He will take no messing. He has a short, shrill voice and a sure understanding of procedural protocol. Also he has the backing of Sentex Security who are present tonight to ensure that the democratic process is strictly adhered to. Also, three unopened video cassettes sit taped up in a shoe box on Coleman Seer's kitchen table. The videos are a *Hot Girls Extra* home-movie production.

Coleman Seer is keen to wrap things up early tonight.

Most people here are content to listen. Community Forum meetings are usually pretty shambolic affairs. It's hard finding someone prepared to take minutes and there aren't many votes taken. Sometimes whoever is Treasurer runs off with the kitty. One time a postholder jumped off a six-storey blackstone. I mean!

This isn't how it seems in my reports back to City Hall, of course. My reports paint a healthy picture of proceedings. They particularly praise the Chairman, Coleman Seer, and the success herein of proactive city consultation.

Most of the time, it's just voices from the back shouting out dumb questions and the Chairman ruling them out of order.

The questions get asked by Sloopy Den Barton and Joe Mole from the back of the hall where they stand with the priest called Daniel. They ask whose fevered mind made up this Beaker Street Oath? And what is the purpose of the curfew that stops them from moving into the city after dark? What are they? Criminals?

Coleman Seer rules them out of order.

Also, they ask, 'Why are these goons here?' and they point at Jason Pound and his colleagues in their neat suits and their badges saying 'Sentex Security'.

Sloopy Den and Joe Mole want to know about the spate of arrests in the quarter recently. What is the council's motive in all this, they ask, and I'm forced to repeat the explanation that these were protective custody orders in light of retaliation by cityfolk going into the east quarter seeking instant justice for things.

What things, they say.

Centuries of things.

There are mumblings across the hall and Coleman Seer has to call for order and demand that the meeting returns to the formal agenda, and the small group at the back subside into quiet and mumble 'turkeyneck' and things.

Just wait, though. Boy, have I got their number.

You want to know which two names were on the report that went in to Corwen Lintock's office? Sure you do.

Sloopy Den Barton and Joe Mole, that's who, that's who.

50

The trickiest part of the evening is when the priest called Daniel makes this dumb speech from out of the double-thickness jawbone hidden under his beard. Don't worry. It's going into the report I will submit to Drucker, all in neat English that points up just what he's up to.

You can just see this priest itching for a big confrontation with the City Leader. You see this as a good finale?

I think maybe.

The priest called Daniel has this neat trick of talking quietly so anyone who wants to catch his words has to strain to hear him.

Clever.

Also, he has this mannerism in his face, a nervous tic each time he finishes a sentence that drives you wild but which serves as visual punctuation for his collective audience.

All in all, he'd get nowhere in city politics but here, in the community centre, in the east quarter, men like Sloopy Den Barton and Joe Mole and other such kurs who think my turkey neck is funny listen in this ear-splitting silence whilst he talks.

He says they should consider sending a delegation to the City Hall to argue the case for the east quarter. To protest against this de facto partitioning of everything beyond Beaker Street which is now fourteen acres of rubble and shit.

Daniel says that they should avoid direct confrontation with the city authorities, that they should pursue only non-violent protest because they know their hand is weak. There are one or two nods and someone else shouts out, 'We need more paint, priest-man, for the City Hall walls,' and Daniel the priest smiles.

He says they should not begin to believe all that is said about them. He says if the city wishes to call them kurs, they should be proud to be so. This way, they will not be lonely and outcast but will be strong like a band of brothers.

And I'm sat there thinking, 'Like it's something to be proud of? Who is this priest?'

Then he tells a story.

Daniel the priest says when he was a boy he looked even stranger than he does now, like he was only half-made. He had this great looping forehead and this thick double-sized jaw that in those days wasn't covered up by fuzzy beard. Also, he had this nervous tic in his face.

He said his parents worried about him looking like that. They were good people, he says, but they were embarrassed by his appearance and worried that he was unlovable and that for all his life he would be a lonely outcast in a world setting great store by how men look to each other. So they did the single kindest thing they could think of doing for him.

What was it that they did for him?

They made up a story, that's what, on the eve of his being sent away to the seminary. They told him that he wasn't their natural child. Anyone could tell that from how he looked, they said. They said they had plucked him out of an orphanage and offered to bring him up despite everything.

That's what they said. Despite everything.

The priest says: 'You know why they made up that story?' He says they made it up to prove that even someone like Daniel could be loved enough by good people like them to be picked out and brought up as though he was their own.

He got one thing right, this turbulent priest who threatens to face up to Corwen Lintock and rock the city's boat. We fear nothing like we fear loneliness. It's true, it's true. It's nothing really, I've been there. It's like missing your connection in a town you don't know, didn't want to be in. It isn't that you don't know how to get away or anything. Just that you're usually happy, given the choice, to offer up things sometimes if it'll hurry up the bus before nightfall.

51

It was Christmastime, I remember, when my mother walked out of the house to go over to the Church of St Mary's as part of the church's weekly cleaning rota and never came back.

Christmas Eve. A sod of a time to go walking out of people's lives.

What follows I have since been able to piece together from her diaries. Unlike the collected volumes of Kegan Laurie Wold, my mother's notes to posterity were left in cold and open English. Odd that, since she had increasingly spoken nothing but Polish in her later years.

They were written in a Woolworth exercise pad. A comment on her worth to the world. I surmise this. It's not something you can know absolutely, is it?

My mother's diaries were undisguised in their reflections on the love and the hate and the loss she had known from schoolgirl in Warsaw to housewife on Beaker Street in the city's east quarter.

The line between mitigation and revenge was a narrow one for my mother in filling her Woolworth exercise pad with her sparse English phrases. It cost her dear at her weekly confession to Father Keam at St Mary's and it echoed through her diaries on each pencil-scratched, marginless page.

'Dear Diary,' each page began, and you wondered into whose eyes she dared to look as she spoke her words onto the paper in the privacy of the kitchen. Did she see a face or merely toss out her English words hopefully?

I wondered about that until I reached the final page and saw whose face she was looking into, saw that she was writing them to me. Oh Christ, oh Jesus Christ Almighty.

'Dedicated to my son, Harni,' it said on the back flyleaf, 'who is better than all of this.'

Someone said that you only come to know your parents after they have died on you. I always liked that as an idea. Amongst other things, it gets me off the hook of not knowing her until she really did die.

In all her life my mother had loved one man. It was just that my father had the misfortune to marry her before she met and then lost the partisan Kadosh Schmeickel in the outback hills of Rajska.

Kadosh Schmeickel was the de facto leader of the rag-bag group of rebels and gypsies and strays which the refugee Brogdan Zelenewycz with his tattered Polish army greatcoat and his child bride Rivka, chanced across as they pulled their wooden-wheeled cart south to God knows where.

Schmeickel was not a good-looking man but he had this self-possessed air about him that conferred on him the aura of leader without a word having been spoken of it.

The group of partisans (they were hardly that) took in the refugee Zelenewyczs. This was a brave thing to do since the countryside was full of spies but Schmeickel was a good judge of men.

The Zelenewyczs stayed a year with these people in the hills. It was known by some that Schmeickel and Rivka had become lovers, but it was never spoken of. To have history in your possession was unwise.

They moved camp each week. They raided farms for food. Sometimes they raided trains. At night they sat round the campfire, singing 'Kde Domov Muj?' into the flames in slow, sad voices led by the Czech Schmeickel.

They managed to stay one step ahead of the Germans until one day when the whereabouts of the partisans were betrayed and they were cornered high in the woods by a brigade of troops despatched from the garrison outside Rajska.

Brogdan Zelenewycz managed to escape the ambush in the back of a stolen army van with his wife and three of the women from the partisan group.

It was the van in which I, the infant Harni Zelenewycz, would be born as it tore south on dirt tracks.

Down in Rajska, the remaining partisans were rounded up. Those with bad blood were trucked north of the village to the gas ovens of Auschwitz. The leader of the group, the Czech Kadosh Schmeickel, they beat up with rifle butts then crucified to a tree upside down.

Schmeickel had these strange ears, wide like trophy handles. The garrison captain nailed these back to the bark of the tree in front of the gathered village and the blood lipped down over Schmeickel's turkey neck and onto his stiffening body.

At night my mother would dream of him.

They had only fleetingly been lovers. In the aftermath of war, Rivka Zelenewycz believed it might be enough to see her through. To keep alive this strange spark he had lit in her.

In those early months on Beaker Street the thought of him warmed her like a blanket but it could never be enough. She felt that to set out her life neatly before her was her only salvation. That way she would see it coming.

Words, clean English words, stacked up like boxes for her, but grief was the space between all those broken thoughts, and increasingly she took refuge in a silent mysticism of her own making and in the language and hope of her youth. She saw statues cry. She felt herself to be the reincarnation of Our Lady of Kocjelska.

A starter for ten, therefore. Of the four people who have known real love herein, only one has been nailed to a tree.

Who? Who got nailed to a tree?

Kadosh Schmeickel, that's who.

That was a tough one.

Like I say, she went off at Christmastime, apparently to the Church of St Mary's as she always did at that same time each week, but she was not seen again alive.

I know what her last words were because she wrote them in the Woolworth exercise pad which was found nearby. The one with the dedication in the back to me which seemed to want to say that I was her last hope. I always wondered if she had second thoughts about that since she wound up throwing it to the wind in a hundred pieces. Maybe she was only testing my resolve.

Her last words were these, before she threw herself off the blackstone outcrop and into the path of a passing subway tram coming slooping out of the tunnel, sung with a sweet and sure cry:

'Kde Domov Muj?'

These were the words which she sang out into the Christmas air.

This was her Christmas song.

And then the subway tram.

Hell, I sure wish my father hadn't lied so much.

Shuckety puck, shuckety puck, shuckety puck.

52

It was felt important, by the Council Leader amongst others, that any architectural merit the city might have should be enhanced by the new arrangements for the east quarter.

Whatever life may become, art should remain above it, don't you think?

An architectural practice up from London was drafted in to supervise the design around key areas of the project, notably the main exit point at the bottom of Beaker Street where the quarter faces the city proper.

A gaggle of architects bestrode the city before putting their designs and site recommendations on paper. Only local materials were to be used. The familiar blackstone brick of the city, polished leather brown by the damp winds, was to be used to create the effect of a medieval wall. The plans won praise for their aspect.

Corwen Lintock is well pleased by their aspect. Also the pipe-sucking Drucker smiles a lot and has an artist's impression on the wall of his office in pastels.

The wall is up for awards, and there is much debate about it in architectural circles. I know this because I got the job of chaperoning this London gaggle with the dull suits around for a week. It should have been Fitsimmons's job but he was busy on weightier matters. That's his version. Me, I reckon Corwen Lintock was offering me a chance to make good again after the pukka berry supply fiasco.

I heard these men from London saying that the architecture they would practise in bequeathing this tercentenary monument to the small blackstone city was art brought to life. It seemed like a dumb thing to be saying because I figured everyone knew that art was a stuffed crocodile. I stay clear of art myself like I stay clear of religion. My concerns are only for the living. I'm no lover of dead crocodiles.

The architects went around for a week looking at the sites where Corwen's wall would run, saying things in public like, 'Boy, it rains a lot here.' The damp climate that made cotton king didn't go down well with the dull suits.

One time I told them, 'My father was an artist. He carved from blackened beech and things but then he burned them one by one on the hills.'

With the trial going a little better these days, Corwen Lintock has been able to take a more active interest in city affairs. Some people have said that he's turned the court proceedings on their head, made it a witch hunt. Corwen Lintock just smiled when he heard this. 'Heck,' he said, 'in my book either you're for witches or against them.'

The work on the wall which encircles the east quarter has pleased him. The architects are paid up and gone to drier climes clutching their awards. The Leader has examined their work and seen that it is good.

Maybe Aaron Wold will bless it in the name of Jesus for a half pound of pukka berries to keep the evil eye off it now it is done.

It is true that for much of the perimeter line around the east quarter, down by the river for example, the architecture gives way to simple barbed wire fencing, but money is money even when you're stuffing a crocodile.

The vision of a wall to contain the city's problems within the east quarter, to exorcise its ghosts, is Corwen Lintock's. It's alright dreaming at night, like my father in his silent rooms, like Coleman Seer in his stockinged feet, like Vernon Smitts in his basement empire, like my gaggle of architects dreaming of stuffing more crocodiles.

They are harmless enough but they make no history, unless it's at someone else's bidding. I know this from the Woolworth exercise pad.

Government needs people who can dream in the light of day. People like Corwen Lintock. Sure, and people like Harry Angel too. I feel that these days I am increasingly trusted by the City Leader. The pukka berry incident was maybe an aberration. I got the plum job of chaperoning the architects for the wall after all.

The wall is one such dream. One such restless urging forward. There are others in the pipeline. Soon the city will have no problems left at all. After that, Corwen Lintock will be able to attend functions like this, the official opening of Stage One of the wall, without the converted golf cart in which he sits at present.

The metal badge on the front of the vehicle says 'Sentex Security'. Inside, the Leader is shielded from the sweat of flesh and the abrupt cries of the city which distract him from the work still to be done. Also it helps him get about. He's not fully recovered from the stomach bug he had. He still needs a little help on his feet. Fortunately for us, though, his vision remains intact.

The glass-plated buggy is washable against graffiti. Also it has lights inside. Corwen Lintock is afraid of the dark. Also it has been consecrated against having the evil eye put on it.

Mostly, though, it is just bullet-proof.

The best of dreamers are practical men.

Since Stankill took over the Housing Commission hearings, Corwen Lintock has judged it wise to take precautions until the rooting-out process has been completed. The Housing Commission's task is pretty straightforward. It is to root out all those kurs who have infiltrated city life here across the East River and put them back where they belong before they succeed in bringing Corwen Lintock down and doing some real damage. Sorting out the wheat from the chaff as I think Aaron Wold put it when he stood in his clearing in the City Park.

I myself have already been screened. It was a necessary process before my being entrusted with the care of the architects from London. The Commission asked me about my father in the sanitarium on the edge of the city. I said my father was a crazy man whom I visited irregularly out of pity. They asked me about my mother. I said she fell off a subway tram going shuckety puck, and now she is dead and gone.

They said, 'What about your wife?'

I said that I married the most English girl I could find in the city, and that now I fill my silences with pukka berry tasks.

Shuckety puck.

The wall went up in four weeks, that elegant part which has won awards for its aspect.

Whoosh!

Cement and bulldozers and hod carriers and classic blackstone cobbles everywhere.

The hod carriers were mostly men from the east quarter. Men like Sloopy Den Barton and Joe Mole who hang around the priest Daniel Daniel. Job creation. Work, you see, is harder to come by in the city proper these days if your identification is set out on a yellow card.

It was my boss Daulman's idea to recruit the labour for the work from the east quarter jobless who queue at the Beaker Street Gate each morning at dawn. I just got the task of supervising the project. Another mile walked on the road to recovering my reputation in the eyes of the city.

As for Sloopy Den and the like, I reckon the wages, what there were of them, would be welcome to help meet the increased rent. After all, the protection which kurs have won from the construction of the wall has to be paid for somehow.

Of course the round-roll wire fencing went up overnight. It drops out from coils compressed on the back of special wagons. I had six of them ordered specially for the job. Each one lays double-length steel mesh with butterfly barbs at a thousand yards an hour in the dark.

The wagons trundle down the road unwinding their coiled load and making an instant fence for you like you were making an instant milk whip or something. And there you have it – three and a half miles in circumference sketching out the perimeter of parallel habitation.

Ingenious.

Lord knows how they managed to lay the lines in Kegan Laurie Wold's day in his Belgian flower fields. Maybe Aaron Wold can tell me if he ever makes it to Volume Eighteen.

I got this official invitation to attend today. The success with the round-roll wire helped, I'm sure, but I think the assistance I gave to the architects was the clincher as far as my invitation went, although the architects to a man did seem to take comic exception to the way my shirt collar rolled into rope around my tie however hard I tried to straighten it.

Of course I didn't quite make top rostrum today, but then Corwen Lintock's golf buggy takes a fair amount of room up there. I sit with Coleman Seer who is invited as Chairman of the East Quarter Community Forum.

Coleman Seer gets to make a speech too.

He makes a good speech in his funny careful little voice with sweat beads spiking his forehead. Some say it is a speech of atonement.

Coleman Seer pays tribute to the past glories of the city when 'Jerusalem' was sung over the clatter of a thousand looms and India was clothed with the dhootie cloth of our mills and sweated labour.

He recognises the need to revitalise the city. In achieving this, he knows, says as much, that the east quarter cannot expect to leech off the city forever. He uses that very metaphor. He knows the east quarter has to learn to stand on its own two feet.

Then he steps back. Enough is enough.

Before he had stood up to speak at the opening ceremony, Coleman Seer had turned to me, asked me, 'Are you sure it will be enough to get me out?'

I said sure. Heck, this was plenty far enough to straighten things out. Just leave it to me. Now that he has finished his little speech I tell Coleman Seer he has done well.

Guess what!

Soon I will accompany Coleman Seer to the River Court Hotel.

Soon, with Harry Angel as escort, Coleman Seer will collect payment.

53

Stankill's Housing Commission sat initially down in the City Hall Basement, in what had been at one time the Municipal Housing Enquiries Office. I had known it well in my formative years.

The committee reviewed cases in the open-plan office where Councillor Nan Lintock had cornered poor Vernon Smitts that stifling summer of 1964 when even the subway tracks buckled.

Just as it was then, the queue waiting to be seen by the committee stretched back along the dimly lit corridor. Maybe they had rats in the cistern and damp in the walls but they didn't tell that to the Commission.

Now, the hearings take place in a more formal setting in the City Council Chamber. From the two public galleries the TV cameras watch the proceedings each day unblinking, eating streams of video tape dumb as mutes. Stankill tells people to be patient. Everyone will get a turn.

Stankill chairs the sessions. He brings to them all the application of F. W. Taylor's theories of Scientific Management. Stankill has the application of a stakhanovite. This I have noted before. On one side of him sits Aratakis. He makes notes and says little. Figures Stankill can do the talking. Knows of his being unsound. Is joined on the committee by others depending what day it is. Daulman likes doing Tuesdays for example.

Down in the Basement they had run two hundred and twelve hearings a week. The schedule was Stankill's. At fifty-six hearings a day, this came out at one per eight-and-a-half minutes during the time set aside for hearings which included the need for each contestant to swear allegiance to the city in Corwen Lintock's new tercentenary oath if they were to pass.

After eight-and-a-half minutes, the interview was concluded, the panel made a decision, a box was ticked and the next hearing commenced. Thus was the city to be cleansed at eight-and-a-half-minute intervals.

Shuckety puck, shuckety puck.

Aaron Wold has said this to Corwen Lintock on the mound by the City Park clearing after dark after the traditional weekly blessing:

'Don't suppose that I come to you to abolish the Law.'

'No, no,' Corwen Lintock has said. 'Go on.'

'I tell you this, so long as heaven and earth endure, not a letter, not a stroke will disappear from the Law until all that must happen has happened.' You can just see Aaron Wold trying frantically to remember his lines.

'Fine by me,' the Leader has said. 'No place for trouble-makers in my city.'

Aaron Wold has said, 'If any man sets aside even the least of the Law's demands and teaches others to do the same, he will have the lowest place in the kingdom of heaven. I think.'

'Bingo,' Corwen Lintock has said. 'That sounds like kurs to me.'

It was after this that Stankill's Commission was switched from the City Hall Basement to the Council Chamber where the TV cameras could fix on the proceedings.

One thing Corwen Lintock has figured, or maybe it was Fitsimmons who worked it out for him up there on the Fourteenth Floor, is that there's no point hiding your light under a bushel. Not when it comes to defending the law and the city and the blessings of the Jesus in the navy anorak and stuff like that. Also it pays well. Wouldn't you know it, these hearings where every resident in town gets eight-and-a-half minutes in the hot seat now get higher TV ratings than anything including the old format game shows. Also, what the TV stations put up in cash pays for three new public works a week.

I have to agree it makes good entertainment. Like all good game shows it has everything that real life has: drama, human interest, neat conclusion. Also you get to belch whenever you like and nip out to brew tea during the breaks.

Contestants stand first to give the Tercentenary Oath. I swear allegiance, so it goes, to whomsoever carries the badge and flag of the office of Leader in the City; and, forswearing all other allegiances, reject and abhor those who would bring down, repel, or advance upon the ancient and rightful promises and duties prescribed by the City and its sundry Authorities. So help me Jesus.

Nothing to it really, although some have refused to take it. Taken a stand. Of course for that they win the booby prize.

I watch the old Stankill game show myself when I'm home in the apartment, especially now I've no pukka berries to attend to. It helps take my mind off bigger things, like the preparations for the circus and the fireworks and the laser lights for the tercentenary. Heck, if all my planning comes off, will it be a ding-dong!

Life is undoubtedly tougher without the reassuring time-table that the pukka berries brought to my days. At least the drama and so on of the Commission's hearings are keeping out the voices in my head which read my mother's Woolworth words to me over and over again at a distance. Some nights I can block their female whining right out.

Some nights not.

54

Stankill is in his element during the Commission's hearings. Maybe he knows about being unsound. Maybe he sees this as his route to salvation. He leans over his desk in the hot glare of the TV lights and chews his pencil to the butt and says, 'Are you now or have you ever been active against the laws of the city?' Boy, he loves it.

Stankill's lank hair hangs on his brow. He sweats evilly. The grease on his forehead makes his skin shine grey. The stenographer's fingers click on the key pads. Stankill consults the papers spread out on his desk again.

'Speak up,' he will say. 'The city can't hear you. Are you now or have you ever been active in supporting kurish plots to undermine the city?' I tell you, the TV audience must be on the edge of their seats. Wrong answer means it's off to the gunge tank. Here is the game show of the year. Here is Stankill weaving in and out of the questions he sets and the answers he receives to the applause of the public galleries above them.

Some believe it can be good for a man to hear a different drummer's beat. Stankill knows better. Stankill knows that Thoreau never had to save a city. Stankill knows that herein lies the way, the truth and the light. Also there is

TV exposure and a memo of appreciation from Fitsimmons on the Fourteenth Floor and a warming smile from Drucker, while losing candidates trail off to wait for their transfer across the bones of Beaker Street. There, in the community centre, some people, my daughter Sonja amongst them, will give them blankets and new papers for identification and tell them what's what in the east quarter.

Stankill and the others sit at the long low Recorder's table. The individual being screened for citizenship sits up a level, where the Mayor's seat is positioned when the City Council is in session. It's a joke. Stankill calls it the hot seat.

'Don't worry, it's not plugged in,' he says, as the next contestant enters the room from the long dark corridor outside and emerges into the TV lights of the Council Chamber.

I watched Sloopy Den Barton and Joe Mole on TV when they were contestants recently on the game show of the year.

Their starter for ten was this:

'Are you now or have you ever been active against the law in the city? Members of the infamous council of kurs, stuff like that?'

Now they are in protective custody.

Stankill said, 'What do you know about the oath that kurs take to undermine the city?'

They said, 'We watched Corwen Lintock hold it up like some scraggy piece of paper someone wrote out in pencil in a hurry one dark night.'

Stankill said, 'What do you know about Coleman Seer's dog?'

They said, 'It doesn't bark any more.'

Stankill said, 'What do you know about Sam Pound?'

'He's dead,' they said. 'And dead men don't tell tales. Unless they've left some legacy of words behind in sealed envelopes so others can speak for them.'

The truth will out, as truth will.

Afterwards I switched channels. I'd seen the ending to this one before.

55

The three men whose apparel says 'Sentex Security' stand by the blackbrick arch that marks the exit point into the city on Beaker Street. Coleman Seer waits for me nearby some yards from the striped barrier across the road. 'It's alright,' I'm saying to the men, smiling, 'he's with me. I'll sign him out for the night.'

We drive down by the river towards the River Court Hotel, Coleman Seer's little smile playing on his lips beside me. His jacket and trousers, tight at the angles like a shedding skin on his beanpole frame, have been freshly brushed of dog hairs.

Tonight, the dog that doesn't bark sits alone in the east quarter apartment. Tonight, Coleman Seer is going to heaven, although he'll be back by nine-thirty.

He has an erection inside his suit that makes him wince.

We had to walk across the no-man's land of Beaker Street to get out. I tell you, it's not like it was. I'll tell you how it looks. It looks like some dreaming diagram of how my tongue tells me that my teeth look. The only things that still stand rigid are the old streetlights that had to be left for fear that the demolition would short the power supply to the city. They have that look of tall weeds, starved of the sun. Here and there is dead meat hanging. Sentex traps on sticks to snare the cats which have bred out of control. I'm told it's working.

Last night, Sentex Security bought another thirty-second slot in the middle of some game show or other with the proceeds of their burgeoning city-wide business.

The ad shows black-and-white images of a blackstone city with the broken face of an old woman. Slowly it gives way to the gold and grey of a clean dawn over the moors, then children playing on a green and neatly mown lawn. A collage of people smile into the camera lens. Bright handsome people with strong smiles.

At the end the voiceover says,

'Corwen Lintock: Giving You A Better Future.'

I figured out what it really should have said. It should have said: 'Corwen Lintock: Your Route To History's End.'

Don't you think?

You want to know whose handsome faces were amongst those in the advert, reminding us between game shows and stuff that happy days are soon to be with us again? Sure you do. Pretty faces with wide eyes and snub noses and pale skins and small sour mouths?

Two Pound girls, Hannah and Sarah, smiling strong smiles in the gold and grey of the city's new dawn.

That's who, that's who.

Blonde hair now shining like wheat in the Coral Suite of the River Court Hotel as they wait for Coleman Seer's arrival and his hour on the stairway to heaven.

We nod to the doorman and I take Coleman Seer up two storeys in the lift. He looks down at the ground and shuffles. He keeps licking his lip.

Oh boy, oh boy!

Anticipation grips his light and dizzy stomach.

I bang on the door of the Coral Suite and Hannah answers.

She wears a simple red cotton dress and high heels. From inside the room comes the sound of some warm country music played low. The singer is telling Coleman Seer there are blue skies in Tennessee.

I leave Coleman Seer with her at the door. I will be back for him in an hour's time. The door closes and I walk down the corridor and round into Room 162.

Aratakis opens the door. Inside the room, Corwen Lintock sits in a wheelchair by the two-way screen, can see the unfolding drama in the Coral Suite through the glass, can see right into the clubhouse so to speak.

56

Aratakis says, 'What has he done to deserve this?'

Corwen Lintock smiles his boyish smile from thickened lips, sat in the wheelchair. The buggy wouldn't fit in here. 'He spoke up for the people,' he says. 'Forswore all other allegiances. Abhorred those who would repel the authority of the city.'

Stankill gets no invitation to the show. Stankill has the application of a stakhanovite but he is unsound.

Inside the Coral Suite, standing over Coleman Seer who sits on the edge of the bed, Hannah has peeled off her simple red dress but left the heels on. She has cool pale flesh. She has a body that is sixteen years old and holds the bullfrog Aratakis beyond the screen with rabbit eyes.

She cups her high curving breasts in her hands and brushes them faintly against Coleman Seer's mouth. Her blonde hair obscures his expression from Aratakis and from the smiling Corwen Lintock and from the taxi-driving Harry Angel.

There is another forty-eight minutes before I must knock on the door of the Coral Suite and collect Coleman Seer for home. The taxi-driving Harry Angel has an erection that makes me want to weep.

Through the glass we can see that Sarah, who wears yellow football shorts and white ankle socks, is knelt between Coleman Seer's legs. She is shorter than Hannah, smaller breasts and wider hips. She is doing little things to his erect penis with her mouth, with her tongue, with her small white fingers.

Coleman Seer is dribbling from the side of his mouth. Unaccustomed as he is to public speaking, he is making small animal noises as he lies on the bed.

In Room 16, I ask Corwen Lintock, 'Why are you here?' The pounding of blood around my flesh has given me toothache. I picture the crevices of rock on Beaker Street. Oh my traitor tongue. Corwen Lintock says he's here because he likes watching losers. It reminds him of what not to become. All he ever wanted he says was to be Eddie Melon; to be a winner in that effortless way that some men just seemed to have.

He asks me if I reckon we have got our money's worth from Coleman Seer, whether the city has done well by his efforts.

I say, 'It depends how much you figure it cost us.'

He thinks that is a good answer. He laughs. It seems to cost him in the way his chest heaves. Maybe you can count the cost of it in minutes off his life.

I wonder if maybe I've redeemed myself. It would be good to gain redemption. I watch the action for a little while through the glass, until I notice Corwen's laughing painfully some more.

I ask him, 'What makes you laugh now?'

He looks through the glass at Coleman Seer and the Pound girls and says he is laughing because he knows the punchline.

Eddie Melon, hero of the football field in Corwen Lintock's childhood, proprietor now of my father's sanitarium on the hill, was early on his own particular stairway to heaven. Remember – his father lied to him. Eddie Melon, bow-legged and tousle-haired, could dribble and push and punt a tennis ball around the city backstreets like it was tied to his shoe. Heck, he could volley a marble clean through the neck of a milk bottle.

Eddie Melon had a real Midas touch in front of goal. When he got the ball, a buzz would go round the ground, as though 30,000 people were passing on a secret. When he ran at defenders the men who had spent all week dutifully weaving dhootie cloth in sunless mills felt the hairs on the backs of their necks stand on end and an electric ripple run through their hearts. Eddie Melon was surely a winner.

Small boys, Corwen Lintock amongst them, clamoured for his autograph and shouted 'Bags I Eddie Melon' as they hacked their tennis balls about between them in the city streets. Old men with memories stretching back bought him drinks and compared him wistfully to Syd Puddefoot and Tom Finney. Young girls shaped like Hannah Pound offered him their sweetly yielding bodies. They knew a winner when they saw one and figured maybe it was catching like a disease or something.

And all the time none of this mattered a lot to Eddie. He was just happy singing his hymn to the universe, volleying marbles through the necks of milk bottles.

When the door opens, Hannah is clothed again in her simple red dress. Coleman Seer's hour is up. Hannah is combing her blonde hair in the doorway with an ivory-backed brush.

Another odd thing.

In the car, on the way back across the city as we drive down past the river, Coleman Seer will cry tears into his long insect fingers.

Standing at the door of the Coral Suite, waiting for Coleman Seer to appear, I smile at Hannah.

I want to say, 'Hannah, you look a winner to me.'

But I just smile, and she glances up at me and gives me this sidelong look. You know the one.

You know what it says.

57

'This is your delegation?' Stankill says.

'Yes.' The priest called Daniel with the wooden jaw sits high up on the Mayor's seat in the Council Chamber. It was reckoned they could get through the priest's hearing at the same time. Assert his right to live with us in the city. That he'd be less trouble over here with us, inside the tent pissing out. Stankill, though, has forgotten to say, 'It's alright, it's not plugged in.' Odd, that.

Stankill will put the questions. The stenographer sits ready over the desk to tap out the priest's words so that they can be cut and jointed before the butcher's day is out. With him is Harry Angel, that's me, the former pukka berry grower, the taxi-driving, architect-chaperoning, pimping confidant of Corwen Lintock. The bullfrog Aratakis and the smiling Drucker watch from the galleries, dumb as mutes.

Fitsimmons is absent. Fitsimmons, of course, is now on the Fourteenth Floor. Fitsimmons with the happy sex life, exchanging fucks for the trophies he brings home each day like promissory notes.

Who knows about Daulman. Maybe he lost the memo.

Fitsimmons has figured out there's a way of identifying your average kur through genetic fingerprinting. I said, didn't I, that he was wasted here. He'd be better out in the real world.

Fitsimmons argues true-bred cityfolk have this different genetic strain, which would explain a lot, don't you think? You know, the evil eye and everything. The process is kind of a genetic litmus test. Aratakis has put money each way with Drucker that the unsound Stankill will eventually register yellow when he's tested. Fitsimmons has calculated that there could be upwards of five thousand kurs hiding out in the city proper, undiscovered, making like they're just cityfolk, making like they own the place or something.

Maybe his wife will let Fitsimmons do it doggy-doggy soon.

'You were going to lead a delegation,' Drucker suggests.

'I was,' Daniel Daniel says, 'but you locked them all up.'

'The law is the law, Father.'

'Yes, the law is the law.'

'I am glad we are agreed.'

'Perhaps,' says Stankill, 'you could say your piece and then we could proceed. There is an oath for you to swear. A formality, for those who would live amongst us.'

Daniel says, 'I want to talk about the east quarter of the city.'

The east quarter is now, of course, somewhat separate from the city which itself rises daily from the ashes of bad history, which benefits daily from the investments of Sentex Construction and the like. Also there is the marketing of the city through Sentex Communications whose new non-executive director is Fitsimmons.

Now the east quarter community must fend for itself, feed itself, clothe itself. The city has its own destiny to meet this side of the Beaker Street line.

You know what they say – work liberates.

I put that in a committee report. It went down a bomb. The Members figure to use it as a slogan for the self-sufficiency programme of the east quarter under Parallel

240

Habitation. It was one of my better reports. The report was headed 'Enough Is Enough'.

Residents of the east quarter with their yellow addenda to items of identification can no longer work in the city proper without the permission of the Police Authority. Anyone getting the gunge bucket in Stankill's game show of the year usually needs to find work within the east quarter. Needless to say there's precious little of that. Hence I guess the soup and blankets in the community centre there.

Drucker is explaining all this to the priest, that this community is founded on three hundred years of respecting the law. It's all down in the committee reports.

Daniel Daniel with the wooden jaw says quietly, 'Where will you stop?'

Drucker smiles pleasantly on high; who knows what is going through his mind? But Aratakis next to him you can see is thinking: What a dumb question. What a dumb godforsaken question. You can just see it written on his face.

Stankill says, 'We will stop, Father, when the battle to resurrect this town is won.'

'What battle are you fighting?' the priest asks.

Here we go again.

Stankill says we are fighting the battle to win.

'But who is the enemy?' Daniel Daniel says.

'Losing is the enemy,' says Stankill. 'God hates to lose just as much as anyone, so don't get preachy about not wanting our town to win.'

'Heck,' Stankill continues. 'In the lottery of St Mary's, after you've sung your hymns and stuff, the winners get Paradise and the losers burn. At least in our game no-one gets eternal damnation, just the gunge tank and a life across the East River behind the rubble and shit.'

'What moral, then, do you draw from this?' Daniel Daniel asks.

'Don't get drawn with a yellow ticket.'

That's what Stankill says.

Little does he know.

Daniel Daniel asks if he can see Sloopy Den Barton and Joe Mole. He says he believes them to be in protective custody. Stankill feels compelled to give him the unfortunate news. They finished up being fished out of the East River in sacking cloth bags. The price of authorship of the Beaker Street Oath.

Sloopy Den Barton. Joe Mole. Rest in Peace.

The priest is making ready to leave, to go back to the east quarter like he was Father Maximilian Kolbe or something.

'Why not join us here across the river?' Drucker says. He is a PR man at heart. If he can find a way to avoid ruffling feathers. . . you know the rest. Says there's a vacancy for a chaplain to the City Hall. 'Come sing your hymns over here with us,' he adds.

'No,' says Daniel. 'Thank you for the offer, but how can I pledge allegiance to you? How can any man? Can't you see? Your law can only be the enemy of my law.'

And I get this feeling deep in my belly that surely the culmination of this narrative, the moral confrontation between the wooden-jawed priest and the Leader Corwen Lintock, cannot be far away. Who else would be foolish and brave enough to do it?

You get this sense also?

Stankill is telling Daniel Daniel that the priest is naive. Worse, he is wrong. He is an innocent in a world of real lives.

Aratakis should never have belched at just that moment.

58

Making history has all kinds of spin-offs. One is that there's no more howling like a dog coming from the City Park after dark, though you sure can hear it coming out from the east quarter some nights.

In fact, the park is due to feature in Sentex Communications' next thirty-second trailer for the City Leader's tercentenary celebrations. Summer will be upon us soon. Making the park safe is kind of a symbol of things for the Leader. 'Look,' he will be saying, 'I have given you back your park.' The park will be a backdrop to the TV trailer. It will speak of rebirth. Stuff like that. After that people will invest more in the city, good times will be here, jobs will come, land prices on Sentex properties will triple.

The park is the key symbol of this revival. It's where the big tercentenary circus will be staged. Going there alone at night is Aaron Wold's big mistake.

Aaron Wold has come to fulfil his mission in the city, playing out Jesus Christ after ten years' apprenticeship to the role and then spending another ten years in a different wilderness exiled away from his home on Crull.

'Go away and learn how to be this man,' the elders of Crull had said to him when he was originally chosen, probably from a list of names in the phone book, for the part of the man who began a religion and shaped the world and preferred prostitutes to politicians and said so and got nailed to a tree for his troubles.

These days, when he leaves the sanitarium on the hill and goes out into the city to meet with Corwen Lintock and the other unfortunates who choose to believe he is other than Aaron Wold, milkman, Hebridean, crazy man, he is just playing out the part he has practised for. Emptying his heart of all these carefully stacked words. How could he know they would land him in trouble with the City Leader?

He plays out this simple role for his own peace of mind. It is his own small hymn to the universe. He means no harm.

It is a dangerous thing, though, to get rounded up by Sentex Security who clean up the park nightly these days. Ready for the Harry Angel Circus and things. But then even Aaron Wold's role model got himself rounded up in the end.

Aaron Wold has been preaching out in the thin night air. He has stood waiting to rendezvous with Corwen Lintock to earn more pukka berries for the brag games in the sanitarium. But the last time they met, Aaron Wold told him a dumb story about passing through the eye of a needle which worried the Leader. Corwen Lintock cussed silently but said nothing and handed over payment. Half a pound. But you know what – if you're shelling out pukka berries, half a pound at a time, you deserve, surely, the kind of answers you want to hear and not some cockamamy threat about passing through the eye of some needle.

When the Leader got back to City Hall, the City Pukka Berry Attendants, Daulman and Stankill, had to report to him that all the pukka berry plants had died. I think it was the wrong watering times or something, pukka berries are hellish difficult to rear, but Corwen Lintock had different ideas. He figured someone had put the evil eye on him. He reckoned Aaron Wold was a dangerous force to be left roaming round the city. So he set him up.

59

The would-be Jesus Christ performer in the navy anorak and the heavy beard stands waiting patiently for Corwen Lintock to appear. Little does he know that he has cooked his goose. That was a dumb story to tell about the camel and the eye of a needle. I figure maybe it put Corwen Lintock's back up. The Leader is not well, is quick to anger these days, looks like he's been bitten by something in the bushes and left to moulder.

To pass the time Aaron Wold preaches to his imaginary disciples, standing on the mound in the clearing. What does he preach? Something about death and rebirth, I think. Heck, does it matter? It's just the sound of his voice. Then he sits down and smokes a cigarette and soaks up the silence that he welcomes out here because he is outside the sanitarium and he is free to speak and sing and cry out if he so wishes. Tonight he is happy in silence.

Then he sings a quiet hymn and the branches of the bushes around the clearing rustle in the breeze. There had been no brag game at the sanitarium this afternoon. The doctor had been called to come up the hill from the city. Aaron Wold's friend and fellow brag player Bronislaw Angel died tonight.

Bronislaw Angel has died tonight.

He died quietly and with some dignity which is surely all anyone can ask. He died in his room in the sanitarium.

His last words before he died were these:

'*Kde domov muj*, my friends?'

Maybe it was a line he'd seen in some movie. Heck, I don't know. You were never sure with my father.

Towards the end he announced that he really was Father Maximilian Kolbe, the Polish priest who asked to be sent to the death camp in place of those marked out by the

Germans because he preferred prostitutes to lawyers and politicians.

Personally, I think Bronislaw figured that the only chance he stood with his God was to pretend until the bitter end that he truly was Kolbe and not the wretched Brogdan Zelenewycz who lied to me all his life. Only as Kolbe, I think, did he believe he could avoid the gunge tank.

Jason Pound says, 'Where's your crown, Jesus?'

The Sentex Security patrol has picked up Aaron Wold on an anonymous tip-off wandering in the City Park close to the mound where he has met with Corwen Lintock twice a week. Here he has offered the Leader his careful stacks of words and claimed his pukka berries.

Nights like this, Aaron Wold has been glad to get out of the sanitarium, to wander alone in the town, to talk to people who might want to believe he is Jesus Christ, or a former milkman, or a city wino or something. Corwen Lintock has been turning up recently for these rendezvous in his converted golf buggy that Aaron Wold had blessed for him, but tonight he hasn't shown.

We know why. We know Aaron Wold has cooked his goose. Now he will be swept up in Sentex Security's net of protective custody.

There are worse fates perhaps to be had this night. Across town a short line of people are stepping down from six converted round-roll wire-dropping trucks. No-one says much. They walk quietly under the architects' carved wooden escutcheon leading into the east quarter. Each has been allocated a yellow identification card. Each will get soup and maybe blankets from the community centre.

'They sure must have had it coming,' Daulman is prone to remark.

Me, I'm at least glad you can walk in the City Park again at night and not be fearful or hear howling like a dog and not have the evil eye put on you.

60

Jason Pound says, 'So you're Jesus, are you?'

Aaron Wold says, 'It's you who said it.'

'Ha!' says Jason Pound. 'So if you're Jesus, where's your crown?'

Famous last words.

The boys from Sentex Security have found him a crown to wear. Jason Pound has cut and ringed it with his quick ferrety fingers from the stalks of the privet bush by the mound in the clearing. They have jammed it on his head, on his thick black hair, and Aaron Wold has shuddered with the pain.

'What you going to do now, Jesus, put the evil eye on us?'

Sure, sure, I know. Games with rules.

Before he left the sanitarium tonight, Aaron Wold had spent time translating another page and a half of the eighteen-volume works of his grandfather, Kegan Laurie Wold. Today, draped in the shadow of the death of Bronislaw Angel, has seen him complete the translation of Volume Four of the eighteen-volume work. Progress.

Volume Four concludes with Kegan Laurie Wold leaving his regimental base at Khartoum. He had at this point met and was living with the Dinka tribe of East Africa.

The Dinkas were the oldest tribe in Africa, the original inhabitants of the Serengeti, Wold discovered. They were a tribe ten thousand years old before anyone on earth got nailed to a tree and he loved them for it. Kegan Laurie Wold had resigned his commission in the aftermath of the colonial plan of forced labour for the tribe. The tribe's initial protest against the plan had cost them a hundred thousand lives in the Maji Maji rebellion. It persuaded the Dinkas that forced labour was maybe okay for them to accept, after all, in helping the colonials to advance the cause of progress, but Kegan Laurie Wold didn't see it like that.

The Dinkas, Volume Four ends by contemplating, are the oldest of the peoples on the planet. If lime mulch and subway trams and city government represent the end of the line, here is the beginning of history.

The last sentence of Volume Four reflected on the Dinkas' hymn to the universe which each Dinka father taught his child to sing on the Serengeti Plain under the baobab tree, and which they had taught Kegan Laurie Wold during his time with them. The song went like this:

'Man is born, and dies, and does not come again.'

Shuckety puck, shuckety puck.

61

When the sanitarium was first opened up by Eddie Melon, the ex-football star and failed TV game-show host, Aaron Wold was the very first resident to be invited to live there after he'd arrived on the doorstep one night, silent and unannounced.

They came after that singly, like refugees and exiles from lives they couldn't fathom. The end of history was killing them.

The building had been a lunatic asylum and a workhouse and a fever hospital by the time Eddie Melon came to buy the place.

By then he'd had a breakdown of sorts. It was a quiet unobtrusive event for the planet beyond the shrieking inner world that was Eddie Melon. He got it expensively treated and that was that. There was money for the treatment left over from his footballing days and from the TV game show called *Take Your Shot* that they let him host until the ratings fell after his breakdown on TV.

Even Eddie's magic touch couldn't pull the ratings round. Heck, the viewers asked, who was this Eddie Melon? The young kids kicking balls, pthuck pthuck pthuck, against apartment walls didn't know who the hell he was. Other heroes had replaced the forgotten Eddie Melon on the football field. Also, older people didn't like the way he smiled in close-up on TV. Volleying marbles counted for nothing if your close-up on TV made people feel like you were putting the evil eye on them.

Eddie hired nurses with thick stockings and pumps and blue cardigans over white aprons. He hired a gardener to cut the lawns and trim the hedges and prune the poplar trees. He hired decorators to paint the high rooms cool and green. He had separate apartment rooms refurbished throughout the building and he took Room 23 for himself. He had tossed up for a better room and lost, which pleased him no end.

Then he had an ad placed in the city paper. It said simply: 'Do you need refuge in a place of safety? Here at the sanitarium on the hill you are welcome. Truly.'

Over the main entrance to the building it said nothing except, 'Welcome. Truly' in very small letters. Inside, there were no signs and no rules except for the three separate lines written in the first page of the visitors' book. These said:

'Don't wreak violence.

'Don't frighten the others.

'Don't go round trying to burn the place down or something.'

That's all it said to each new guest as they arrived to take up residence alongside Eddie Melon and the first-to-arrive destitute former milkman from Crull, Aaron Wold.

62

Eddie Melon set up the sanitarium as a way of advertising for kindred spirits. He cried with joy the first night after a figure turned up at the door under the sign saying 'Welcome. Truly' wearing a navy anorak and a heavy beard.

Eddie Melon made him some tea and the stranger, who would not speak a single word but who wrote messages down on sheets of paper, wrote to him that he was a former milkman from the Hebridean island of Crull who'd been drummed out of the community onto the mainland for fouling up the decadal Cycle of Mystery Plays.

'How goes it with you?' he wrote to Eddie Melon after that, and he listened whilst Eddie told him and they drank tea together.

In the sanitarium there was no money. Decision-making was shared by everyone, including the cook and the gardener and the nurses who lived in. They too had tossed up for rooms. They met together each Monday evening in the main lounge with its cool high walls and its hearth fire and its bookshelves lined with a roomful of volumes, each one stacking a universe of words in different kaleidoscopic patterns of sentences.

At these meetings they went through humdrum routines like sorting out the shopping order for the week and reviewing the sanitarium's accounts, and sorted out the problems that cropped up.

They took turns chairing the meeting. The taciturn Aaron Wold used a home-made semaphore and it kind of worked but not very efficiently and sometimes they got crazy with each other. All in all they were more bothered about the route than the shortcuts which made for a lousily inefficient system anyway.

For myself, when I learned of all this from my infrequent visits to the crazy palace to see my father, I had this thought: Just think of the mess the city would be in if we ran things like that.

The craziest man, I figured, would be left running the show.

One more thing.

When Aaron Wold and Bronislaw Angel and the Glaswegian swindler Father Keam and Stanley Kubrick started playing serious five-card brag each afternoon in the main lounge, they had to play by staking something pointless and without value in order that no-one could get corrupted by the exercise. Which is why they chose pukka berries.

63

The young Corwen Lintock couldn't volley marbles through the neck of a milk bottle to save his life.

He tried. Heck he tried.

He thought maybe he could catch some of the magic from his hero on the field, the one he watched lead the team's attack every other Saturday afternoon from the children's benches down by the asphalt track which circled the touchline.

One time he queued for the autograph of his footballing idol, the young prodigy Eddie Melon, who was leading the team and the whole town with it to glory in the eyes of the outside world. Heck, they won two FA Cups and the League Championship in that time, before the slide started and the rot set in.

Eddie signed the autograph book of the young Corwen Lintock. So when the boy was exiled to the cupboard under the stairs for peeing on his bed again, the autograph book went with him, clutched to his chest like a talisman or a holy relic whilst the boy prayed and prayed in the pitch black.

Funny, that. He never prayed for the light to come on. Or to be let out of the cupboard. He prayed to be able to volley marbles through the neck of a milk bottle.

I remember it being said that my great idol on the pitch, the flying Preston winger Tom Finney, could do it too. Volley marbles through the neck of a milk bottle.

It was like having this umbilical cord to God or something. It seemed so of Eddie Melon who could do it so perfectly time after time. It was as if in reaching perfection he was touching some sorcerer's stone. That's how it seemed to us as we watched from the sidelines wishing like crazy that just a bit of that magic would rub off on us.

Here was this hero, this talisman for us, what with two FA Cups and the League Championship for the city. Of course when he retired he just became this man who could volley marbles through the neck of a milk bottle but it was a heck of a trick and at least he got to present TV game shows and get well paid for it. Which was a handy trick to have because by then the dhootie cloth trade was crumbling like it was dust and there was not much work around and the town was starting to crack in places like the face of an old woman.

Coleman Seer in Galbraith's India Mill was still saying the trade and its incumbent wealth should last here another thousand years but we all knew. We knew. Someone had put the evil eye on us.

Heck, a dying dhootie cloth trade and no more championships.

64

Bronislaw Zelenewycz, who lived the last years of his life in Eddie Melon's sanitarium, not wreaking violence and not frightening the others and not trying to burn the place down, is safely planted in the ground.

My daughter Sonja was here for the funeral. I got a day pass to allow her out though she was obliged to wear her yellow badge. On the form is a space to give the reason. Someone had written 'Death'. She held my hand.

Bronislaw was born, now he's dead. He will not come again. Unlike me, he hears no voices ringing in his head. What he hears is nothing. Amen.

At the burial, the priest Daniel Daniel has spoken words which suggest otherwise, but Bronislaw and I have each in our time recognised this as pish. We came to know too much of life, Bronislaw and I, to reckon there could be anything meaningful to follow, that praying to a God in the sky for help is like asking an empty car park for forgiveness.

Now he is planted in the ground. A few more weeks and for him it's lime mulch season. The priest has said prayers about eternity but Bronislaw and I both know it ends here in a hole in the ground.

I expect the Dinka tribe of the Serengeti knew that. Maybe that's why no-one got nailed to a tree for so long.

I expect Aaron Wold knows that too, having got as far as the end of Volume Four of the collected works of his grandfather, Kegan Laurie Wold. How he must be looking forward to the painstaking translation of the remaining fourteen volumes.

The Dinkas heard voices too. That's what Kegan Laurie Wold reported. They believed them to be the spirits of the earth and the elements. The Galswegian Father Keam believed such voices in my head to be the voices of angels, but then he started off nearer to the end of history than the Dinkas. It was an unfair contest.

Me, I knew the voices to be those of women in a men's world where the principal by-product is sometimes seen to be the accrual of human bonemeal.

Now the funeral on the cemetery hill above the town is over and Aaron Wold, Bronislaw's compatriot from the sanitarium, stands on the edge of the summer-warm field playing some Gaelic lament on the pipes.

He would not stand with the small band of mourners led by Eddie Melon and Stanley Kubrick. Some nurses were here also and they have cried.

Aaron Wold will not look me in the eye. He plays prettily on the pipes for a man who once more will not speak words. To anyone. Not a single meaningless animal grunt. Oh God!

After his ordeal in front of Stankill's Commission, the pipes are his only lament for his friend Bronislaw Angel who was my father Brogdan Zelenewycz the pilgrim Polish soldier and weaver and speaker of four languages and father and carver of blackened beech.

Daniel Daniel the priest with the wooden jaw shakes me by the hand. He says my father was a good man. I have this urge to say 'I know, I know!' Instead I say to him, 'Yes, but I could have done more in his later years.' I am relieved to find that he doesn't disagree.

As we stand in the vestry he is folding away his vestments and the apparatus of the burial service. He says he is made melancholy by death, an odd affliction for a vicar of Christ. I tell him my father was made melancholy by life.

He says, 'You have had an extraordinary life in some respects.' He means in this bizarre century of ours. He talks of the legacy of my parents, of their ordeals, of their flight to a new life across an apocalyptic Europe, of the extremes of good and evil into whose faces they had looked through their lives.

It has made for an extraordinary heritage, he says.

What lessons I must have learned from this life of mine!

65

Aaron Wold's protective custody order ended with his hearing in front of Stankill's Commission in the Council Chamber at City Hall.

Stankill said, 'Are you now or have you ever been in league against the best interests of the city as defined by its duly elected representatives?'

Aaron Wold, in his navy anorak and his heavy beard said, 'I go my own way. Heck, I have never much cared for treading the path of others, whether they believe me to be a crazy Scottish wino or Jesus Christ himself.'

'You were caught chanting incantations in the City Park after dark. Why were you doing that?'

Aaron Wold said, 'I was singing my hymn to the Universe.'

'Bullshit,' Daulman said. 'You were giving out the evil eye, and just when the circus is coming to town.'

Daulman is all fired up thanks to Fitsimmons's absence. Daulman these days feels odd, I think, when Fitsimmons is around. Kind of cold. Kind of absent. He can't put his finger on why.

Stankill said, 'Some have said of you that you are Jesus. What claim do you make?'

'I make no claim,' Aaron Wold said. 'Some people say I am Jesus Christ and give me pukka berries to use at the brag table. Some say I'm an itinerant Scottish wino. One or two, like Harry Angel, believe I am a former milkman from the Hebridean island of Crull fallen from the grace of men. So be it.'

'Either you are a crazy man or you are Jesus Christ come to claim the city,' Stankill said. 'I ask you again. Have you come to be Leader and cause trouble in this town of ours?'

Aaron Wold said, 'I guess I'm just here to bear witness to the truth.' Daulman wanted to know what kind of pisspot answer that was. Daulman suggested that maybe Aaron Wold really was just a crazy man. Aaron Wold shrugged. 'It's a mystery to me,' he said.

They asked him if he could turn water into wine.

He said no.

They asked him if he could volley marbles through the neck of a milk bottle.

He said no.

They believed he was too unpredictable, too crazy to be let loose in the east quarter. In there, any fool could be forgiven for thinking he was Jesus Christ or something and they had no need of a rabble rouser. Especially with the finale they had in mind for the east quarter.

They had a better idea.

When the security men from Sentex were called into the room, the figure of Aaron Wold stood with a cardboard placard round his neck which said this: 'King of the Kurs'.

Aaron Wold was jibbering. Jibbering. Old Testament frothing at the mouth.

'You know who this is?' Daulman said to the two young men with respectful haircuts and Sentex uniforms.

'No, sir.'

'This, boys, is Jesus Christ himself.'

They whistled under their breaths, 'Fucki ...'

'Watch your language boys or you'll get zapped by a thunderbolt. He'll put the evil eye on you.'

They said, 'What do you want us to do with him, sirs?'

Aaron Wold's face was twitching like he'd been zapped.

Aratakis said, 'Take him out to the city dump. But wait till after dark. Don't go frightening the neighbourhood. This is a peaceable town.'

'What do you want us to do out there, sirs?'

Stankill said, 'Why, crucify him of course.'

They left him, as they had been instructed to, at the city abattoir after dark. They were taking no chances about the albeit remote possibility of crucifying the Son of God just when Corwen Lintock's town was getting straightened out.

When they left him propped against the oak-beamed door they had found in the yard, hammers at the ready, Aaron Wold was no longer jibbering. He was dumb as a mute.

'Plumb perfect,' Daulman said. 'Just plumb perfect.'

66

When I was a boy and living on Beaker Street with my mother, even before my father arrived on these shores, in these damp little hills, to be with us from his small heroic war, the voices of angels were singing in my head. You remember, they went away for a while, quieted by the rolling cogs of history and the satisfactions of each new Football League season.

They are back now, of course, those bleak contralto voices that sang to me then and sing to me now in words that slide through my dull fingers. Women's voices, slipping, sliding in my head like marbles rattling round a milk bottle now that the pukka berry tasks are gone from my life.

Sometimes I doodle away in the margins of newspapers or the blank squares of committee reports to try and quell them. It doesn't work. They come and come again.

You know where they were born, these voices, these sweet bleak singing voices in my head? Singing to Harry Angel?

Of course you do.

They were born in the back of a van running south from Rajska being driven by Brogdan Zelenewycz.

They came from the women in the back who nursed my mother through her rattling, rolling agonies of labour which would produce the infant Harni. From these women with oval faces and saucer eyes. When the one who talked opened her mouth her teeth were black.

Uurgh!

She had a green ribbon tied in her hair.

You don't believe newborns can remember the details of their birth? I remember. I remember. Either that or I read it in a Woolworth exercise pad. One or the other.

I was born into this world bloody and bleeding in the back of a straw-bedded van, and the women with their saucer eyes and rugby skull heads looked on like some Greek chorus and sang. Only the Green Ribbon spoke whilst my mother gave birth to me, but all of them sang.

Can you believe that?

What a start in life.

They all have dumb stories and they too are in that work of art which my mother finally dedicated to me, an act which would surely have placed an unfair burden on any man. Most of all me. Most of all Harry Angel. At least my father had the good grace to burn his own creations when their use was done.

Why me? For Christ's sake, why me?

The Green Ribbon is a Salonica Jew. We are heading for Salonica, remember, in this straw-bedded van. The destination is her idea. The Salonica Jews are known across Europe. They are tenacious and ferocious and thieving in their attempt to cling to life. They live betwixt and between two languages, Spanish and Greek, and half a dozen cultures. The Salonica Jews were some of the first into the death camps. They are nearly all exterminated by now as we drive in haste in the year of my birth, despite their appetite for life. In the camps they were known as singers of songs.

The Green Ribbon was asked by my mother in one of her more lucid spells how she had survived so long.

'Kleptiklepti,' the Green Ribbon said.

The second has been a civilian worker in the Buna, in the Ukrainian lager. Before she was finally trawled, she had hidden in a farmer's cellar with her family for a year and a half. Each night one of them in turn crept out to hunt for food. She returned one time to watch the farmer shaking hands with soldiers. It seemed so well-mannered a transaction. Then she watched them drag the family out and send them on their way to heaven one by one, blow by blow, bleeding and, who knows, uncontrite. When they were done they packed up and went.

The third was a captive of Birkenau, brought on one of the interminable cattle wagons from Vienna. Her father was a dentist. Oh sore and sacred teeth. She was fifteen.

All three survived death by becoming prostitutes of the soldiers and getting shipped out to Rajska beyond the compound to service the garrison full time. All three fluked their escape. They were being used by a handful of off-duty guards, I choose my verb carefully, when Kadosh Schmeickel and friends struck out at the village for food or glory or some such thing one starry night. The soldiers, they killed. The three women tagged onto the rag-bag group led by Kadosh Schmeickel.

In the camp of the partisans they did what they do now in this van, which is to say nothing much apart from to sing their sweet bleak chanting songs. Friends and neighbours of my mother on Beaker Street might have thought of the three of them what they thought of my mother which is that they could have made more of an effort.

As they sing they make simple movements with their hands in a careful sequence, touching first lips, then head, then thumbs, now rocking back and forth three times. Then lips, then head, then thumbs, now rocking back and forth three times.

And so on, and so on.

As though one simple wrong move in this life-preserving rondo would cast them down into the waters of hell and leave them drowning.

These songs, sung in the hills of Carpathia and in the back of the van in which I was born and on the steamship bound from Salonica, were the songs that haunted the infant Zelenewycz.

The Glaswegian Father Keam told me once that they were the voices of angels that I heard in my head and I figure that maybe he wasn't far off.

67

Corwen Lintock has said that he wants to reward me, Harry Angel, public servant, for my services to the living. A little treat, the memo says, for all my work on his behalf. For the celebrations and the circus which are imminent.

You want to know what it is?

I'll tell you, I'll tell you! I will.

I only hope it will help ease the pain of having no pukka berry tasks, no simple rearing of plants to feed my soul with happy repetitions.

It's a kind of going-away present. You want to know why? Corwen Lintock is a dying man – it's official.

Whodunnit? Wait and see.

'A new era of contentment is abroad in the protected east quarter.'

This is the opening line in the monthly report I am constructing. In my report I make reference to the re-opening of the great but formerly derelict Galbraith's India Mill which is now the industrial flagship of Sentex Industries.

In fact from where I stood with Daniel Daniel the priest on the cemetery hill I could see the steady smoking of the mill's chimneys. It was, I suggested to the priest, a handsome sight. It was good when people who were once lost were now active again in the creation of wealth for the community under the stewardship of Sentex Industries.

Four hundred and fifty men from behind the round-roll wire have been commissioned to work there. At dawn they are taken to the factory. Each evening they return to the east quarter in lorries. In between times they generate dhootie cloth and other such things for the world and the wealth of the town which pays for the security of the east quarter community and so on, and so on.

And so on.

Of course the circus elephants arrived early, due to some breakdown in communication. Oh God, the commotion. I think one of them is sick. She has pus leaking from the edge of one reddish cornea. Like Corwen Lintock, looking death in the eye.

Corwen Lintock's memo to me offering me reward for my efforts on behalf of the city sets out the time and the place. In the game show of life, some may have drawn the gunge tank but circus-man Harry Angel is a winner, Harry Angel has won an elevator ride to paradise with Sarah and Hannah.

But you know what. I can't get it up much these days. Maybe it's the toothache. Maybe it's the other things.

Then again, there's the elephants.

68

Dumb Dooley Pound is a salesman. He couldn't settle out in the city and he came back to live his days in the familiar courtyard streets of the east quarter, armed with his ten-gallon hat and his cowboy book of the world. He knows my daughter Sonja who is back now from Bronislaw's funeral, handing out soup and blankets to new arrivals from Stankill's game show. Sonja who I'm trying to pull strings for to get her back this side of the river. Dooley hangs out in the community centre. I asked him to keep an eye out for her. He shrugged. 'Like John Wayne?' he said.

Sure, I said. Like John Wayne.

He makes his living selling magazines and videos. Each night he sneaks out through a hole he knows about, across the no-man's land, and into the town carrying his rucksack of goodies for the cityfolk.

Some of Dooley's offerings are newly made, with fresh attractions. Making a living is hard when your identification is stamped in yellow. Other videos have older favourites. Like who? Like Sarah and Hannah.

You want to know about Teenage Twins Sex Lust? You want to know what was in *Hot Girls Extra*?

Sarah and Hannah Pound, that's what.

Twins?

Just a little poetic licence to stoke up the marketing potential. A tenner a go, that's what Dooley flogs them for out in the town. Rumour has it that Stankill has an interesting library. Corwen Lintock has little use for them where he's heading.

Each dawn Dooley creeps back, happy to be home again. Knowing that a roll of sweet cash under his belt makes him king in cowboy country.

Dooley knows all about the circus coming to town. What else does he know? He knows that after the circus is over, the Injuns are coming to get him.

What lessons I must have learned from these circumstances of my birth and upbringing! This is what Daniel Daniel was saying.

The priest had packed away the tools and vestments of the burial service. Tomorrow he was due to bury two more. On Sunday a christening. Life went on. The circus had arrived. There was the overtime to sort out and where the grandstand was to go. And so on.

Bronislaw was fertiliser in the ground. Rotting vegetation. Alive only in my head. I walked with the priest who had come to see me off.

The priest asked me if I would miss him.

I think that I will miss what he was rather than who he was. He wasn't really my father. He was just an innocent.

He never saw it coming.

'Yes,' I said to him before we parted and he returned to the little cemetery chapel on the hill, 'I learned a lot from my life.'

What did I tell him?

I said that I watched fate kick the shit out of crusty Coleman Seer and poor old Vernon Smitts. It's odd, but I sure seemed to learn fast around losers like that.

69

You know what.

Old Bronislaw lied to me. No, not just about being my father.

He was no hero. He was a little man in a bigger tide of history than he could comprehend. Sure didn't see it coming. He thought that to save grace in the eyes of the boy so nearly his son he had better lie a little, but truth will out as truth will.

Bronislaw Angel the Polishman joined the Polish army. When he was Brogdan Zelenewycz. I grant him that.

He fled south from Rajska as a raggle, taggle partisan, driving the stolen army van in which I, the infant Harni Zelenewycz, was born. That much also is true.

He arrived on Beaker Street from Palestine when the festivities were over and the lime mulch had run out, to join us. Correct.

Heck, and not much else.

You know why he lied to me?

He was ashamed. He believed himself unlovable without the smudge of fiction. He created a new history for himself by touching up the edges here and there.

Starting a new life on Beaker Street in post-war England he wanted to give me, to give all of us, a clean start. He said.

I know that from the Woolworth exercise pad.

Every September 1st he told me his intricately woven tale of reluctant heroism. He thought I believed him. He thought it would help me to respect him. What could I say? How could I reveal, after my mother passed on and I saw the Woolworth exercise pad, that I knew the truth of it after all those years of smudge.

Bronislaw, Brogdan, take your pick, knew there was no greater gift from God than to believe in your country. Trouble was, he got off to a bad start by having to watch his country pack up and move out, one handcart to a family, after the Polish cavalry charges were outsmarted by battalions of German tanks and the dive-bombing Stukas.

This is how it goes:

Brogdan Zelenewycz pushes his handcart south, eighteen years old and wearing his ten-day-old army uniform and a dog blanket he shares with the lice to cover up the fact that he is a soldier. Rivka, his wife of two weeks, walks alongside. Each time a German staff car or supply truck speeds up the road, the convoy of refugees has to shuffle off into the field, and Brogdan Zelenewycz has to crouch down amongst the litter of women and old men. Buildings smoke. Children cry. Wooden wheels smack against the ruts in the road, forcing the contents of Poland on the move to shake and belch in their unwieldy handcart heaps.

In the Zelenewycz cart, buried out of sight in the heap of useless family treasures the couple have brought, is the portrait of the young soldier Brogdan Zelenewycz, done six months ago. It shows the seventeen-year-old Brogdan stiff in the army uniform he had scrounged for the occasion. His aunt from Poznan knew a man who was passing through and who could do his portrait in uniform for a very reasonable fee, the artist being a patriot himself.

Brogdan had told everybody that he had applied for a post in a cavalry regiment. Rivka loved horses. When they turned him down he had been unable to confess the news. He had a weak chest and bad eyes. He wasn't cavalry material.

Oh, the imagined disgrace! Always the uniform and papers would be arriving in the next few days, he was forced to explain to his family and his fiancée. He kept up the pretence for nearly six months before the Third Reich's invasion finally saved him the bother any more. Phew!

The offer of the military portrait almost saw him undone at the outset of the pretence. To get round the dilemma Brogdan was reduced to confessing his secret to Rivka's father. He borrowed an old cavalry uniform from her father who agreed to the loan for fear the incident should reflect on his daughter. It was a Great War uniform from 1915, three sizes too big for the young man.

Afterwards, Brogdan Zelenewycz's flesh itched for a month where the uniform had bitten him. He figured his prospective father-in-law had given him a living uniform purposely, though the man wouldn't live through the blitzkrieg long enough to laugh about Brogdan's rash.

Brogdan explained away the uniform to the patriot artist from Poznan by saying there was a delay in new cavalry uniform supplies. The uniform wasn't his, didn't even fit, but he wanted the portrait done anyway because he was proud of being a soldier, willing to fight on horseback for Poland, God and Christendom. And so the deal was done and Brogdan's portrait was painted for half the standard fee in a tunic that hung like turnip sacking and which he shared with the fleas who breakfasted upon him even as he struck a pose.

On the eve of the German invasion, the infantry took Zelenewycz, weak chest, bad eyes and all. By then the military were taking anyone who could hold a rifle. Almost by the time the portrait was framed, the painting seemed an honourable representation of the truth, but by then Brogdan Zelenewycz's father-in-law lay dead in some mown-down street or other, believing his daughter's future husband to be a fool and a fraud.

Brogdan was angry at his new wife's suggestion as they made ready to flee Warsaw in the face of the invasion. She said that they should throw the portrait out and not carry the stupid thing with them to God knows where.

He would not budge, though. He insisted that he would take the picture with them when they fled the German advance. He told her as if she were a simple child that there was no greater gift from God than a love of one's country. She said nothing after that, just looked at him as if to say, 'You're a fool, Brogdan Zelenewycz.'

The story continues so:

They find work on a farm in a small town three days south of Warsaw and are grateful for it. The farmer is uncurious about them. Labour is hard to come by. He teaches Zelenewycz to milk the cows and dig ditches and such like. He shows Rivka how to feed the pig and the chickens. She cooks on the kitchen stove for the three of them. At night the Zelenewyczs sometimes make love in their attic room. One floor below, the farmer listens.

It's a small farm, a quiet place. The farmer is a widower, has no children and a bent leg. In the small town where few outsiders have come before, the exotic Zelenewyczs from Warsaw are commonly believed to be Jewish. Heck, what is a Jew if not a foreigner arrived in the midst of familiar faces? For a few months they are tolerated. They learn to keep away from the town whenever necessary, only to go in for provisions, not to draw attention to themselves. When a child of the town goes missing, Zelenewycz goes along with the farmer to help the locals search the nearby woods for signs of the girl. She is found, and the town is happy again.

Eventually, the farmer is visited by members of the Town Council. They tell him that the two strangers from Warsaw who work on his farm should leave, that their presence is jeopardising the well-being of the townsfolk. He says, 'How will I manage afterwards with no labour?' and they agree to find him a village boy who will help out.

As Brogdan Zelenewycz and his wife push their handcart over the brow of the hill the townsfolk raise a white flag on the pole in the market square, signalling that the town is at last free of Jews.

70

Sure, sure, the Zelenewyczs then stumble across Kadosh Schmeickel and his rag-bag of partisans four, maybe five days later. Here the versions of truth converge for a little while. The group feed them, let them tag along. Brogdan keeps his portrait wrapped in a blanket and sleeps with it as a pillow. His wife falls in love with the group's leader. Around the campfire they learn to sing songs as they pass their days in the hills. Down in the valley, the wheels of the boxcar trains heading for the terminus at Birkenau-Auschwitz just up the line sing, 'Shuckety puck, shuckety puck, shuckety puck.'

Sometimes they need to scavenge for food. Brogdan Zelenewycz's favourite spot is down around the railyard in Rajska. The garrison of soldiers leave binfuls of scraps. Except that one night he falls over one of the metal bins, the alarm is raised, and he finds himself taken prisoner by the soldiers on guard. It is Brogdan Zelenewycz who betrays the partisan group to the Germans.

Brogdan Zelenewycz flees not from the Germans but from his fellow outlaws. Under interrogation he has told the Germans where the partisan group are hiding out in the hills. Who knows what they did to get the information from him. Sure, he came out unmarked and with all four limbs intact, but who knows what they said, whether they wondered aloud if he was Jewish or gypsy or full of the evil eye or something and did he fancy a one-way trip in the boxcarts that sang 'Shuckety puck, shuckety puck' on their way to Birkenau-Auschwitz station along with his wife?

'What about me?' Brogdan Zelenewycz asks. The sergeant laughs so much his belly aches and points to a battered supply van in the courtyard. Do a runner in that, he says, before maybe I decide to shoot you.

'What about my wife?' Brogdan asks. 'She is due to give birth any day now.'

The sergeant takes him to the barricaded cells and opens a door. 'Which one?' he says. A group of women and old men sit silent in the room; they look up when the door swings open. Zelenewycz points. The sergeant pulls her to her feet. Zelenewycz puts her in the van, drives off. Nothing is said. There is nothing to say.

On the mountain road they are stopped by three women standing in their path, last remnants of Kadosh Schmeickel's partisan group. One, the Salonica Jew with a green ribbon in her hair, aims a pistol. They climb aboard and tell him to drive. With a pistol to his head, Zelenewycz drives clean through the two roadblocks they meet. At the first one, Brogdan Zelenewycz swears that the soldiers in the roadside hut are laughing as the old supply van from Rajska hammers through the gate. In the back of the van his wife is in labour.

Zelenewycz drives on, too much in a hurry to stop. His wife screams. Zelenewycz pushes his foot to the floor. Behind them, the remainder of the partisans are being rounded up. The leader Kadosh Schmeickel, turkey neck and ears like trophy handles, they will nail to a tree.

Shuckety puck.

71

You think that was all? No way!

With his wife and son stowed away on the hashish-smuggling chugger boat in the Greek port of Salonica, Brogdan Zelenewycz, nineteen and alone in a strange but equally war-torn country, needed to survive.

The fuel-less van was useless. He sold it. After two months' scrounging round the docks he was rounded up and put in a holding camp. With the Germans busy hunting live human flesh to stock up the boxcars on the shuckety puck line to the metal spoon and lime mulch factories, Zelenewycz invested the last of his money in the uniform and papers of a dead Canadian soldier. Since this was a familiar ruse of fleeing Jews and gypsies and possessors of the evil eye, Zelenewycz posed as a mute, shell-shocked imbecile of an Canadian soldier to fool his captors. For two and a half years he fooled his German gaolers who left him be in an Allied POW camp outside Cracow. For two and a half years he uttered no intelligible sound for fear of giving himself away to the camp spies.

He taught himself to carve with a penknife on broken rafter splints from the camp huts. Sometimes he heard voices in his head.

But truth will out, as truth will.

When the war ended he risked transportation with the other troops back to Canada in his mute, shell-shocked imbecilic role. So he came clean to the Allied forces who immediately locked him up in a detention camp as a possible camp lackey for the Germans and a potential communist spy. So he confessed to being Jewish to explain his need to conceal his identity and was moved off to await shipment to Palestine where men with round eyes and oval faces waited with him and feared his obvious physical health as a trick.

Once there, he confessed to being Brogdan Zelenewycz, Pole, husband, father of the infant Harni. The authorities sent him up to Jaffa to a rehabilitation complex. Someone there gave him an old set of Egyptian carving chisels. The glare of sunlight on the orange roofs and white houses hurt his eyes. Some days he cried, for no obvious reason. He was put in touch with a woman from the refugee agency which had an office in Jaffa. It was she who finally traced his wife and son. After that he dreamed of England.

All this I know only from the Woolworth exercise pad my mother left behind, the one she dedicated to the one uncorrupted soul she knew.

I gave him a kind of soldier's funeral. The priest from the Ex-Servicemen's Association did the sermon while Daniel Daniel looked on. I thought maybe Bronislaw would have liked a soldier's funeral. Who knows for sure? Who knows anything about a man who reinvented his life and made a different home to please a kind of son? He figured I would despise him if I knew the truth.

72

And then the circus came to town. Brought in on twenty-three trailers from out of the witchy hills, come to celebrate three hundred years.

Children gripped pink fists as if to hold the day fast and not to let it loose. If they lived to be as old as Stanley Kubrick they would remember this day and the circus coming to town, pitched in the open air of the City Park.

They would remember.

Men working know the morning will burn away into a hotter day. The hottest day since pavements baked and the overland subway tracks buckled in that summer of 1964. Harry Angel knows that the residents of the sanitarium will see the fireworks explode across the city sky tonight from behind tall windows on the hill.

Dooley Pound, swanning around the east quarter, knows something. Knows that, afterwards, the Injuns are coming.

The day dawned an age ago, it seems, gentle on the hills. Dew weighed down the cool grass but circus men ploughed on to get their work done early, wary of the dog-day sun ahead. Animals prowled, nervous, in cages. They knew something was up. Big men in threes and fours, practised and somnolent, levered posts and poles into positions agreed between the circus man Harry Angel and the owners weeks ago. Unshaven, they have cussed with sounds that slapped the air, hammered steel pegs into the hardened summer earth; built grandstands and fixed firework struts and pounded billboards into place. Good men going about their plain and simple business. Tomorrow they move on.

Folk have watched on their way by, off on their own daytime errands. Off to make bread or buildings or bowling alleys under the noonday sun. They will be back later, know places are booked for them in the amphitheatres of seats. They have tickets and everything.

Daulman and Stankill, damp at their armpits and the 'V' of their backs, are lieutenants of the day. The jangle of Stankill's change inside his cotton socks spooks the lions as he walks past time and again. They tense at him like he was bad meat.

Fitsimmons, heir to Drucker's empire, good teeth, well sexed, has watched across the park at City Hall. Fitsimmons doesn't sweat. Never has. Watches the jigsaw pieces of the day bolted together. Smiles, knowing all is well.

Only Harry Angel has been missing, playing a dangerous

game as far as Fitsimmons can see.

In their hooded caravans, circus people snooze lightly now. Their turn will come. Raw dogs bark at the sun that blisters the sky and sours tempers.

73

In the sanitarium cool blue light lies over us.

I sit with Stanley Kubrick who is old now, sends letters off to what are maybe car parks in the firm belief that they are theatres where men perform on stages.

We play cards, Stanley Kubrick and I. Aaron Wold will not play. Why not? He stands alone as sentry, mute, waiting for the pharisees to come back for him up the long hill.

Other residents hover at the edge of things. Refugees from the cauldron day outside. A quiet scene. Ah deception! There is drama in our hearts.

I moved into the sanitarium a week ago. Maybe more. The voices in my head were getting worse. I had this need to answer back and plead my case, what there was of it. They got worse almost as the very day of the circus approached. I figured they didn't like circuses.

I moved into the room of the old Polish soldier, Bronislaw Angel. The man whose lifelong telling of untruths included the fact that for forty-eight years he went on like he was my father or something.

Now he is buried and summer has come and I have taken residency of his room in the sanitarium owned by Eddie Melon.

Eddie Melon has been taken. Gone with the Sentex Security team who called on us today. Gone to the circus and the gathering of men downtown.

Me, I've done my circus business. Seen the troupe safely arrived in the City Park. Signed the contracts. Booked the overtime. Left it all to Daulman and to Stankill who, it seems to me, are most themselves steering between sweating men saying where crates and caravans should go.

I am most myself sat by tall windows, a little bowed maybe, a little fixed, looking out alone into the garden. Looking at nothing much. Like I went and hid my soul on a hill and may not ever find it.

I never took up Corwen Lintock's offer, the free ticket to the Hannah and Sarah Show at the River Court Hotel. What point was there? I couldn't get it up any more, couldn't quiet that engine hum.

Time passes, don't you find? Days come, days go. Time ticks away for sure for Corwen Lintock, slowly poisoned to the verge of death by the eating of quantities of my pukka berries.

I pass my hours up here when I'm not working, my ticking hours, sometimes playing cards, sometimes idly practising how to volley marbles through the neck of a milk bottle out in the garden.

Days back I caught a single volley out there just so perfectly with the instep of my leatherbrown shoe that I let out a cry. Felt this small electric ripple run through my bones. P-ting, it cracked into the back of the glass. But no more, no more. I figure I could live to be a hundred and not carry that one off again. Heck, that could turn out to be the best sweet little thing of my life.

Retreat is a harsh word.

But who am I to judge? I am happy, more or less, to play cards with the eponymously named Stanley Kubrick and with Aaron Wold when he comes down off the roof. Just the turn and pitch of the cards on green baize. Hot tea on warm days. The drawing of breath. Simple things to keep the hours at bay. Besides, this is where the elephant is stashed, out back.

74

The elephants of course arrived early, nine of them, a week ahead of the main circus convoy. It caused me no end of concern. They were delivered by a freight company to the renamed George Steen Porch of the City Hall where once Queen Mary took the cotton crowd's applause at the grand opening of the building. What do you do with nine grey elephants? I rang Fitsimmons. 'What a peach, what a peach,' he said.

Corwen Lintock's office promised they'd ring back. I'm still waiting. Stankill just twisted his long white bloodless fingers round and round. 'Elephants, you say?' Meanwhile the elephants just shat and shat. No respecters of history, they.

I settled in the end for putting them in the City Park. I had them tethered to large summer trees close to the lake so they could drink. Close to the clearing where Aaron Wold came to perform his Mystery Plays to an audience of one. Where the giant TV screens were due to go up. On circus night these screens would carry the diseased face of Corwen Lintock, favoured son of the navy-anoraked Jesus Christ, giving his farewell speech.

Every morning at dawn I came down off the sanitarium hill to check how the elephants were doing on the way through to City Hall where the shit had been shovelled away from the steps by men from Cleaning and Supplies, Vernon Smitts's old department.

I would pat them, rub their trunks, feed them peanuts given me by the elephants' foreman. Even the sick one that wouldn't take her food, hung back away from the others, blinking pus out of her sickly eye and watching me from over by the hawthorn bushes.

On the fourth day the elephant foreman came across to say he'd had the circus vet down, and that the lone elephant who watched me was a write-off and they needed to get rid of her before the other animals arrived for the show. It might be catching. It seemed like the last thing we needed in a city briefly famous for some decapitated polar bear was an elephant dying in stages in the City Park. I agreed she certainly looked sick to me.

I was told to get hold of a Council trailer van and ship her to the self-same knacker's yard where once Bronislaw Angel had stationed his Polish Second Brigade when he was General Sikorsky for the day. Having the elephant put down in the park in full view of everyone would distress the sensibilities of the passers-by it was decided. A good thing, surely.

I booked the van and drove it up at dawn the next day, but I couldn't go through with it. Just couldn't. She had this look, like maybe a bit of loving would see her through. So I hid her from the abattoir, brought her here. No-one saw. No-one cared. It was just one sweating elephant less from the Noah's Ark down there.

There's been some help for me in nursing the elephant through.

I get Dooley Pound up here each day at the moment. He treks over the top road like some east quarter pied piper, stray cats hanging loose around him. He's good with dumb animals. He helped.

He's fed the elephant, found some rotten swelling stump of tusk and smacked it out, brought her round on aspirin and temazapan. It's the stuff he deals in back home beyond the Beaker Street rubble where light from lamp posts turns the broken ground to moonrock.

He's a handy man out there. Back and forth every day across the moon, bankrolled by the Hannah and Sarah Show which is proving a gilt-edged investment.

As for the elephant, she looks out at the hills from the garden up here seeming happy enough despite the heat. Her eyes have cleared up. The pus has gone. She's big mates with Dooley Pound for sure. All in all it could have been worse, could have finished up a fifty quid dead-weight kind of tale.

Corwen Lintock's dead-weight soon. Remember, he has sour blood thanks to all the pukka berries he ate that turned out to be poisoned. Well, hell, I was in an awful state round about the time when my wife left me for her better life, taking our daughter Sonja with her. How was I to know I'd been growing the wrong variety?

My consolation is that at least the Leader has hung on long enough to life from his pukka berry poisoning to see his good name cleared in court, albeit on a technicality.

What? You didn't know? The news has kind of been swamped by the arrival of the circus and the heatwave and stuff, I agree. The charges against him have been dropped. It seems that the police hadn't filled in all the necessary dates on the search warrants before impounding documents from the bottom of the bathroom cupboard in Councillor Lintock's southside maisonette. That's what the court has said, insubmissable evidence, about a fat bundle of key documents. Notably a pile of *Hot Girls Extra*.

See what I mean. Gilt-edged!

The law is the law, the judge said. Besides, it wasn't like there was some star witness for the wobbling prosecution waiting in the wings to be produced with a flourish like a rabbit from a tall black hat. Someone like Sam Pound, say, who's dead and gone and has no more to say. Dead men don't tell tales.

The case wound up in some disarray. On the steps of the city courthouse the contingent of Corwen Lintock, acquitted, passed the prosecuting team.

Lintock, being wheeled down in his chair step by step, bump-ti-bump-ti-bump, acknowledged his adversaries as if to say 'No hard feelings'. As if to offer a healing hand.

'You must have been sick as pigs in there,' he offered.

'Win some, lose some,' the bullfrog Aratakis said.

Children have got the day off school. Heat presses against their bare skin. Traffic has stopped in the steaming streets. Corwen Lintock is exonerated in the eyes of his fellow men and the circus has come to town.

75

Staging the circus day in the City Park shows a dominion won over darkness, over spirits that once howled like dogs at the moon from in here. It'll be a good time for all.

The bad part will be the delivery of the news that Corwen Lintock is dying. Some things even the love of Jesus can't shelter you from. He has that bitten-by-a-puff-adder look about him at the moment. He is going to tell them in his speech tonight that he is dying. Maybe he'll tell them that partings are sweet sorrow. That they leave business unfinished.

Corwen Lintock, I know, doesn't hold me responsible for his imminent death. This much has he confided to Fitsimmons. Apparently. He feels I've been used. Betrayed. Much like himself.

But I know this much, again from Fitsimmons. I know that someone's going to cop it. Someone'll suffer tonight when the news is heard; when the fireworks are all shot and the bears have finished dancing and the beer's run out and there's still a skein of salt blistered on the mouths of half-drunk men.

No, Corwen Lintock doesn't blame the dupe Harry Angel. Not like he blamed Sam Pound.

Sam Pound, who'd gotten himself subpoenaed to the Corwen Lintock trial. Happy to be lined up with the prosecution telling tales of his time at Sentex Construction. Reckoning he had no choice but to spill the beans on Corwen Lintock's little deals. That's why Sam Pound finished up in a sack at the bottom of Caspar's Gorge one starry night.

76

Now Eddie Melon is gone, I guess I'm kind of left in charge for a while. Eddie was met here by Jason Pound and a neatly suited Sentex Security team early this morning. You should have seen Aaron Wold's face when they showed up at the door. Thought they'd come for him. The man with no name who once drove subway trams just shuffled away going 'Shuckety puck, shuckety puck.'

They had their orders. They had wanted to clear out all the residents from the sanitarium into the east quarter for the day. Just for the day they said. Easier to keep an eye on our movements there, on the far side of the moon. Didn't want some crazy man going messing up the city's big day. Going putting the evil eye on it. Offered tea and biscuits in the community centre over there where Daniel Daniel used to hang out.

Eddie did this deal with them. He agreed to go back down the hill as Corwen Lintock's star guest. Sign autographs, pledge allegiance, that kind of thing. In return, he got a deal to allow the residents to be left alone here if they consented to remain housebound for twenty-four hours. By which time the city would be safely embarked on another three hundred years.

Sentex Security have finished their clear-up of the streets. Vagrants and ne'er do wells and the like. Now everyone who might go mucking things up is safely lodged on that far side of the moon. Fitsimmons has been taking no chances. Doesn't want trouble. Can't afford it. He instructed Daulman to make sure the troublesome priest was picked up a few days back. I was there at the time. I saw Daniel Daniel being led away.

When the order had come, Daulman had eyed Fitsimmons with his round uncurious eyes, grinned stubbornly.

Daulman knows when he's a beaten man. He wonders if it's halitosis.

It's fair to say there isn't much of a future for the sanitarium. The Planning Committee meets next week to consider compulsory purchase of the only suitable site within the city boundaries for the proposed Lintock Institute which the architects from down south were recommissioned to design. The only suitable site turns out to be the land occupied by Eddie Melon's sanitarium. Shuckety puck.

The contract was won by Sentex Construction. Half of the £42 million will be put up by Sentex Holdings PLC, the other half by the City Council under its Tourism and Development Programme.

All the residents of the sanitarium will go before Stankill's Housing Commission. It shows in their faces round here. In the way they move. In the way some speed up, some slow down. Some, so to speak, are on the roof. Like animals in cages, knowing something's up. Still men, though, don't you think? Surely that.

The day is airless now. Closed upon itself. Dripping. Corwen Lintock sits in Room 162 in the hotel, watching Hannah and Sarah who are like dancing bears, like seals, to Corwen Lintock through the two-way screen. The noise in the park, the heat, are too much for a sickening man. He'll be wheeled over there later, in time to give his shortish speech.

They know he's there, the girls. They are amused and curious and empty, like their souls were hidden away and buried on a hill that someone might dig out as treasure but not for a thousand years. Lintock watches, a little breathless, as if there is not air enough to breathe whilst they perform, maybe to tease him, maybe to cause him some small hurt in the catching of his breath.

77

It was an accident that I was in the community centre when the Sentex Security men came in for Daniel Daniel. I'd gone to see Sonja, to warn her of what might occur in the east quarter streets after the fireworks and stuff.

It did no good, of course. She said she'd stay. They'd both stay. That they belonged here now. That their IDs were embossed with yellow stamps throughout. She pulled one out, a driver's licence I think, dropped it on the table like she was trumping me. Like she was proving something.

She seemed more worried about me. She said word was that Fitsimmons had set me up. Suggesting that my poisoning the Leader was deliberate. That I was maybe in on the conspiracy. She said they all knew. Drucker. Daulman. That the raid on my apartment wasn't just for pukka berries. That they were watching me. They thought I maybe dreamed kurish dreams.

How could I bring myself to believe her?

I said I could speak to Fitsimmons on her behalf and on behalf of her . . . of Drucker's wife. I could speak to Corwen Lintock even. Get them to turn a blind eye if I could get her out like I got Mary Pound out one time. Get them to pretend that she was maybe one of us. Oh the words just came spilling out.

When they came for Daniel he never made a fuss. Like he was expecting it. He gave some quiet orders to one or two who were staying on to run things. To Sonja. To the woman. To dumb Dooley Pound who feeds the cats and unbaits the Sentex Security meat traps. Smiled. Then went. Like he'd never existed here. Like we'd turned the TV station over.

Plick!

The contracts are already drawn up, I understand, for the Lintock Institute. Fitsimmons has seen to that. Fitsimmons rising. On the board of Sentex Holdings PLC. Money rolls in. Four thousand contracts for jobs are expected. Fitsimmons risen like the sun.

The Lintock Memorial Library will form a key part of the project. Four million titles carefully chosen by a task force sitting under someone or other. Stankill thinks it's him. Ha! It won't be Corwen Lintock, that's for sure. He'll be gone, planted in the summer-dusty earth. They surely wouldn't wish to stock the eighteen volumes in Aaron Wold's collection or my mother's Woolworth pad. I hear the slogan over the Library will be this: 'It's the books that we reject that make the Lintock Library the best.'

78

What did I think when they took the priest away? When he nodded to me? Smiled? When people in the hall looked round as if to say, 'Harry Angel might have something to say about this.'

What did I think? Nothing.

Nothing.

There were no thoughts in my head. Just a big blocking zero keeping the train I was riding steady on the track.

Shuckety puck.

Oh sure, sure, there were words whizz-banging around. Some tossed green salad of words. Of things. Chairs and tables and faces all shaken into words that sounded, round, in my head.

Station announcements for some other platforms.

But there was no pushing or pulling; saying 'Do this, do that, Harry Angel.'

No sir.

Just a calmness. A nothingness in my face, the one my daughter watched, they all watched, as the Sentex boys led Daniel out into the street to who knows where.

Was it unpleasant? No, no.

It was something like death. Like the wind had gone and there was no land in sight. And I could only observe that this was most truly me, sitting by tall windows, a little fixed, watching and waiting for something outside. A movie, maybe. Something. That was me. And my mother shouting in my head, 'Jump, Harry, jump.' I know I should do something but it's so hard to jump from a speeding train.

Like I say, this one time out back I hit this volley.

P'ting.

Smack in the back of the glass, but no more, no more.

I guess the circus will be in full swing about now in the boiling basement city. I pulled it together, you know. This I told myself. Sorted the elephants out. Plotted the sites. All that stuff. Corwen Lintock, nearly dead, was surely grateful.

Myself, I stayed away.

Stanley Kubrick and I have a small wedge of dried raisins laid out on the table in front of us, to be used to wager bets during the game, the game on which my mind is not too set.

We're all out of pukka berries these days. Small sour things. More trouble than they're worth. We found raisins in the pantry.

I've been looking out of the window. Like there was something out there but there isn't. I'm drawn back in, study my cards, flip another pair of raisins out into the no-man's land between us.

'Call,' I say, a little zip in my dull old heart at the prospect of a winning hand, but Aaron Wold is semaphoring by the door, he wants me over. Boy, he looks upset. Wants me over no messing. I shrug at Stanley Kubrick, fold in my hand. I can't help noticing that Stanley would have won hands down.

Phew!

A moment later Aaron Wold is pointing out that there are intruders in the garden.

It's okay, I tell him. They are for me, and for a minute I think he's going to kiss me.

The night that Sam Pound came to me I did some staring out of the window, I can tell you.

He came slooping in out of the dark one evening, knocking at the door of my blackstone apartment after the last of the kids had slid away with their ball to TV land, to darker places. He said he'd been subpoenaed to give evidence in the Corwen Lintock trial. Got the letter a few days before and had sat on it, not told a soul. Now he'd come to tell me. It was busting out inside of him, he said.

Heck, I said, that's a big deal, Sam.

He asked me whether he should agree to appear in court.

Sure, I said. Just go and tell the truth.

No, he reckoned I didn't understand. He knew things about Corwen Lintock. Sam had been employed by Sentex Construction for a lot of years by then. Knew a lot of ins and outs. A lot of the strokes that Corwen had pulled. He knew he was going to have to spill the beans in court.

'Oh hell,' I said.

He agreed.

He made me swear that I wouldn't tell another soul about it. He wanted to try and keep the subpoena quiet until the day he was due to testify. That way, once the evidence was out in the open there was nothing anybody could do to put it back in the box.

Sure, I said. Sure.

I kept news of the subpoena a deep dark secret between me and the pukka berry plants which grew all around the room. Never told a soul. Except for Fitsimmons, of course. And he just smiled and smiled.

Dumb Dooley Pound is away over by the fence, feeding titbits to the grazing elephant who looks happy to see him.

Dooley has brought Sonja safely across the Beaker Street rubble and over the top road that leads here to the sanitarium. She has come to see me. Wanted to know that I was okay. Feared I wasn't. You see she'd heard that the Sentex boys had been up here. Dooley told her. She'd worried that they might have taken me.

No, I'm fine. They took Eddie, I tell her. Drove him off down the hill to go and perform for Corwen Lintock. But I'm okay. I think she looks peeved. We go quiet.

Really, I say. Figuring she wants some reassurance. I am wrong. Funny, I used to be good at stuff like that. She has that look, like if I reached and touched her she'd just break wide open. I don't remember her being like that. Always thought she was the strong one with her mother's independence.

I tell her I play a little cards, gaze out the window some, take care of the elephant. I've not seen her since the fuss over Daniel the priest a few days back. Does she want to see the elephant maybe?

Dooley's been a big help, she says. He hangs out in the community centre most days. Buys things folk can't afford, can't get. He seems to have this bankroll stashed away somewhere. Sure, I say, he's been good with the elephant. Pulled her through. Gave her aspirin and temazapan, smacked out some sore residue of tusk. Now she's right as rain.

She nods. I nod.

The conversation lurches out of gear again.

79

'How's Elisa?'

Her mother is well. They write.

Good. Good.

That's good.

'I worry over what to feed it. Do they graze or what?'

'I thought you were dead.'

It is an accusation. Stops the turning of easy wheels. What can you say? There's this insect-little scurry of words, chasing, out of reach. I shrug. Picture myself crouched at the window, looking out beyond, a little bowed.

Around us in the sanitarium, the remaining residents are walking on the edge.

Familiar territory, you might say.

Wrapped in postures. In positions of heads and necks and knees and feet. The steady rock of heads and necks and knees and feet. Without end or beginning.

And me? There don't seem to be any exits for the orphan words that sink and die in me. Maybe what I need's a Woolworth exercise pad. Maybe there they'd find a home. But who could I dedicate them to?

I don't understand, she says. Quietly, you understand. Not played for effect. Not angled to get some worked-out reply.

You stand there and watch Daniel get hauled away. Then they come for Eddie Melon. Sloopy Den Barton and Joe Mole get washed up at sea. And Sam Pound all the time has wound up at the bottom of Caspar's Gorge.

What is it with you? she says.

Me? I say. Me? Hell, I saved the elephant, didn't I?

Didn't I?

They were going to chop her into dog food and I saved her.

She says I only saved her out of cowardice because it was easier to drive the van up here. Because the whole damned thing just fell into my lap.

'People have died,' she's saying, 'and you've saved a fucking elephant on a fluke.'

80

You carried me on your shoulders so that I was a giant.

This she says to me. Whispered. I have to bend to hear.

I thought you were a giant. You fought my demons. You told me they were in my head, not in the City Park or on the hills. You made me unafraid.

Did I? I say.

Unafraid. All this before we left, to our different lives. For this, I thank you. For this, I will always love you.

But, you know, it's hard to picture this almost-other man that she carries in her head, drapes in front of me now. So long ago. You think that was Harry Angel?

I think maybe. Maybe. Just so long ago. So far back down the subway track.

Will you take tea with me? I ask.

She says no. She says she must get back. All the world knows what's coming tonight. In the east quarter's community centre they are making what preparations they can. After the fireworks everyone knows what's coming.

I don't get it, I say. This is some silence later you understand. Some bleak silence like a blasted thing. Why is she mad at me? So quiet. So far away. She says this dumb thing. She says she's not the one that's far away.

What do you want from me? What things are you asking for, like the askings of plaintive voices in my head.

You think it's easy? I say. You think it's what I chose. Sitting alone by some window watching stuff go by, a little crooked in the stare and thundering words kept back from my plain face. You think this dumb journey on some speeding train is easy?

I sigh; some small death.

'You think it's any much different for anyone else, Harry?' She's in no hurry now. She knows I'm all spent. You think you're the only one? she says. Just look around you. It doesn't make you special. Look around you, Harry. You and a million others. I have to go, she says. I hope you make it one day.

But I'm still clinging to the wreckage.

'Why don't you go away?' I tell her, still trying to be useful, still being Harry. Get clear of here. There's still time.

I tell her there's still time. Do I know her well enough to plead with her? She said she loved me.

That's right, she says. There's always time.

But no. She will not run. You run, Harry Angel, she says. They're out to get you, Harry. I've heard it said when you're not around. They'll get you like they got Sam Pound.

You want me to run? I say.

What else is there to do? A man like you.

Run, Harry, run.

When I look round, later, she is gone. Hours? Minutes? I don't know. I just don't know.

Words still blow like litter around me. I remember how before my wife left me she went to the City Park and cried and howled like a dog, and I think 'Comrade, comrade.'

81

Music spins men's heads till they are dizzy. Sweating, they drink beer from tents providing some shelter from the sun. Not much. Beer that dries to vinegar on crusty tongues. On the edge of the noise's expanse a subway tram goes slooping out.

'Shuckety puck, shuckety puck.'

Then it's gone in the flood of other sounds.

On a hill, a man called Harry Angel stares and stares. Sees himself seated by a closed window. Sees ribbons of words trail away like night trains. If you too stood, stared long enough, you would see Stanley Kubrick come out of the house, say some small words to him, see him stand and return to the house that is a sanitarium. Inside, tick tick tick tick, he calls some residents together in the high lounge, knowing there's this one thing he can do before he leaves.

Grandstands of people watch the lions roar, see elephants stand on fat hind legs, trapeze artists swing in wide arcs under the sky flecked with summer stars.

Somewhere in the crowd Drucker sits and watches. Admires the lightness of his touch. In his pocket, I know, is a letter that arrived today. A letter of appointment. Drucker is to be a City Commissioner, is to move on to the place where architects live and breathe, leaving barely a trace in the sand. Smiling, sweetly smiling.

Nearby, Fitsimmons, ochre beard shaved close to his unblemished cheeks, sits poised to succeed him. His wife doesn't like circuses. All straw and shit, she says. She waits at home.

All the town is here. Some happy, some drunk, some mad that Corwen Lintock's light is fading fast. There are torches and clubs stacked somewhere, someone knows, ready for later, for after Corwen's parting speech.

Just a few Sentex Security boys are scattered round the edge of town, keeping tabs on the curfew in the east quarter. Checking IDs. Keeping bad men off the street. Waiting for the relief so they too can head to the giddy lights before the fireworks start.

82

Here's a picture for you:

An hour on or more; the light has slipped past the hills, the noise from the City Park seeping out into this higher place as through a tunnel or a hundred sheets of glass.

Sonja, Drucker's used-up wife, three maybe four feet apart. Standing on the edge of the no-man's land by the Beaker Street crossing. One of them smokes, the other looks at the stars. They breathe. You can hear them breathe. I guess. It's how I see it.

The used-up wife says maybe she'll head back in. Turns. Walks slowly, like this is after the battle. Which of course it isn't. Leaves Sonja to her own moment. Alone.

The swelling of lights, the circus, are from another country, Sonja thinks. Up here on the lip of things it's last light. First dark. A middling gloom.

Something else.

She sees a single figure.

In the distance. Just a single figure under an immense sky. A simple thing. Coming down off the dark moors road. Then another, two steps behind. And another. Single file. Noiseless, not covert. An almost silent convoy breaking the curfew rules. Lost souls playing one final hand.

83

They are sober and nervous and small beneath the continent of stars. Down in the valley is the shriek of carnival and of life. Up here these four sound just a low music of footfall. Four of them. Harry Angel, Stanley Kubrick, the man with no name and Dooley Pound who leads the elephant at the rear. Harry Angel and Aaron Wold, we carry packages like they were frankincense and myrrh, which they are not. They are going-away presents. We are leaving town. Missing out on our appointments in front of Stankill's Commission next week. Maybe my daughter was right. Maybe there are worse things than regret.

I like to think she sees us approaching on the night road down from the hills like Mary must have seen the Magi, but I think not.

I think what she sees is four dumb men come from the crazy palace on the hill leading a half-sick elephant, come to find a moment of reprieve. Whatever. She hugs me. Greets my fellow travellers. Looks me in the eye like I was something she needed her whole life.

What you got? she says. She means the packages.

Surprise.

And so she feeds me tea and tells me things. Others come round us; men, women, Dooley's cats, out of the blackstone courtyards. Coming slowly, reluctant, from lookout posts like we are maybe spies or saboteurs.

We move out across the no-man's land of rubble that once was Beaker Street and stuff like that. Astronauts in space looking down at other men's worlds. We are two miles, maybe more, from the City Park where all life is being celebrated and the odd fist fight has broken out. Close enough, some might say, to put the evil eye on Corwen Lintock's day. Instead we break bread, drink tea, gather round the spit of flames like lost men on an open night. Last things.

84

I remember something.

Christmas was coming. The geese were getting slain. Out on the escarpment where the shuckety puck trams come slooping out of a blackstone tunnel Harni Zelenewycz was bent against the breeze. Scurrying this way and that. Retrieving loose pages that lay scattered around on the ground.

His mother was dead. People had come and gone. Had confirmed her death. Been testimony to the fact. Some had spoken to the driver of the subway tram who never saw her coming.

What was he doing, this Harni Zelenewycz?

Gathering up the pages of a Woolworth exercise pad the jumper had left behind carelessly to the world and the weather on the hill. Policemen watched him, amused, like he was wrestling with the wind.

Harni Zelenewycz was rescuing them one by one. Would store them ever afterwards in a tin biscuit box under his bed. Would spend his nights wondering why his mother's dedication on the final page was to him. Would reassemble the pages on dark nights into some kind of order after the wind had rifled them. Some kind of order from a wreckage of lives that ended on the hill with a siren sound and a cry of shuckety puck.

Come meet the travelling circus of Harry Angel. Strolling players. We four and one stray elephant. Plus Dumb Dooley Pound.

We're going with Stanley Kubrick to stay at the Grand Theatre with Stavros Kouros, his lifelong friend. We'll give elephant rides and stuff. Teach children tricks. Do recitations. Aaron Wold knows some cute old lines. And Stanley Kubrick. Maybe there'll be some bit parts for old Harry Angel, too.

Anyone can join. There's only three rules which are these: don't go wreaking violence, and don't go frightening people, and don't go trying to burn places down as we move from day to day on the way to Stavros Kouros's place.

A simple dream. What else was there for us to do? There was a week's notice to quit the sanitarium. Stanley Kubrick knows the way. Knows the address, over some dozen seas of hills. Another town, another town on, still more. It's somewhere out there. Somewhere.

Of course, first, there is this one last errand to perform in service to the city. You see, that night Sam Pound came calling to confess he'd been subpoenead, he left three sealed envelopes with me addressed to three wise men. He told me this: if ever I was to desert this small blackstone city for good, to burn my bridges, to go tilting at windmills somewhere away over the hills, I was to hand over these three envelopes. Meantime, he said, keep them safe in some well-lodged biscuit tin, Harry. Don't want you winding up at the bottom of Caspar's Gorge one day. He had this orphan look as he said it.

What's in the envelopes? All the evidence Sam Pound was due to give against Corwen Lintock in court. Everything.

Everything. It's no big deal. Corwen's just some guy who did some wrong things in the hope they'd make things right.

If anything ever happens to me, Harry Angel, he said, if ever they find me at the bottom of some river, hand these over to the three wise men whose names are written on the envelopes.

Sure, Sam, I said, sure. I kept them in the biscuit tin under the floorboards along with the Woolworth exercise pad.

Coleman Seer wants to know how we plan to beat the curfew. I tell him we're joining the circus. We could be late arrivals to the fray. We'll get by, I say. The Sentex lads are drunk. They'll let us pass on the necessary detour to deliver Sam Pound's envelopes to three wise men who live and breathe smack in the city.

Someone wants to know how we propose to get them to take the envelopes seriously. Us! How will they know it's not some mealy-mouthed trick. Who, I say, Harry Angel? Turkey neck and ears like trophy handles? Maybe I'll just tell them I put the evil eye on Corwen Lintock. And I can smile, a big broad grin, so deep and wide it fills my face.

Sonja's not grinning. My daughter has a face ebbing and flowing with woes, but then she's not joining up with the circus, not off to join up with twice-nightly Stavros Kouros. She has this shorter smile that now and then breaks. I tell her not to worry.

Aaron Wold sits storytelling with small boys. Together they watch flames spit and picture Hebridean dawns and cold ironstone roads at the edge of the world. Women fold cloth, cut ribbon, improvise the Harry Angel touring circus. Pack food for our approaching journey.

Coleman Seer has gone. Who knows where.

85

With a faraway whoosh and a noise like city traffic the first fireworks go up. The cries of children carry them, thrown from the earth, until they splinter and bang, pouring little twists of light above the town.

Beyond the Beaker Street no-man's land, they know it as the signal.

What is it you would see if you were here?

A pantomime, perhaps. The air flicking with ribbon and the colour of eiderdown and linen, and hornpipe reels played by Aaron Wold.

A circus. For surely a circus it is. Led by the callipered Dooley Pound.

Tall hats and sad-faced clowns and loony tunes with rattles and drums, and a bag over each shoulder hanging like a dead dog to march with down to the town and then over the barbarian hills.

You would see this: Harry Angel, Stanley Kubrick, Aaron Wold, Dooley Pound and a man with no name, led by a half-dead elephant ready to go delivering late mail to three wise men whose names sit on the envelopes in Sam

Pound's handwriting: Drucker; Aratakis; Fitsimmons. Off
to spill the beans on Corwen so that the wise men entrusted with them can put things right. After that we're on
our way. Where to? I don't know the way like Stanley
Kubrick does. Aaron Wold knows a song about sailing to
Skye in an apple pie. Dumb Dooley Pound says there's
blue skies in Tennessee. I wonder if it's important when all
you're really after is to jump down from the speeding train.

Sonja takes from us the presents that are not frankincense
and myrrh. One of them is Kegan Laurie Wold's eighteen-
volume journal wrapped in red-leather binding. The other
is a Woolworth exercise pad, sellotaped back into some
kind of shape, safely kept in a tin biscuit box.

Take care of them, the man called Harry Angel says.
Save them. They're all we have. They're everything.

What she whispers is this, over and over, so quiet she's
maybe barely thinking it: 'You dumb stupid man. You
stupid, stupid man.' She kisses me. I drown in warmth, like
this was a beginning.

Picture this too:

The elephant snorts. Circus pipes play. Small flags wave in
the streams of air. Laughter and lanterns say this is no covert
mission, led by Aaron Wold astride an elephant. Headed
for some electric amphitheatre that is the City Park.

Here now is the one last picture I will leave you with;
beyond this point I go alone to do my last thing for the

city, for poor Sam Pound, for Brogdan Zelenewycz, for my mother who held a stubborn faith in me almost to the end that you might call love; for Harni, blond hair and squinting fringe and getting ready to run a million miles from here – the music of sticks and pipes, following the small band of men down the hill. Fading. Fading. Leaving silence like a hole around the woman called Sonja.

Cool air. Bare mountainside. A child cries.

No more. No more.